CHAPTER 1

I'm the Vice President of Lawson Corporation, and I still need to finish college. My father talked me into doing this when I should have said no. So now, I'm sitting in finance class at New York University, waiting for the other students to file inside. Most students are wearing jeans, shorts and ratty t-shirts while I have on a business suit, making me uncomfortable. I'm fiddling with my phone when I look up at a young woman who picks a seat one row in front of me.

I forget my emails to gaze at her. She's beautiful and looks very familiar. I'm not the only one who notices because I see other guys eyeing her. It's obvious she knows what she does to men. Her long blond hair parted to the side in a sexy wave, and she has sapphire blue eyes, which I focus on when she smiles up at me.

She's wearing a tight blue skirt that frames her shapely ass. I get a great view of it when she bends over to take her notebook out of her bag — my cock twitches. I would love to take her out some time, but it would only be a one-time thing once I got her into bed.

I'm not the relationship kind of guy even though my father said I should settle down like my brother, JC. But he was lucky, he found the woman of his dreams, not once, but twice and finally married her. Now he lives with his wife, Lexi, and my nephew, Johnny, in a large apartment overlooking Central Park.

That's not for me. I like variety and normally find a new lady each week to fuck. I don't need the attachments. Anyway, I'm so swamped with my position at my father's company, Lawson Corporation, and now school, that I have no time to play house with someone. I know plenty of twenty-six-year-old men who do the same thing.

I'm daydreaming when I hear a soft voice and feel a tap on my hand. It startles me, and I jump a little.

"I'm sorry. I didn't mean to scare you."

I look at the woman in front of me, and I'm tongue-tied. *Say, something dummy.*

"It's okay. I was thinking about work."

She nods and holds out the paper in her hand. I smile and take it from her, then she turns around and pays attention to the professor in front of the auditorium. The sheet she just handed me is for attendance, I must have missed the instructions, but it looks like students have checked off their names.

I do the same and hand it to the guy a seat over from me. It's then that I realize I'm semi-erect. For fuck's sake, this isn't high school when the turning head of a pretty girl could get you hard. I think horrible thoughts, and my cock goes back to normal.

I'm half-listening to the professor because this is corporate bullshit I deal with day in and day out, budgets, economics, fiscal spending. The only reason I'm here is to complete the business degree I didn't finish four years ago. My father needed me, and I answered. It's his fault I don't have my diploma, now he insists I get it.

At the end of class, I'm itching to get out of here. It's warm, and it feels like they turned off the A/C, it's eighty-eight degrees out, and the suit I'm wearing is making me overheated. I need to go back to the office as soon as I'm finished with class and don't

2020©MJ Masucci

This book is a work of fiction. Any resemblance to actual persons, living or dead, or actual events is entirely coincidental. Although every precaution has been taken to verify the accuracy of the information contained herein, the author and publisher assume no responsibility for any errors or omissions. No liability is assumed for damages that may result from the use of information contained within.

All Rights reserved. No part of this publication may be reproduced, distributed, or transmitted in any form or by any means, including photocopying, recording, or other electronic or mechanical methods, without prior written permission of the publisher, except in critical reviews and certain other noncommercial uses permitted by copyright law.

ISBN 978-1-950175-11-6

want to do it all sweaty. I gather my notebook and pen, slipping it into the soft black briefcase I brought with me and turned to go.

"Excuse me."

I turn to see the beautiful girl who was sitting in front of me. Now she's gently tugging at my sleeve.

"Uh, hi. Do you need something?"

"You could give me more of what you gave me this summer."

Now it's my turn to be surprised. "Excuse me?"

"I want you to fuck me," she whispers.

I wrack my brain thinking of where I know her. A woman like this, I would definitely remember. She is not unlike most of the women I sleep with except that she is. There is a quality about her. She smells wonderful, and I lose myself in her scent for a minute.

"Did you hear me?" she says a bit louder.

"Yes, but I'm sorry, I'm at a loss."

Her plump red lips turn down slightly as she frowns. Why can't I remember where I know her? Surely I would.

"Are you serious?" she says with annoyance lacing her voice.

Most of the students have filed out of the auditorium except for a few stragglers standing with the professor near the podium. It's safe to talk in normal tones because the room is so large, no one will hear us.

"Please forgive me. I definitely would remember someone like you, but I don't."

"Montauk. Fourth of July weekend."

It starts to dawn on me. This beautiful creature I met on the beach when I was renting a house on Montauk for the week with some of my buddies. She was wearing a bright yellow bikini. Her friends had rented a house not far from ours, and she was visiting for the weekend.

I met her the evening before the holiday when we had a small fire on the beach. My friend Matty dared that I couldn't get her to sleep with me. It wasn't that complicated when you look like me.

That might sound arrogant, but it's true. I've never had much of a problem finding women to fuck.

They love running their fingers through my thick sandy brown hair, which I spike up when not in the office. If that doesn't get them, then my eyes the color of milk chocolate or my cleft chin usually does. I spend several hours a week in the gym, sculpting my body with weights and cardio.

"I remember now. Would you like to get some coffee?"

Her frown grows deeper, and lines sprout on her forehead. "I don't think so."

She walks past me in a huff, and I sit there gaping at her ass as she walks up the stairs to the double doors. She doesn't glance at me as she walks through them. I've missed my opportunity to get her under me again. I think hard and try to remember what it was like to fuck her.

When I do, I start to harden. She was wild and very skilled with her mouth. We spent several hours in my bed, and when I woke up, she was gone. In fact, I never saw her again that entire weekend. I ended up sleeping with another woman the next night, but I've thought of her on occasion.

Now I'm wondering what her name is. As I'm heading back to the office on the subway, I search my brain. Her name began with an A, I think. Allie, Alison, Annie, Alaine. I go through a bunch of names before it comes to me, Aurora. I don't think I called her that, though. I think she used a nickname.

I enter the office all sweated up. The short walk from the train in the heat left me with sweat stains on my shirt, so I can't even take my coat off. I plop down in my chair and enjoy the air conditioning for a minute before my father is contacting me on my cell.

"Dad, I'm back. I'm in my office."

He hangs up without saying goodbye, and in two minutes, he's sitting in front of my desk.

"So? Are you going to finish your degree by December?"

"Yes. I have just the two classes, and I'm done."

"Good. I want you to be prepared for when I retire."

"And when will that be?"

"Not for a while, but you still need to be ready. Your brother is so stubborn. I wish he would take my offer and come to work here."

JC is smart. He decided not to take my father's offer and go to work in advertising. He's good, and he once told me that not working under our father was the best decision he ever made. I didn't want to work my way up. I wanted it all from the beginning, though I had to sacrifice finishing my degree.

Maybe if Jonathan Camden Lawson the third weren't such a dick, people wouldn't quit. He's mellowed in the past four years, but he still can be a bastard.

"Are you joining us at your brother's this weekend?" Dad asked.

"I'm not sure. I have some work to do."

"I'm sure your boss can give you some time off," he chuckles.

"Dad, I can't. I have homework."

"Try to make some time."

"I will."

He leaves my office, and I boot up my laptop. I wonder if I can find out where Aurora lives by searching the student directory. I would love to spend the weekend in bed with her. Though it seemed like she was turned off when I said I didn't remember her. The information on the student website is sparse, and there is no address, only her university email. I prefer to wait until I see her in person rather than send her a message.

I spend the rest of the day pouring over figures for the next Lawson planned merger. It's a small construction company, but he wants it, so it's going to keep me busy for the next few days, at least. I find it hard to concentrate because my mind keeps wandering to Aurora.

Since it's Friday, I think I'll head over to one of the bars near the university. Maybe I can get Matty to go with me. It would be nice to have a wingman as good looking as I am. I shoot him a text, and he's game though he wants to go to some of the bars in midtown where there's an older crowd.

I tell him that we'll stay just a little while and then head over to Flanagan's, which is one of our favorite bars. They have draft specials on Fridays, and after the week I've had, I need to unwind. When five rolls around, I'm out to the elevator like a shot. If I stay in my office too long, my father will nag me about going to see JC and his family this weekend.

I love JC, Lexi, and Johnny, but I don't want to get strapped down with boring family time. I'd rather hang out in the park and kick around the soccer ball. Ever since my brother became a father, he never has time to do that anymore.

I meet Matty at one of the bars near campus after eight. It's crowded, and the bar is two-deep for drinks. We finally get our beers and head to the corner in the back of the bar where the pool tables are. There are a bunch of college women too young for us but still plenty hot, trying to shoot pool.

Just my luck, Matty has a black eye and a cut on his cheek. He had a bad time in the ring with his trainer and got leveled. I keep telling him to lay off the boxing before he gets his brains scrambled, but he loves it. It makes him look too tough, and women don't want to be bothered. No one wants to mess with a troublemaker.

However, sometimes there are a few that like a bad boy, which Matty really isn't. He's a real estate agent who usually shows seven-figure properties. His apartment is swankier than mine and right on Central Park West near JC's.

"Nice shiner, tough guy," I say.

"Lucky shot," Matty says as he gives me a light punch in the arm.

"Lucky or you were looking for your in?"

He grins. "I was looking for my in. Bastard hit me before I could read him."

"Isn't that the point?"

"Yeah, I guess it is. As I said, lucky shot. There are no women here. It's a total sausage fest."

I roll my eyes, taking another sip of my beer.

Matty keeps bitching about there being no action here, and then I see her. Aurora. She looks even hotter than this afternoon. She's exchanged her blue skirt and a sleeveless blouse for a slinky black dress that hugs her sexy curves. Just looking at her makes my dick twitch. Matty recognizes her from the beach this past summer.

"Isn't that the girl you fucked on that bet I made you?" he whispers.

I nod. "Yeah, it is. She's in my finance class. I saw her today, but when I didn't remember her, she got pissed."

"How the fuck could you not remember her? You told me she was great in bed. Plus, she's totally hot."

"Because I fuck a lot of women. It's kind of hard to remember all of them."

"You should lay off that for a while."

I shake my head. "Hell no. I can't be you and date one woman for months."

Matty just got out of a two-year relationship with his girlfriend. She was moving to Florida for her job, and he didn't think a long-distance relationship made sense. If you ask me, I think she was hoping for a ring to stay here, but Matty isn't ready for marriage.

"You might want to rethink that one of these days."

"What? Fucking the same pussy over and over. I like the variety."

I do, but shit, if Aurora would want to work out with me in bed for a few days, I'd take it. I play it cool and sip at the remainder of my beer, waiting for her to catch my eye. When she finally does, she turns away and ignores me.

"Ha, looks like she remembers and wants nothing to do with you," Matty says.

I wink at him. "Really, watch this."

Aurora is waiting two-deep at the bar, trying to get a drink. Is she even old enough to be in this place? She looks young, and I could swear she told me she just turned twenty when I saw her in Montauk. But a lot of college kids know where to go to get fake IDs. I bet she has one. I walk up behind her and lean into her ear.

"Hey, do you need help getting a drink?"

Fuck, she smells incredible, even better than this afternoon.

She looks up at me. "No, leave me alone. I'll get my own drink," she growls.

"Come on, Aurora, don't be like that."

She doesn't look at me, waving her hand at the bartender. "Why should I talk to you? You don't even remember who you fuck."

The guy next to me turns his head to stare at the two of us. I give him a smirk, and he turns away. He could be thinking one of two things, one, I'm a total dick or two, good for me because Aurora is gorgeous.

"I'm sorry. I had a lot on my mind this afternoon. I had to go back to work after class. I'm working on this big merger."

"Really? Why are you taking a finance class if you're already in the game?"

"Because my father wants me to finish my degree. I have two classes to go, and I'm done. Tuesdays, Wednesdays, and Fridays, I'll be on campus. So I can see you at least two days a week."

"Who says I want to see you?"

"You don't?"

She looks up at me and smiles the widest smile, and I decide she looks even more beautiful when she's happy.

"Maybe."

"Let me buy you a drink and take you out for some dinner."

"I'm with my friends."

She gestures over to a couple of women, one brunette and the other blonde. They're pretty but can't hold a candle to her.

"Bring them along."

"I'd kind of like to be alone with you."

I brighten because maybe this is going to be my lucky night with her again. But then something happens to me, something that I never felt before. I start to realize I like this woman. I don't want just to take her to bed and forget her.

I put my hand on her arm. "Let's have some dinner. My friend Matty can take care of your friends."

From the corner of my eye, I see Matty watching me, and I gesture for him to come over.

"This is my friend Matthew. Matty, this is Aurora."

"Rory. Only my parents and grandmother call me Aurora, and that's usually when they're angry with me."

"So, if I'm angry with you, I can call you Aurora?"

"No!" she strokes my arm with her thin fingers, which sends shivers down my spine. Oh, I like this woman.

"What happened to your face?" she asks Matty.

"I box and my trainer got a little cute when we were working out."

"Call your friends over. Let's introduce them to Matty," I said.

Aurora's friends are Veronica, a cute little brunette with long pink-painted fingernails, and Ellie, a pretty woman with long blonde hair. I see the look on Matty's face as he grasps her hand, holding on longer than necessary.

When everyone is acquainted, we decide to go to a small Italian restaurant down the block. It's a bit busy even though it's well past nine. I volunteer that we should order a couple of pies and share them. Everyone agrees, and we squeeze five chairs around the small round tables. It's tight, and Rory's knee keeps banging against mine.

While we're waiting for our order, we talk about class. She's very intelligent, and she tells me that she's graduating at the end of December. All through college, she took extra classes even in summer, piling up her workload so she could graduate before four years. I'm impressed and tell her if she's looking for an internship, Lawson can offer that.

"You work for Lawson Corp.?"

"I not only work for Lawson, I am a Lawson."

Her face turns sour, "Is that how you got your job?"

"It is, but I work hard. My father doesn't give me any breaks because I'm his son."

"But, you would never have such a job at your age if you weren't his son."

"How do you know what job I have?"

"You don't remember shit, do you?"

"What don't I remember?"

She glances over at her friends who are engaged in conversation with Matty and not paying attention to us.

"You told me a lot about yourself before we fucked, except your last name and the company you worked for," she whispers.

"If I remember, you didn't tell me much except you attended college in the city."

"I wasn't in your bed for conversation. I just wanted to get laid."

I raise my eyebrows because she sounds like me. That is exactly something that I would say. I've silenced many a chatty Kathy with my mouth or an orgasm.

"Well, excuse me for wanting to talk about myself."

"It seems like you do that a lot."

Is she looking for an argument?

"Sometimes but not always. You can tell me about yourself if you like."

Rory screws up her face. "I don't think you're interested in what I have to say."

"What gave you that idea?"

"I saw how you looked at me today when I handed you the attendance sheet. I bet you were looking at my ass when I bent over to get my notebook."

I can feel my face start to flush as I turn crimson because she's right. How the fuck did she know? Probably because half the freaking guys were sporting hard-ons from that gorgeous ass of hers.

"How could you possibly know that?" I retort.

"Because I do. You think I don't know when guys are looking?"

"I didn't mean anything by it."

"I bet. You don't mind objectifying women."

"Me? What about you. You're not exactly dressed like a nun. If you didn't want to attract men, why not wear something a little less provocative?"

She gives me an icy stare, and I see a fire in her sapphire eyes.

"You're such an asshole. And to think I actually liked you."

This is news to me since she disappeared from my bed before I even woke up. If she liked me so much, then why didn't she stay around? I want to say that to her, but the waiter shows up with our pizza, and our conversation ceases.

I'm starved and practically inhale two slices in about five minutes. It's a good thing we got two large pies because Matty and I finish one on our own. Rory isn't even looking at me while we eat, and I can feel a chill coming off her. She's angry, and the fucked up thing is that it's a major turn-on. If we weren't here with other people, I'd take her in the bathroom and fuck her right now.

I was hoping we could hang out after, but our previous conversation has put a pall over our night. The other women want to hang out with Matty, and I promise them that I'll see Rory home. By the time she starts to protest, they're already half a block away.

"Do you live close? Can we walk?"

"I don't need you to escort me home. I'm fine by myself."

"Hell no. What kind of asshole would I be to let you walk by yourself? It's after ten."

"You are an asshole, and I'll be fine, so go home."

I follow behind because I have no intention of putting her in harm's way by allowing her to walk home by herself at night.

"Stop following me."

"Rory, stop."

I grab her elbow, and she wrenches it out of my grip, speeding up to get away from me. I walk faster and meet her stride for stride in a manner of seconds.

"Hunter, leave me alone, or I'll scream."

I start laughing because I could see her screaming bloody murder.

She stops, crossing her arms over her ample breasts. "Don't laugh at me."

"You're adorable when you're mad."

And she is. She's downright sexy when her eyes flash fire. It makes me want her even more. She flips her blonde hair and starts walking fast again. How the hell can she walk in her heels, they must be five inches high. But she does it until she comes to a building several blocks from the restaurant.

"This is my building. You can leave me now."

"When you get inside."

"You don't need to watch me like I'm a child."

"How old are you, Rory? You're not old enough to be in a bar."

She glares at me. "I'm old enough."

"For what? What are you old enough for?"

"To take care of myself. Now leave, or I'll tell the front desk you're bothering me."

"Fine. Have it your way. I'll see you in class on Tuesday."

"Maybe not. I might drop it."

I whirl around. "Why? Because of me?"

"No. I think I took too much this semester. I have five classes and three and a half years of this has finally gotten to me. I need to enjoy myself. I can take the class next semester and take it easy."

"You could, but then you won't see me. Or you can grin and bear it and intern with Lawson in the winter."

"I have no intention of interning with you."

"You wouldn't be my intern; I don't have any."

"Why? Are you too good for them?" she said.

"No, my position is too involved, and I work with confidential information."

"You really are full of yourself, aren't you?"

"I'm not. But if you want, you can be full of me."

Rory stares at me. "Fuck you, Hunter. You're a pig."

"Why are you getting mad? I'm only echoing what you said to me this afternoon. Did you not ask me to fuck you?"

"Well, after the way you acted, I've changed my mind. I wouldn't give you the time of day."

"You already did by having dinner with me."

"And I gave you too much of my time as it is, now go home."

I cross my arms and stand there as she walks into her building, but as the door is closing, she looks back at me and smiles. I'd love to spend the weekend with her in bed, but it's her choice, and it looks like she's made it.

CHAPTER 2

I start looking for a passing cab so that I can go home. She's made me all hot and bothered, but I would rather have her satisfy me than finding someone else to do it. I could always call one of my friends with benefits, but I decide against it. Normally, I would do it without hesitation, but Rory has gotten under my skin.

I start walking, and I'm two blocks down when my phone rings. The number is unknown, so I let it go to voicemail and put my phone in my back pocket. A minute later, a text comes in, and I fish my cell out to see who it is. Rory. How did she get my number? Then I realize probably the same way I got her email. I think I put it in the student directory a few years ago. I still have the same number for business.

You gave up too easily. Do you want some dessert?

Now I'm not quite sure if she means dessert as in pie or cake or her, and I'm seriously hoping it's her because my cock is aching to be inside her.

Are you offering?

I just told you I was. I let the desk know you're coming. Just tell them who you are. My last name is Barton.

I know it's Barton. I remember seeing it on the attendance roll but only her first initial, A. I wonder if she saw my name on the roll as well.

I'll be up in a minute.

My cock is now hard as a rock, and I need to realize that I'm getting ahead of myself. We might not have sex at all. I'll take what I can get though I would prefer we end up in her bed.

The lobby of the building is nicely decorated with marble floors and light plaster walls with colorful tapestries hanging against them. I nod at the guy at the front desk who's dressed in a suit.

"I'm visiting Aurora Barton."

"Sure, apartment seven D."

"Thanks."

The ride up in the elevator takes forever because several people came in the car with me. They all seem to live on floors below Rory. A guy in jogging shorts gets out on two. Really? You just went running, and you can't walk up one flight of stairs?

When I arrive on her floor, Rory's waiting at the door for me. She's changed from her sexy black dress to yoga pants and a tank top, both of which frame her body beautifully. It's the first time I notice her slightly muscular arms, which has me thinking she works out.

"You got changed pretty fast."

"I wanted to be comfortable. I can change back into the dress if you like."

"No, I want you to be comfortable."

She invites me in and gestures to a small table in the corner of her apartment near her kitchen. The living area is painted in a soft beige that sweeps right into the hallway. The walls are decorated with reproduction paintings by Salvador Dali, Monet, and Picasso. I go over to examine one of them and slyly turn my head to see down the hallway to the bedrooms.

"Would you like a tour?" Rory asks.

"Sure, I guess."

"Follow me."

Gladly because I would follow that beautiful ass anywhere, I can't stop myself from fixating on it as she shows me her roommate, Ellie's bedroom, then hers. Rory's bedroom is the smaller of the two but still has a queen-sized bed taking up most of the wall space. She has a small dresser and a nightstand with a blue and orange lava lamp. The wall is painted a serene light green with a duvet cover to match.

"I used to have one of these when I was a kid."

"What are you implying?"

"Nothing. I just had one. I liked to put it on at night and shut all the lights out."

She

giggles. "I do the same thing."

"Rory, can you be straight with me?"

"What do you want to know?"

"How old are you?"

"I'm twenty. I'll be twenty-one July first of next year."

"So, you're just barely twenty."

"Is that a problem?"

"Sort of. I'm twenty-six."

"I've dated men older than you."

My eyes widen because it's shocking to me that she's dating men seven, eight, maybe ten years older than her. She's barely out of her teens, but I'm glad to know when I had sex with her, she was twenty, not nineteen if even just barely. She's not for me. She's a child, and I'm the vice president of a big corporation. I should be with someone who's at least legally able to drink.

"I should go."

"Why? All of a sudden, you don't want to be here. You were practically begging me before."

A lock of hair fell seductively over her forehead, and I smoothed it away with my thumb.

"You're too young for me. I shouldn't have had sex with you this summer. I'm sorry."

"Do you think I was a virgin? I've fucked men other than you."

"Why, Rory?"

"Because I like sex and sex gives me control."

"Do you like to control men?"

"Not particularly, but I have very little control over things in my life. That's the one place where I can call the shots. Haven't you noticed, men fall all over themselves when I'm around? You did."

"You shouldn't do that."

Rory frowns. "Don't lecture me. You fuck women indiscriminately."

"You don't even know me. How could you say that?"

"I do know you. You're the guy who thinks he can fuck any woman he wants. The guy who loves when women drop their panties when he's around. How many women have you fucked in a bathroom?"

"It's not like that. I don't do that."

"But you fucked me and moved onto the next woman."

"Rory, you left without leaving your number. I never saw you again that weekend. What was I supposed to do? Did you want me to hunt for you?"

Rory chops down on her lip. "You should've. I felt used."

"What about all the men you've fucked?"

"Who said I fucked a lot of men?"

"You did."

"I never said that. I said I like to have control in bed."

"Well, your behavior this summer tells me that sex is just an act for you. You like it, you do it and move on."

Her eyes flash fire, and I know she's getting ready to tear into me.

"You're an assumptive bastard."

"Rory, I'm sorry, but you said you had sex with men other than me. How did you want me to interpret that?"

"I've had sex with two men other than you."

I'm curious when her first time was because she was very skilled when we had sex this past summer.

"You said men. You had sex with men other than me."

"I meant two men. I've dated several men but didn't have sex with them."

"I'm sorry, but when was your first time?"

"When was yours?" she counters

"I was fifteen. My friend's older sister, she was seventeen. Your turn."

"I was sixteen, and he was twenty-three."

My mouth drops open, and I really don't know what to say. Some asshole took advantage of her when she was only sixteen. She could have him arrested for statutory rape. I don't know what to say, but I have to say something.

"How did that come about?"

"It's not important. My parents don't know, and I want to keep it that way."

"Your parents should've been watching you, not allowing someone who I can only term a predator get his hands on you."

"He was kind, and he taught me things. He was also married. My father wasn't in the picture until just before I was seventeen. My mother was busy."

This whole conversation has put a major damper on what I thought I'd come here to do. I no longer want to have sex with Rory. My heart hurts for her having been taken advantage of by a man much too old for a teenager. What an asshole.

"I should go."

"You don't want dessert?"

So there really is dessert. I'm curious what it is.

"Sure. What do you have?"

"Coconut cake. I like to bake, and Ellie won't eat this stuff. She said it doesn't agree with her hips."

"I'm not worried about my hips, so I'll take a big slice."

I'm hoping she's a good baker, or I'm going to have to choke down the entire slice she places before me. I watch as Rory cuts a huge chunk of cake. The coconut flakes onto the counter as she hands me the plate. I take a small forkful, and it's delicious. She stands there, watching me eat with her eyes shining.

"This is fantastic. You're a really good baker."

Rory grins. "You're not just saying that?"

"Nope. I love it. You can make it for me again."

She smiles, and it makes me feel just a tad better about what she told me. It shows me that she's vulnerable and sweet. I feel like a major shit because now that I know her virginity story, it makes me realize I took advantage of her. I feel guilty.

"Or you can come over tomorrow night for study time, dinner and cake."

"Study time? We just started class this afternoon."

"Yeah, but did you see the syllabus. We have to read eighty pages by Tuesday. I heard the professor likes to give pop quizzes."

"Fuck, I can't believe this. I hate quizzes."

I shouldn't worry because school has always been a breeze for me. I'll skim the chapters and do fine, but I'm not telling Rory that. Any chance to spend some time with her is okay with me, even if it's just to study. I want to take things slow, get to know her. It's silly since we already had a night of sex, but I want to. I really like this woman.

I can't wait for dinner with her. The night before, after I finished my cake, I kissed her soft cheek and left with aching balls. The first thing I did when I got home was jerk off to the image of her mouth around me. It wasn't a fantasy since it's one of the things she did when we were together this past summer.

Since last night, I've done it twice more. This is a rarity for me, having a woman get so deep into my brain. But she's barely an adult, and I need to be careful since I think she's more fragile than she lets on. Rory texted me that Ellie is going out with Matty, which means we have the entire apartment to ourselves. It's news to me since Matty doesn't date much since his breakup. He must've had a good time with Ellie the night before.

I wonder what I should bring. Usually, I'll take a bottle of wine to dinner I attend, but she isn't legal, and that would be inappropriate. I could bring a dessert, but that would be insulting since she wants to make me a full meal. Maybe a box of candy would be nice. There's a wonderful little chocolate shop near where Rory lives. I think I'll get some truffles, and hopefully, she'll let me feed her one.

I have no idea what to wear since it's been forever since I went to a woman's apartment for dinner. I decide on a light blue oxford shirt and a pair of dark blue jeans. At 5:00, I head to her apartment. The Uber driver I summoned is outside my building when I get down there. He's driving a Mercedes. A freaking Mercedes! I like the luxury, but geez, if you have to chauffeur people around, then you can't afford a Mercedes.

I ask him to drop me off at the chocolate shop, which is only two blocks from Rory's house. The place smells wonderful, and it's crowded. As I wait in line, I search the display cases for just the right chocolate. I pick two types of truffles, one cocoa-dusted and the other with toasted coconut on the outside.

When I get to her building, the same guy is at the front desk as the night before. He waves me to the elevator, and I press the up button. A woman with a small dog comes in, and I can see her eyeing me in the gleaming steel of the elevator doors. If it were any other time, I would strike up a conversation with her, but I want to see Rory.

The doors open, and I step aside, letting her enter the elevator first. She's young, maybe a bit older than me and very pretty. I give her my million dollar smile before she steps out on the third floor. The elevator continues up to the seventh floor, and when I come out, Rory is waiting. The front desk must have called her.

She looks gorgeous dressed in a short skirt that shows off her curves along with a tight halter top that frames her shapely breasts. Added bonus, her back is bare. Her hair is up, and when I get to her, she smells terrific. I want to bury my face in the ivory flesh of her neck, but I resist and hand her the chocolates instead.

"You didn't have to bring anything."

"That would be rude. I always bring something."

"Did you bring your books."

"You were serious?"

"Of course. I guess we'll have to share."

The apartment smells heavenly, and my stomach starts to rumble at the aroma emanating from the kitchen.

"What's for dinner?"

"I hope you like steak."

"I love it, but I didn't expect you to make that."

"Would you prefer something else?"

"Not at all. I just thought because it's warm out, you would make something lighter. I don't see you like a steak and potatoes type of girl."

"Really? How do you see me?"

"As a salad and yogurt one."

"I have a fast metabolism, so I eat whatever I want. I also workout at least four days a week, sometimes more."

"It shows."

She narrows her eyes at me. "What's that supposed to mean?"

"It means I can see that your arms are toned."

Rory looks over at her bare arms and smiles at me.

"You can sit on the couch. Dinner should be ready soon. I made potatoes au gratin and green beans almondine. I hope you like those."

"I sure do, but you're spoiling me. I didn't want you to go through all this trouble. I could have taken you out to eat."

"We have to study after, so this is perfect."

Rory goes back to what she was doing, and I pick up the finance book sitting on the table. Truth be told, I haven't even picked it up from the bookstore yet. I was planning on it before class on Tuesday. I'm not concerned about the professor's pop quizzes. I've spent so much time in the past five years immersed in finance; I could probably teach the class better than him.

I page through it anyway, smiling as I read through. I know this stuff, and it shouldn't be a problem for me, but I won't tell Rory. I want to be close to her, and if it means faking my way through, then I'll do it.

"Do you want a glass of wine?" she calls.

I do, but how did she get alcohol when she's underage.

"How did you get wine?"

"I have a fake ID, silly. You can get them all over the city for a price. They look pretty authentic, too."

"You shouldn't do that. You can get in trouble."

"I don't want to sit home on the weekends, and most of the clubs will only let you in if your twenty-one."

"Clubs are overrated. You can find something better to do."

"When was the last time you went to a club?"

"A few months ago."

"To find women to fuck?"

"Rory, I don't go to clubs for only that. If it happens, it happens."

She plops down next to me, and her eyes are wide and sad. I think my revelation hurt her.

"Why do you go?"

I don't want to sound nonchalant about it. I find women to satisfy my need to fuck, but that would be too harsh to say.

"I don't do it intentionally. I go, and women come to me. And before you get on me about sounding arrogant, it's true. I'm not a predator. I don't hunt women down and drag them home. They come willingly."

"But don't you feel cheap when you do it?"

"Do you?"

"No, because I do it so rarely."

"So you're saying I'm one of the few one-night stands?"

Rory shakes her head. "I'm saying you're the only one-night stand."

"Before me, you never slept with someone you didn't know?"

"Yes. I haven't slept with a lot of men. I told you that."

"Yesterday, you made it seem that you did."

"I haven't. One man taught me a lot."

My blood starts to boil at the mention of that asshole who preyed on her. Unfortunately, my curiosity gets the best of me, and I ask her.

"How many times did you sleep with him?"

"Quite a bit. He was kind to me."

"He preyed on you and took advantage."

"He didn't. I wanted it as much as he did."

I can see that this conversation is agitating her because she won't look me in the eye, and she's playing with some invisible thread on the hem of her skirt. I can imagine how much this man wanted her. I'm sure even at sixteen, she had gorgeous curves and full breasts. He probably lusted over her for a long time, and when he saw the right time, he seduced her.

"Rory, I'm sorry. I don't want to upset you."

"Dinner should be ready."

She walks away, and I can't help feeling sorry for her. Her first time was with some asshole whose marriage was probably falling apart. He used her so he could feel better about himself. Where the fuck was her mother during all this?

I continue to page through the finance book and skim about thirty pages when she calls me to the small table in the corner. It's nicely done up with a white linen tablecloth and two place settings. My stomach is growling because the last time I ate was at noon, and it's nearing six.

"The table looks beautiful."

"Sit, I'll serve you."

"Can I help?"

"No. You're my guest."

I sit patiently waiting for Rory to serve me, and when she does, the plate looks great. She sliced the steak and watched me while I take my first bite. Wonderful. She must have marinated it because I can taste some spices.

"Everything is great. Thank you."

She smiles and daintily takes a small forkful of potatoes into her mouth. Oh, that mouth. I would love to kiss her and not just there. But then I think about that asshole and concentrate on my food. We're quiet while we eat, barely speaking during the meal.

When dinner is finished and the dishes cleaned from the table, I take over washing them since Rory was so gracious with cooking. We sit down on the couch and share the finance textbook.

Our knees touch, and I feel butterflies in my stomach. I haven't had them since I was a teenager when it comes to girls.

Rory asks me a question about a graph, and I'm not paying attention.

She touches my hand. "Hunter?"

I look up at her. "Oh, sorry, I was thinking about something at work."

"Is this boring for you? Would you rather be doing something different?"

"Not at all. If you want to study, it's fine."

"I didn't ask you that. I asked if you wanted to do something different."

"Like what?"

She takes the book out of my hand and places it on the table, then tips her face toward mine, softly kissing me. I want her more than she knows, and I place my hand on the smooth skin of her back as I deepen the kiss. She moans into my mouth, and I immediately start to harden.

"No, Rory," I say as I pull back. I almost let myself go.

"Why not?" she pouts.

"Because I don't want to seem like I'm taking anything from you."

"You're not taking; I'm offering."

"And the answer is no. You deserve flowers, candy, and dates. I'm not sure I can give those to you."

Rory narrows her eyes. "Why? You've dated before, haven't you?"

This is where it gets sticky because, in my twenty-six years, I've never had a steady girlfriend. I've had women I fuck regularly who escort me to functions, but they could never be termed a girlfriend.

"Define dated?"

"A woman who you take out on dates and spend time. Someone you're monogamous with. You know, a girlfriend."

"Uh, no."

She raises her eyebrows. "Seriously? You've never had a girlfriend?"

"No. That's my brother's thing. He had girlfriends. I have fuck partners, and I don't want you to be one of them."

I realize when the words come out of my mouth, it's the wrong thing to say. Not only because of how harsh it sounds but from the gasp I hear from her. I'm in for a battle.

CHAPTER 3

"How dare you. You don't want to fuck me? You choose now to be chivalrous?" Rory screeches.

I hesitate, staring at the angry blush on her cheeks. I better start explaining before she throws me out. "That's not what I mean. I meant that you deserve better. I don't just want to fuck you."

Rory frowns. "You don't?"

"I do, but that's not the point."

"Please explain the point."

She's angry, and I can see the already familiar fire in her beautiful sapphire eyes.

"The point is that I don't just want to fuck you. You're the type of woman who needs to be dated, taken to dinner and outings. Not just thrown on the bed for some man's pleasure. I don't want to be that guy."

"I don't know if I should be flattered or disgusted."

"Why would you be disgusted? I just said you should be dated. That's not a bad thing, is it?"

"No, but don't I have a say in what I want done?"

"You do, but you're special."

"You think I'm special?"

"I do, and that's why I don't want to fuck you."

"But you don't want to date me either, do you?"

"It's complicated. You're young. You should find someone your own age, not a jaded jerk like me."

"You're not that much older than me, only six years."

"But it's six years of experiences that you haven't had yet. You're very innocent."

"I'm not innocent. Innocence refers to virginal, and I'm not. You of all people should know that. Why the sudden turn around? You had no problem taking me to your bed this past summer."

"Because I know you now. I never would've taken you to bed if I knew you."

"And that makes it different. My body is still the same. Aren't you attracted to me anymore?"

"Rory, I'm more than attracted to you. You're beautiful, intelligent, and sexy. I just don't think this is going to work. I'm sorry. I don't know how to be a boyfriend, and I would just hurt you trying to figure it out."

I rise from the couch before this conversation gets ugly. She looks at me, confused, and I bend down to kiss the top of her head, drawing her scent into my nose as I do. It's intoxicating, and I need to get out of here before I do something I shouldn't.

"I'll see you on Tuesday. Please don't be upset."

She says nothing as I leave her apartment. I feel like crap. I know she's hurting, but I can't give her what she wants. She needs someone close in age and experience. She's better off staying away from me.

It's nice out, and I decide to walk a few blocks before I either hail a cab or summon Uber. On the way, I see a bar I used to frequent when I went to NYU. I guess I'm a hypocrite since I used my brother JC's ID to get into bars when I was underage. I shouldn't tell Rory she can't go to them.

The place is packed, but I'm able to work my way to the bar

and order a whiskey sour. I need a good stiff drink after spending time with Rory. I'm finding it hard to get her out of my head. I just want to have a drink and head home, but I bump into a woman as I turn away from the bar. Some of my whiskey sloshes onto her dress.

She's pretty, but no Rory. Is this how it's going to be? I'll compare every woman to her now. I want to be polite, and I offer the woman a napkin, an apology, and buy her a cosmo. We strike up a conversation, and I introduce myself; it turns out that she works for a company that's done business with Lawson Corp. before. What a coincidence. Her name is Loretta Swann, and she works for the acquisition department at Banover and Sons.

We find a small table just vacated by a few college kids. We slip into the seats and continue chatting. I didn't realize it, but by the time I look at my watch, it's after ten, and we've been talking for three hours. I'm tired, and I want to go home, amazingly, without her. Something has come over me, and I'm not in the mood to just fuck any random woman.

I excuse myself letting Loretta know I need to go home. She seems disappointed that she won't be coming with me, but it wouldn't be a good idea anyway to take someone to bed for a casual fuck who has done business with us.

Outside, the weather has turned, and it's now drizzling. I hail a cab and give him my address. I can't wait to get home and put this night behind me. My mind keeps drifting to the look on Rory's face when I told her I couldn't get involved with her. I feel like a dick.

Sunday, I mope around most of the day. I was supposed to go to JC's for brunch, but I don't feel like it. I text him to let him know that I won't be coming, I use the excuse that I need to read for class before the workweek starts. I'm sure he thinks I have a woman in my bed that I prefer not to leave. He's always getting on my ass about settling down.

In the evening, I sit down and page through the three chapters the professor told us to read. Thanks to the internet, I found a site that had the book in PDF form. I'm not sure how legal it is, but I was able to read the book on my tablet. I probably won't have time tomorrow since my father found a small steel company to take over. He wants me working on the paperwork for the acquisition as soon as possible. That should take up most of my day.

By the time I go to bed, I'm exhausted though I didn't do much all day. I should've at least left the house, but I feel melancholy, and I'm not really sure why.

Monday drags even though I'm so busy that I work in my office all day. I order lunch in and have my assistant bring it to me. My father wants the paperwork sent to legal first thing tomorrow. Plus, I have class tomorrow morning, and I won't be in the office at least until eleven.

I can't wait to see Rory, and I toss and turn most of the night. The next morning I wake up with a raging hard-on, more than likely because I had a dirty dream about her. I need some relief and find it when I go into the shower. I'm excited to see her though I know she probably hates me. I hadn't heard from her since Saturday night when I walked out.

I decide to take a cab from my apartment to NYU. I prefer not to be sandwiched in like cattle on the subway. It also gives me time to enjoy my coffee and bagel I picked up at a deli not far from my house. I wish I could've worn jeans, but since I need to go to the office after class, a suit is in order.

When I get to the auditorium, Rory is already there, and she's not sitting in the seat she sat in on Friday. She's sitting several rows down from there and me. There's a guy with short inky black hair sitting next to her, and I shoot daggers at the back of his head. She keeps turning around, and when she spots me, she puts her hand on the guy's shoulder. *Real mature, Rory.*

Now I'm annoyed, and I concentrate on the last of my coffee and the emails that keep chugging in on my phone. From the corner of my eye, I can see Rory continuing to glance back at me, but I ignore her. If she wants to act like that, then I was right in my assumption she was too young for me. She's acting like a middle school girl.

The professor comes in holding a bunch of papers, and I hear someone whisper behind me; it's a pop quiz. I'm not worried because I skimmed the book on Sunday, and I remember most of it. He hands the stack of papers to the front row, and they pass them back until we all have one, and he collects the extra.

Rory gives me one last glance before she bends her head over the desk to work on the quiz. I check out all the questions and whiz through in five minutes, then start playing with my phone.

"Uh, Mr. Lawson, is it?"

My head shoots up, and the professor is pointing at me and holding the attendance roll.

"Yes, sir?"

"Are you cheating?"

"Absolutely not. I'm finished."

"You're finished? Well, why don't you come up here and let me grade your quiz."

The last thing I want is to become a spectacle, but I have no choice but to bring him my quiz. I slowly walk down the stairs to the podium with all eyes on me and hand him my quiz. I look over my shoulder and see Rory staring at me until I meet her gaze, then she looks away.

I wait for the professor to grade my quiz, and I'm not surprised I get a perfect score. It was easy, and I do this crap every day. This class is going to be a cakewalk for me.

"Very good, Mr. Lawson. Please keep your phone in your pocket on quiz and test days."

"Yes, sir. Thank you."

Rory looks up at me, and I smile widely at her as I head back to my seat. The quiz lasts fifteen minutes more before the professor collects them, and I'm bored. This class is boring. I wish they had a test I could take to pass it and get out. If not for the attendance policy, I would skip it and just come in for quizzes and tests.

So now I'm not only pissed that I have to be here to learn material I already know, but also watching Rory flirt with this poor unsuspecting bastard. She's doing it to get me jealous. She keeps touching his arm or shoulder and glancing back at me. I keep my eyes on my notebook and draw while the professor is talking.

At the end of class, I quickly gather my things to get out of there before I have to deal with any more of Rory's nonsense. I don't want to talk or look at her. Luckily we don't have class until Friday. I get three days away from being around her.

I hurry out of class, and as I do, I hear her laughing. I don't know why it ruffles my feathers, but the last time I heard it, it was for me. A wall of heat hits me as I head out on the street, and I remove my suit jacket as I look for a cab. I hope it's air-conditioned. My father has been blowing up my phone about a paragraph I wrote into the merger paperwork.

It's not like this is the first time I've done this. He can correct the paragraph if he doesn't like the wording rather than pissing me off. I think for now on when I have class; I'm dressing casually. As long as we don't have client meetings, I can wear jeans and a dress shirt.

Wearing suits to class when everyone else is in shorts and t-shirts makes me feel strange. Like I'm so much older than these other students. I battle a professor for a cab that just put on his "on duty" sign. Fortunately, the driver is blasting the air conditioner, and I lay with my head back against the seat and enjoy the cool air wafting back. Traffic is light, and I'm at the office in a matter of fifteen minutes. When I enter, my father is in a mood.

"What's the problem?" I ask as I settle into my chair.

My father crosses his legs and puts his arm behind the back of the chair. "The deal is dead with Richard Bancroft. He had some financial constraints. We don't have the capital to move ahead since we have so many in-progress projects right now."

I sigh. "It might be for the best. That property needed a lot of clean up."

My father grumbles. "But it's waterfront. Do you realize the potential?"

I lean back in my chair. "I do, but our finances won't allow it unless we can find another partner."

"I'm well aware, Hunter, that's why I'm the boss. You need to change the wording on the merger paperwork. R.C. Fields will not sign off without it."

I nod, not paying full attention. I often question whether I have the stones to take over this business. Sometimes I feel bad for the companies we swallow up. Most of the time they're small second or third generation with a good client base. They fall on hard times, and instead of picking up the pieces, they sell. My father is like a piranha; he can smell blood in the water. I think he's even more astute than some of the attorneys he has working in the legal department.

"We missed you at your brother's this weekend," he says after he bitches and complains about the wording.

"I know, and I'm sorry. I would've loved to see everyone, but I had to study for my class. The professor gave a pop quiz today."

"And?"

"What do you think?"

He raises his eyebrows and smiles slyly. JC and I are the spitting image of my father, except his hair is salt and pepper, and his eyes are blue. We get our cleft chins and square jaws from him. I can see why my mother fell in love with him. He's charming to a fault, and even at fifty-seven, I can see women swoon when he walks in a room.

Not that he would ever cheat on my mother. She's a saint for putting up with him since he can be an impossible pain in the ass at times. She always knows how to calm him after a tough day. JC is like him now that he's married to Lexi. Before, he was more like me, though he did have some long-term girlfriends.

However, I'm stuck on that little brat Rory. All I've done is think about her all weekend and how much I want to make love to her. That in itself tells me I'm in trouble because I usually say fuck. But I don't merely want to fuck Rory; I care about making it a very pleasurable experience for her even if it isn't for me.

My head is in the clouds thinking about her in that tight skirt I saw her wearing the first day I got into class. When she bent over, I thought I would die.

"Hunter? We have that call in the conference room."

"Oh yeah, sure."

As I walk toward the room, my phone vibrates, and I slide it out of my jacket pocket to see who texted me.

Why didn't you tell me you're a genius?

It's Rory, and I'm not sure I want to text her back. I'm still pissed at her immature behavior this morning. I thought I got past this bullshit when I graduated high school. I decide not to be a jerk and reply.

I'm not a genius. I just know the material.

How? You barely touched the book when you were here.

. . .

I don't mean to be rude, but I have a conference call. I'll speak to you later.

I slip the phone back into my pocket and enter the conference room. My father is already there with two of his attorneys, more boring shit. I listen with half an ear because it really is more for the attorneys than me.

When we finish with the call and discussion, it's nearing five, and I'm ready to call it a day. As I walk out of the conference room, I check my phone, and there's a text from Rory.

If you have to say you don't mean to be rude, then you are.

I smirk. She takes things personally. I'm sure if I don't try to smooth things over, she'll pull the same crap she did today. I bet the poor sap she was sitting with thinks he has a chance. Even if she did date him, she would chew him up and spit him out. Rory is very strong-willed and needs someone to keep her in check. Someone, she can't just bat her eyelashes at and get her way. I think I want to be that guy.

CHAPTER 4

The heat outside is still oppressive, even more so with the throngs of people leaving work. I begin to sweat as I cross the street, narrowly getting missed by a cab trying to make the yellow light. He blares his horn at me as he whips around me. I'm in no mood for the subway and raise my hand to hail a cab.

The air conditioning in my apartment is more than welcome. The cab driver had the windows open and refused to shut them. What happened to customer service? I need a drink after all the bullshit I dealt with today, a nice glass of vodka on the rocks with a twist of lime. I strip down and get out of my uncomfortable suit, slipping on a pair of shorts and nothing else. I'm in for the evening, so I deserve to be relaxed. I have several takeout boxes in the refrigerator but don't feel like leftovers.

I make myself some cereal, which is my favorite dinner. It's typical bachelor food, but I have no parents I need to give answers. While I'm eating, I check my student email. The professor has emailed our quiz grades. He shouldn't have bothered since I already knew mine, one hundred. I settle onto my couch, flipping through the channels with the remote and sipping what's left of my vodka.

I'm watching a ballgame, Yankees/Red Sox, when I get a knock at my door. The front desk didn't contact me, which is strange. When I open it, there stands, Rory, the look on her face is not good, and I wonder why she chose me to come for comfort. She's wearing a tiny shirt that shows her navel and a pair of cutoff jean shorts. She smells fantastic.

"What's up? I thought you were angry at me."

Rory bites the corner of her lip. "I am, but I need your help."

"Oh, you want something, so you come to bother me?"

"You're good at this stuff."

"What stuff?"

She barges in, uninvited. I'm amused and follow her to my oversized kitchen in the wake of her perfume. She's perfectly at home and opens the refrigerator to grab a bottle of water like she lives here. How did she even know I had water in there?

"Finance. I studied, and I suck."

"Rory, can you make sense?"

"I got a sixty-eight on the quiz. I need to maintain at least a B+ in that class."

"It's just a quiz."

"But you can only drop two, and the professor gives them all semester. They're worth twenty-five percent of our grade."

"It was jitters. You'll do better on the next one."

"I have to, and I need you to help me. I have such a heavy course load. I can't study all that and this too."

"Why do you have to graduate in December? Why not make your life easy and drop a couple of classes. Then next semester, you can intern for me and take them."

She looks up and stares at me. It's like she just noticed that I'm only wearing shorts because I see her eyes follow the muscles of my chest down to my stomach. I feel like a piece of meat, but I did do it to her. Her dreamy blue eyes fix on mine.

"Because I have to. I want to get my life started. My parents are over-bearing, especially since they married."

"You're parents got married? I thought you said your father didn't come into your life until you were seventeen."

"He did. He was engaged to someone else, and I contacted my uncle, who contacted my father. From there, it was like they'd never been apart. The woman he was engaged to broke up with him, but I don't know what happened, he never said. Anyway, I heard she was married to someone else now."

The story is sounding very much like my sister in law Lexi's life before she married JC. I'm curious, and I ask her what her father's name is.

"Noah Wilton."

I cough. Now I'm freaking out because Lexi told me that Rory was a little bitch and nasty to her. She never mentioned her name, but it has to be her, how many people have the same story? This is not good.

"Why do you ask?"

"Just curious."

"Anyway, are you going to help me?"

"No. I can't. I have so much shit going on that I won't have time."

Rory stares at me like I told her she had a bird on her head, then walks toward me and runs her hand down my chest. I grab her hand because it's just like I said, she'll try to wrap me around her finger to get what she wants.

"Rory, I said no."

"Some friend you are," she says in a huff.

"Oh, we're friends?"

"I never stopped being your friend. You're the one who walked out."

"I walked out because it isn't right that I want you as much as I do. You're too young for me. What about that guy you were with today?"

"He did worse than me. He got a sixty."

"You can't use people to get what you want."

"You did."

"When did I?"

"This summer. You fucked me."

I frowned. "Don't put that shit on me like you weren't into it. I didn't force you, and I'm pissed off you would even imply that I did."

"So, you're not going to help me?"

"Rory, it's best we're not friends. You can probably ask the professor who can help you with some tutoring. I think you should leave."

"You're throwing me out?"

"No, I'm politely asking you to go."

She puts her hands on her hips. "Great. I'm going, but if I fail, it's on you."

"His quizzes are straight forward. Study the text, and you'll do fine."

"Thanks for nothing, Hunter."

I follow her to the door, which she swings open and walks through. I watch as she walks to the elevator, not giving me a look back. I feel bad, but now that I know who she is, it's an even worse idea to get involved with her. If I know that, why do I still want her so badly?

I need JC. He is the only one that will understand this situation and how to handle it. He might be pissed at me for not going to his apartment this past weekend, but I text him anyway.

I need to talk to you. This is something you can't tell Lexi about.

What the hell have you gotten yourself into?

. . .

Nothing bad, at least not yet. It's just that I need my big brother's advice before I do something stupid. Can you get some time today or tomorrow?

I can meet you today. Lexi took Johnny to Megan's, and I'm just hanging out at home. Do you want to go to Central Park and kick the soccer ball around? We could go for a couple of beers if you don't want to do that.

Sure. I'll meet you in the park at 6:00 PM.

I scramble to get to the park since it's nearly six. JC is waiting at the entrance. It's nice to see my brother. We were always pretty close, and I'm glad that I have him to use as a sounding board. We're both dressed in shorts and tank tops, and JC is holding a soccer ball, but I'm not in the mood.

"Can we just sit?"

"Hmm, must be serious if you're declining to kick the ball around," JC says.

We head to one of the empty benches away from people walking around the park. JC plops down next to me. I start digging at the chipping green paint on the bench slat near my leg, not looking at my brother.

"What's going on? You haven't asked my advice for a while."

"It's a girl."

He laughs. "Isn't it always."

"Not always, but this one is a problem."

"Okay, so tell me what the problem is."

I look up at JC. "First, she's young, only twenty. Second, and please keep an open mind, she's Noah's daughter."

JC sighs loudly. "Rory?"

"Yes. She's in my finance class."

"And you want to get her into bed?"

I look at my jogging sneakers. "I already have. The week I was in Montauk for July Fourth. I didn't know it then. I knew her name, and, in my defense, I didn't know she was Noah's daughter."

"How did you find out? Did it just come up in conversation?"

"She told me about her father and mother getting married not too long ago. I questioned her, and she told me her father's name. I remember him from that time we were at Brianna's parent's house in the Hamptons a few years ago."

"You know she's off-limits. Lexi would have a fit if she found out. Move on. You never had an issue with doing that."

"I can't get her out of my head. I want her so much, but I know it's going to cause problems, and I love Lexi. I don't want her to be upset with me."

"Hunter, Rory was not very nice to Lexi. She said some nasty things when her relationship with Noah was ending. I don't need your relationship dredging up things from the past, especially now."

"What's going on with her? Is she sick?"

JC smirks. "No, she's pregnant. We just found out, and we're not telling anyone for a few more weeks. You need to keep it quiet."

I raise my eyebrows. "Congratulations. You're working fast."

"Well, Johnny is two now, and we want more children. Lexi's going to be thirty-three soon, and she wants to avoid complications with having children when she's older. We want at least three."

"I guess if that's the case, then you're going to have some busy times in bed."

"It's not very hard. I love her to death. Maybe one day you'll feel the same way about someone, and you'll get it."

I think I already do. I think I'm in love with Rory. Holy fuck, did I just think that I'm in love with her?

"Hunter?"

"Oh yeah, sorry. What did you say?"

"I said you should find someone older, more suitable for you, not a kid."

"But what if she's the one?"

"I'm sure it's just a passing phase. Find someone in the same career space as you. Rory is young and not for you."

We talk for a little while longer, and I understand what he's saying, but I'm not sure that my emotions do. I need to go home and think long and hard about what I want. I hug him, and we head in the separate directions of our apartments.

∞

At home, I can't get Rory out of my head. Just thinking about how good she smells turns me on. She's always so perfectly coiffed. Perfect hair, gorgeous full red lips, flawless skin, and she dresses stylishly. Who wouldn't want her for a girlfriend or a wife?

Whoa boy! Are you talking about marriage? You barely know this girl. You haven't even dated her. The turn-around in a couple of weeks is amazing. I'm sitting here on a Friday night thinking about her when usually I'm out partying with whoever is free. I need to get her out of my system. Maybe a night out will help. I haven't been for almost a week.

I call Matty, and he doesn't answer his phone. My soccer buddies are at a tournament in Boston for the weekend, so I'm on my own if I want to go out to a club. I don't by myself. In fact, I think it's more that I'm afraid to give in to temptation and take a woman to my bed rather than deal with my feelings for Rory. I have a huge dilemma and three days to think about it.

The weekend is spent studying for my two classes, not like I need it and watching a shitload of sports, baseball, college football, and the NFL. It's rainy out now that the fall is here, and I'm not in the mood to even go around the corner to the deli to get my Sunday coffee and bagel.

I can't get Rory out of my head or the smell of her perfume out of my nose even though it's been a couple of days since she's been here. Tuesday can't come soon enough. I know I won't be able to talk to her, I think she hates me, but at least I can see her pretty face. Of course, if that guy is hovering around her, it's going to get me pissed.

I convinced my father that on days I have class, I don't want to wear a suit. He agreed as long as I keep one in the office in case we have a client meeting. I take extra care to dress today. Tight jeans and a form-fitting sweater that shows off my chest. I spray some cologne on and spike up my hair rather than comb it to the side. It's finally sunny out, and I slip on my sunglasses before I exited the cab.

A vendor is selling coffee on the sidewalk, and I buy a cup. It's my third, but I want to make sure I get to class after Rory's there. When I get into the classroom, she's indeed there and sitting with that poor sap. Today, she has her hair up, and she's wearing little dangly earrings. I want to kiss the back of her neck and inhale her delicious perfume.

I catch her glancing back as the professor hands out another quiz. It seems like each day he's giving one. I finish it quickly and then sit there waiting. He sees me and gestures to come down so he can grade it. I see Rory watching me from the corner of her eye as I stand next to him.

"Another perfect score, Mr. Lawson."

"Thank you, sir."

"You can head back up to your seat."

I give Rory the widest grin as I walk by, and she scowls at me. She's gorgeous even when she's angry. Class drags, and I play with my phone, occasionally doodling in my notebook. Notes are a waste of time. I know this stuff pretty well. I can't wait to get out of here.

"I've posted partners for the project due next month. If you're not aware, please check the syllabus," The professor says.

I wonder who my partner will be. I hope it's someone who works and won't dump it in my lap.

When I head to the front to look at the posting, I'm shocked. He put Rory as my partner. Now I can't stay away from her, and that's not going to work for me. I watch Rory as she runs a black painted nail down the list and stops at her name. She whirls around and narrows her eyes while brushing past me; then, she's gone. I wait for the room to empty.

Professor Stanish turns to me. "Is there something I can do for you, Mr. Lawson."

I nod. "Sir, I can't work with Rory Barton."

He raises his eyebrows. "Is there an issue?"

"I was hoping for someone a little older."

"Mr. Lawson, that isn't a good excuse not to work with someone. Young or old, you're all students and should act professionally. I have a reason for putting her with you."

"And that is?"

"She seems to be struggling, and the young gentleman she sits with is not the best student. I need her with someone who has a good grasp on the subject, and you do. She asked me if I can recommend a tutor. You're turning out to be my best student, so what better tutor than you."

"Fine. I hope she's up for the challenge."

"I'm sure with a little gentle prodding; she will be."

"Thank you, sir."

FUCK, this is my fault. If I just helped her with the quizzes, then she might not be my partner. This project is going to require research, and that takes time; time I don't want to spend with her because I'm afraid of where it might lead.

∽

When I walk into the office a little later, my head is in the clouds, and I sit at my desk daydreaming about Rory until I head to the conference room for a scheduled meeting. Several executives are sitting around the table, and of course, I'm the only one dressed in jeans and a dress shirt. The meeting proceeds with my father at the helm.

"Hunter!"

I look up to see everyone staring at me. My father's face is fire red.

"Are you listening to me?" he roars.

I stutter. "I...what was your question?"

He pounds his fist on the table. "If you're not interested, maybe you should go home. I need your attention."

Gladly, I wish I could say, but I don't. "I'm sorry."

"I want to see you in my office."

I sigh as my father wraps up the meeting, knowing I'm in for a lambasting. I follow my father to his office, trudging along as if I'm heading to a firing squad.

"Sit," he growls as he closes the door after me.

"Dad, I'm..."

He opens his gray jacket as he sits down. "Don't you dare apologize. What's with you?"

"I'm swamped. You gave me plenty of work to do, and with the two classes I'm taking, it's a lot."

My father strokes his chin. "You're up for it. I bet you aren't bothering to study. You could probably teach the class."

"I still have reading to do and now a project with a partner."

"One semester. Try to keep it together, and soon you'll have your degree."

I want to tell him I would've had it if he didn't yank me out of school in my senior year, but once again, I keep my mouth shut.

"I sent you a few requests via email. I need you to get the paperwork to me no later than tomorrow afternoon, is that understood?"

"Yes. I'll take care of it."

"See that you do. Now, if you excuse me, I have lunch scheduled with your mother."

"Enjoy. Tell her I said hello."

∼

Once I'm settled at home and eating my dinner of another huge bowl of frosted flakes, my phone rings. I ignore it and let it go to voicemail. It rings again, and I once again ignore it to read the sports page. When I'm finished, I listen to the voicemails. Rory.

"Did you have anything to do with us being partnered today? I hope not. We can work together, but nothing more."

The second one is much more aggressive.

"I think you did have something to do with today. If you want to get together, tell me. Don't go behind my back and suck up to the professor. Call me so we can work out a schedule. I need a good grade."

I listen to the messages several more times, and when I get finished, I'm hard. Fucking hell, how am I supposed to work with Rory when her voice gets me aroused? I might as well call her and get it over with, then think better of it and text her.

Got your message. I had nothing to do with the professor putting us as partners. Was just the luck of the draw. When do you want to get together?

. . .

How about tonight. I'm not busy, and tomorrow my class starts at eleven.

Fine. You want me to come to you, or you want to come to me?

I'll come to you. Ellie has Matty over, and they're driving me nuts.

I smile. So that's where he's been. They must have hit it off if Matty has been spending all his time with Ellie. I haven't heard from him in days. Matty sure didn't take long to find his next girlfriend.

I'll see you soon. Just come up. I'll let the desk know you're coming.

CHAPTER 5

I run around my apartment, fixing things. I left some dishes in the sink and put them in the dishwasher. The garbage stinks, and I take that out to the incinerator shute. After, I check the hall bath to make sure it's clean. I don't know why, but I check the master bathroom too. Rory isn't going to be in there, but I do it anyway.

The last thing is change from the sweats I'm wearing to a pair of ripped, worn blue jeans and a polo shirt. I'm sitting on my couch reading the paper when she knocks.

I check my breath before I let her inside. "Hi, Rory," I say when I open the door.

Shit, she's gorgeous in tight black jeans and a light green sweater. She's wearing lip gloss, and I want to devour her. Her perfume is driving me crazy, and she just walked in the door.

"Where do you want me to sit?" she asks.

If I tell her the truth, she'll punch me because it's my lap. I gesture to the couch. My heart starts to flutter when we sit down next to each other. I can't stop myself, and I pull her toward me and kiss her softly on the lips. She responds then pushes against my chest with her hands.

"What are you doing?" she demands.

"Something I've wanted to do for the last week. I tried Rory, I really tried. I need you in the worst way."

"Need me how?"

"In my arms, my life, maybe even my bed."

She hesitates and leans back, staring at me. I see her eyes brim with tears.

"Say something?"

"I thought you didn't want me. You said I was too young."

"I tried not to, but I can't. You are too young, but I don't care."

Rory crawls onto my lap and presses her lips to mine. I can taste the flavor of the lip gloss, bubble gum. I run my hands up and down her back, holding her to me. I move my mouth from her lips to her neck, the one that I've wanted to kiss all day. I wish she kept her hair up like this morning.

I deeply inhale her perfume and lick until I get to the hollow at the base of her throat, then I suck. She winds her hands into my hair and gently tugs at the curls near the collar of my shirt. I groan her name. In no time, I'm hard as a rock.

"Take me to your bed," she whispers.

"No, it's too soon."

She pulls back and looks at me. "This again? We've already had sex. Why is it an issue now that you know me?"

"Because you deserve better. I treated you like a piece of meat this summer, and I won't make the mistake again."

Rory bites her bottom lip. "Hunter, I need you to fuck me. I don't care about flowers, candy, and dates. I just want you."

I shake my head. "I don't want you to think I'm using you."

"Maybe I'm using you."

I smirk. "Well, then that's different."

"Please, I need to feel you inside me. I've been aching for you since I saw you in class that first day."

Rory is echoing my sentiment. I want her more than she knows. I lift her in my arms and carry her to the bedroom. She buries her head in my neck and gently bites me. It sends shockwaves down to my balls. I put her down to pull back the covers, and when I turn around, she's halfway undressed.

"Let's go slow."

"I don't want to."

She takes my hand and thrusts it into her open jeans, pushing it down. I curl my finger and slide it into her cleft. She's soaking wet, and now my cock is so hard that it hurts. I can't go slowly; I need to fuck her and make it up to her later. The next thing I know, we're tearing at our clothing until we're standing naked in front of each other. She scrambles on the bed on all fours, but I don't want that. I want to see her face when I make her come.

"Rory, I want to see you, lie back."

She does, and I'm not paying full attention to her because I'm searching around my nightstand drawer for the condoms. I find them and pull one off the strip. There are five left and the way I feel; I'm sure I'll use them all tonight. I place it on the nightstand and turn to her.

I gasp because she looks so beautiful bathed in the soft light of the lamp. Her rosy nipples are hard atop her perfect breasts. I want to kiss them, and I do. I dip down and suck first one, then the other. She moans my name, and it's the sweetest sound I've ever heard. I work my way down her body, kissing and biting, marking her flesh with the brand of my teeth.

I want her to be mine; no one else can have her. Her hands are in my hair, scratching at my scalp. I stop what I'm doing, and I climb back up to hover over her, looking into her sapphire eyes which have gone dark with desire. Her nails rake the muscles of my chest, and she pinches my nipples.

"Hunter, I need you."

I want to taste her first. Taste that glorious nectar I had a sample of this past summer. I quickly get between her legs, kneading the soft flesh of her inner thighs before I touch her with the tip of my tongue. She moves her hips toward my face, wanting to feel more of my touch.

I slip two fingers inside her soaked opening, she is more than ready for me, and I want to be inside her. After a minute of teasing her with my fingers while I suck on her clit, I move away, and she protests with a loud groan. But it's only for a few seconds while I tear at the condom wrapper with my teeth, unfurling the latex onto my cock.

"Sweetheart, are you ready for me?"

"I've been ready for weeks."

I position myself in front of her and thrust until I'm almost fully inside her. I hear her inhale as I enter, and I hope I haven't hurt her. I give her a few seconds to acclimate to my size, and then I begin to move. She feels so snug, and I wish I could feel her without the latex between us.

Rory spreads her legs wide, almost until one is hanging off the bed. I would prefer she wrap them around my waist, but I'm going to let her call the shots on this one. Her eyes are closed, and she's got her lower lip between her teeth as if deep in concentration. Low moans are continuously coming from her until she grows close, then I hear my name several times.

"Hunter, Hunter, Hunter…"

She tightens, and I know in seconds, she's going to explode around me. I work my hips hard, and the room is filled with the slapping of flesh as our hips come together. I feel her pulse, and Rory begins to climax with my name spilling loudly from her mouth. I press my lips against hers, spearing my tongue between them.

I try to make it last, but as soon as she comes, I'm done. I begin to pound into her as I release, taking several strokes until I empty myself into the condom. I don't know if it's the euphoria or needing to get out what I've wanted to say for a while, but I say it.

"I love you, Rory." I can't believe I'm telling her my true feelings. I barely know her, but I can't deny the truth. She's claimed me.

She keeps her eyes closed and says nothing, but I can see a tiny smile blooming on her face until I can see all her perfectly straight teeth. She opens one eye, then the other to look at me.

"I knew it."

I'm annoyed because I expected to hear it back. I pull out of her a little too roughly, and I hear her gasp because I'm still hard.

"I'm sorry. That wasn't the response I expected."

"What did you expect me to say? That I love you too?"

"Maybe."

"Well, don't worry, because I do. I think I've loved you from the first time I saw you this summer on the beach, maybe before."

I grin. "So, love at first sight?"

"Yes, for me. I'm sure it wasn't that way for you."

"I'm not sure, but does it matter? I love you now. You're irresistible."

"Funny, but you didn't say that this afternoon."

"How could I? You had that poor sap all over you. I couldn't say a word without him following after you like a puppy dog."

"Bauer is just a friend."

"Rory, he likes you, and you were leading him on to get me jealous."

She looks away from me. "Just a little. But he knows I only want to be friends."

"Does he? You need to be careful. Sometimes guys are aggressive to get what they want."

I climb off the bed to throw the condom away. When I come back, she's on her stomach with her head on the pillow. Her shoulders and upper back peek out of the sheet, and I lean down to kiss them, inhaling her scent. She smells like perfume, sex, and something I can't put my finger on, but I like it.

"Come to bed," Rory mumbles into the pillow.

"Sweetheart, it's only 7:45. Are you sleeping over tonight?"

She turns onto her back as I climb over her and slip under the sheet.

"Do you want me to sleepover? Are we a thing now?"

"I told you I love you. Do you think this is a thing? Do you want this to be a thing?"

"I do very much, but I know you're gun shy. You were very resistant last week, and it hurt me."

"I didn't mean to. I just thought you should be with someone less experienced."

"You mean at sex?"

"No, I mean at life. I have six years on you. I've done a lot and seen a lot."

Rory turns on her side to look at me. "What have you done, and where have you been?"

"I've been to Europe, Africa, Australia, South America, Canada, all over. I've been skiing in the Alps and hiking in the Outback. I ran with the bulls in Pamplona, not the smartest thing, but it was fun. I've done many things."

"I've been all over from the time I was a freshman in high school. My mother wanted me to become worldly, so we took trips everywhere. I've skied and snowboarded in the Alps, too. So don't let my age fool you."

She glares at me, and I smile. I'm in awe that someone so young has had the same experiences as me.

"So, what's your verdict? Are you staying?" I ask.

"Yes, I brought a few things with me."

I start to laugh because Rory knew what I thought before I even thought it. I wanted her to stay with me.

"Should I give you a drawer?"

"Maybe in a few weeks. I don't want to shack up with you."

"What do you want to do with me?"

"I want you to make love to me again."

So now we're no longer saying fuck, we're saying make love.

"I can, but I want to go slowly this time."

"I also want to discuss a few things like former partners."

"Why is that such a problem for you? I haven't been with many."

"Rory, I'm not questioning how many men you've been with, but if you've ever been tested for STDs. You never know."

"I was several months ago and haven't been with anyone else since July when I was with you. What about you?"

Now it's my turn to look away. "I'm not going to lie. I've slept with quite a few women, and I usually get tested every few months. This might be selfish to say, but are you on birth control?"

Rory frowns. "Why is it selfish?"

"Because if we're monogamous, then I want to make love to you without a condom. I hate them but wear them because I don't want a disease."

"It's not selfish. I've been on birth control since him."

She won't say the name of her first love, which leads me to believe it might be a little traumatic since I brought up that I thought he was a predator. But I'm curious if the son of a bitch took her so he could fuck her without a condom.

"Did he take you to the doctor?"

"No, I went to the clinic in Boston myself."

I think of a beautiful, innocent Rory going downtown to a clinic by herself because this asshole wanted to have his way with her without a condom. He didn't care if he infected her. I feel myself getting angry and think that if I ever see him, I'll punch him square in the nose.

Rory strokes her fingers over my cheek. "Hunter? Say something."

"I just think it sucks that your first time wasn't with someone you loved."

"It doesn't matter. It was over four years ago."

It dawns on me that she was barely sixteen when this guy seduced her. I try not to show my annoyance, but she sees it written all over my face.

"I was sixteen. Stop thinking about it. You might meet him someday."

"And if I do, I'm going to confront him. Is he still with his wife?"

"No, they broke up a couple of years ago."

"Good, he deserves it."

"Can we not talk about this? You mentioned something about making love to me again."

"My, you're a demanding little one."

"I know what I like."

"I'm going to teach you to love it," I growl.

She looks at me with innocence as I move toward her.

CHAPTER 6

I throw back the sheet and get in between Rory's legs. I want to taste her. I have her scent on my fingers, and I don't think I want to wash them. I start by teasing her, kissing and licking her inner thighs. She is anticipating, and I keep glancing up at her face. I'm fascinated by the little landing strip she has on her pubic area. She has a little heart shaved into the sparse hair, and I'm not even going to ask how she managed that.

I kiss it and work my way down to her smooth outer lips, kissing and nipping. She hisses as my tongue strokes her folds then withdraws. She tastes better than any dessert, and I keep teasing until I hear her whimper, then I move in. I insert my tongue into her now soaked opening, fucking her with it. She murmurs my name, and it makes me smile. I want to be the only one to make her come from now on.

Her breathing is getting heavier, and I can't get enough of the taste of her. I take long licks from her opening to her clit, tickling the tip with my tongue. Rory is making these loud moans, and my cock is aching to be in her again. But I want her to come before I do that. I know she's growing closer with each stroke of my tongue.

I finally concentrate on just her clit, circling the swollen nub with my tongue. She bucks with each swirl then I feel her hands in my hair, pushing me down against her as she starts to orgasm. She's moaning my name, and it's so erotic to hear it come out of her mouth.

When she finishes her release, her hands relax but remain in my hair, stroking it. I lick whatever nectar I can, and she shifts her hips, pulling away because she's sensitive. I back off and climb her body to look at her gorgeous face.

She's lying there with a cute little smirk, and I softly kiss her lips.

"You've done that before, haven't you?"

She says it so seriously I thought she meant it until she starts to giggle.

"Of course, I've done it to numerous women. It's how I've become so good at it. I know what gets a woman going."

"You're silly."

"Looks like you have a problem you need to deal with," Rory says as she points at my erection.

Her small hand encircles my dick. It throbs at her touch as she slowly strokes it.

"I'd like to return the favor."

Rory starts to sit up, but I gently push her down. I prefer to make love to her then have her give me a blowjob. The change in me is profound in such a short time. Normally I would welcome a blowjob, but I feel I'm disrespecting her by allowing her to do it. It's too early in our relationship.

Her face clouds. "What's the matter? You don't want it?"

"I'd prefer something else if you're offering."

She raises an eyebrow at me, "And what is that?"

"I want you on top, but only if you're comfortable."

"You don't have to ask me twice; I want to do it."

I move onto my back and reach into the drawer to get another condom. I'm about to rip the package open, but she takes it out of my hand and straddles my legs. It's erotic to watch her slowly tear it open and roll the latex over me. Her touch makes me want to cry out; it's so sensual.

I grip the sheets as she positions herself over me, then sinks. The feeling as she engulfs me is hard to describe, but this time I can't control myself, and I groan. When she takes me down to my base, I'm trying not to get rough though I want to pound her.

I let her find her rhythm as she moves over me. My eyes close, and when I open them, her head is back, exposing her elegant ivory-skinned neck. I resist sitting up to kiss it but watch her intently. I hear small moans escape from her as she works herself up and down. I can't contain myself anymore.

"Fuck, Rory, you feel unbelievable."

Her eyes flutter open, and she looks at me. Her cheeks are flushed, and her nails dig into my stomach as she leans forward, picking up the pace. I grabbed her hips and thrust into her. She pushes my hands away, and I move to her clit, gently rubbing it. As she picks up her pace, so do I with my fingers, moving harder over her until I feel her clench and begin to climax.

Rory doesn't let up and keeps moving hard over me until I begin to explode. Once again, I grab her hips and pound upward until I'm spent. I release her and pull her arm to bring her against my chest. Our bodies are misted with sweat, but she still smells incredible. Post-coitus, I want her close to me as our breathing returns to normal. I have to ask the question to myself, what the fuck has she done to me?

"That was good," she mumbles into my chest, sounding like she's half asleep.

"Sweetheart, do you want to sleep?"

"It's still early."

She's right; it's only a little past 8:30. We've done absolutely nothing with our project, and I think it's going to be a battle to get anything finished. If I want Rory going forward as much as I want her now, we're going to get an F. I promise myself to buckle down and work on the project for at least half the time we're together. Whether I keep that promise remains to be seen.

"So, what would you like to do?"

She slides off me and lies by my side. I sit up to remove the condom and take it to the bathroom. When I come back, Rory is asleep with her hand tucked under her chin. She looks so angelic. I don't want to get into bed and disturb her, but I want to be near her. As soon as I do, she wakes.

"I thought you weren't tired."

"I'm a little worn out."

I chuckle, and she kisses my chest then places her head on it. This is the way we fall asleep, and when I wake, it's well after midnight. I'm not sure if she wanted to stay, but I have no intention of waking her up. I wouldn't let her travel home by herself, even if she did. I shift, and she snuggles in deeper against my chest.

"I love you," I whisper, not expecting an answer.

"I love you, too."

I raise my eyebrows. "You're awake?"

"A little. What time is it?"

"After midnight. Did you want to go home? I'll take you."

"No. I want to stay here."

"Do you want me to set the alarm for you?"

"Why? We can travel to school together. Didn't you say you had a class at eleven? I do, too."

"I just thought you would want to get fresh clothes."

"I brought some with me."

I begin to laugh because that means she was coming over to seduce me. It wouldn't have been hard because I wanted her so much.

"Rory?"

I hear nothing but her even breathing. She fell back to sleep.

The next morning, I wake, and Rory is not in bed with me. I look toward the bathroom and find the door open. Worried, I slip on my boxers and go looking for her, hoping she didn't go home. I find her in the kitchen and on her cell. I smile when I see her wearing my shirt from the night before. I assume the conversation is with her roommate since I hear her say, Ellie. She looks up when she hears me and waves.

I give her privacy and head to the master bath for a shower. I love my bathroom, and it's one of the reasons I chose this apartment. The shower is twice the size of a usual enclosure, and I can change the spray to eight different settings. My arms a little sore, probably from holding myself above Rory when we made love. I put the setting on massage. I'm halfway through when I see Rory come into the bathroom.

"Can I come in with you?"

My dick starts to harden, just thinking about her body being wet and soapy.

"Absolutely."

She discards my shirt. When she opens the door, I'm at half-mast, and I turn away to rinse my hair. I feel her hand touch me, and I'm rock hard in no time. Rory strokes me, and without a condom, it's the best we can do. I need to get tested because I want to feel her without one.

"What are you doing to me?" I say as I make cup her face.

"I'm jerking you off if you haven't noticed."

"No, I know that," I reply huskily. "I mean, what are you doing to me overall?"

"Is there a problem?"

"I never felt like this about anyone before. You're making me into a mush."

My breath hitches as she strokes me faster. My orgasm is building fast, and within a few seconds, I'm coming onto the shower floor. She continues to stroke me until I finish. After she releases me, I pick her up and hold her against me with her legs around my waist.

"Is being a mush such a bad thing?"

"For me, it is, but I'll allow it because it's you."

We laugh together, and she grabs the body wash from the shelf. I wonder what her friend Bauer is going to say when she no longer sits with him.

"Do you want some breakfast?" I ask as she finishes washing the soap from her body.

"You're going to make me breakfast," she asks as she wipes water from her eyes.

"I can cook."

"Usually, I just have some coffee and don't eat until lunch."

"Do you mind if I have breakfast?"

"Go right ahead. As long as you make me coffee."

I chuckle as she squirts shampoo in her hand, lathering it into thick suds. I can't stop watching her as the bubbles cascade over her delicious curves.

After we dress, I leave Rory in the bathroom while she does her hair and makeup. I've now seen her without it and believe me; she doesn't need it with her natural beauty. In the kitchen, I pop a pod in the Keurig and wait for her to come out. I poured a huge bowl of frosted flakes and put in some milk. When she finally enters the kitchen, I have my face stuffed with cereal.

"Seriously? That is some bowl."

I nod, swallowing what's in my mouth. "I love cereal. I have several boxes because I eat it all the time."

I get up to make her coffee and hand the mug to her.

"You want milk or sugar?"

"Nope. I drink it black."

It dawns on me that she hadn't eaten much in my presence even when we had dinner at the Italian restaurant. She ate half a slice of pizza. I hope she isn't one of those women that won't eat in front of a guy. She's thin enough and shouldn't be afraid to eat.

Besides, I'm not one of those guys who would mind if she gained a little weight.

"You sure you don't want anything for breakfast?"

"No, stop worrying. I'm fine."

I shovel more cereal into my mouth and look through my emails. Several were from last night when I was indisposed. It concerns the acquisition I'm working on. My father's tone doesn't seem nice, and I'm sure he's pissed because I didn't answer him right away. I have a life outside of work, and he's the reason why I have the added responsibility of finishing my degree.

I look up, and Rory is doing the same thing with her phone. She furiously taps what I assume is a text. I don't hear them come in, so she must have her cell on silent. I stare intently at her full lips as they hug the rim of the coffee cup, leaving a slight stain of the red lipstick she's wearing. She catches me watching.

"What are you staring at?"

"Your lips. I want to ravage you, but we have to leave for class soon."

"We could have a quickie."

I put down my spoon. "No, if I start with you, we'll be late for class. It will have to wait until later. By the way, how is this going to work?"

"You mean sleeping arrangements?"

"We don't always have to spend time sleeping at each other's places. It's something I never did before."

I raise my eyebrows. "You never slept at a guy's apartment before?"

She takes a deep breath. "I've only slept with three men before, and you're one of them. You know that."

I'm still shocked. "Really?"

"I told you, I don't sleep around."

"Then why me this summer? You seemed like you were into that kind of thing."

"Are you implying that I'm a slut?" Rory growled.

ADDICTED BY LOVE

"Rory, you're reading into it. No, I'm saying that usually women who sleep with men they barely know have done it before."

"Well, I haven't. There was something about you, and I couldn't help myself."

"Oh, the love at first sight thing?"

"I was in love with you before that weekend."

"Excuse me?" She has me confused because I don't ever remember meeting her before this past summer.

"How were you in love with me before this summer?"

"Lexi had pictures in a box in the closet. I found them one afternoon when she and my father weren't home. I looked through them and found yours. I took it and kept it in my wallet."

I smirk. "Were you stalking me on the beach?"

"No, that was just a coincidence. I had seen you in magazines about Lawson Corp."

"You never said Lexi's name when you told me about your father's fiancée. Did you know she's married to my brother now?" I said.

"Yes, I heard my father mention it to my mother."

"Then, you know it could be a potential problem."

"Why? She's happily married."

"Rory, your father hurt her deeply."

I wonder if I should mention what JC told me in the park. How do you tell your girlfriend that she was a nasty little brat?

"I know, and I'm sure I had some hand in that also."

"How so?"

"I wasn't very nice to her for the brief time I knew her. I'm sure Lexi won't be happy to meet me again if it comes to that."

"What do you mean if it comes to that?"

"Now that you know I was watching you, do you still want to be with me?"

"I'm in love with you. I can't just shut it off even if you were nasty to Lexi. I love her too, and we're going to have to work this out somehow when the time comes for me to introduce you to my family."

"I'm sorry I created a problem for you. I should have stayed away from you this summer. Maybe it would've been better."

"No, it's not better. What's better is you being with me. Don't let the details bother you. We'll deal with them as they come."

"Thank you."

"For what?"

"For not judging me on what I did in the past."

"What kind of hypocrite would I be? I haven't exactly been a saint."

Rory looked at her coffee cup, averting her eyes from mine. "But this involves your family, and I'm sure they're important to you."

"They are, but so are you."

"Can we discuss this another time?"

"Sure. Let me clean this stuff up so we can leave for class."

I put the milk away, and when I turn, she's at the sink washing my bowl and spoon. I love that she automatically pitches in.

"Tonight, we have to work on our project. I want to have something before our next class."

"Okay. Can we go over the graphs and notes from the last lecture? I can't afford to get another bad quiz grade."

"Not a problem. You'll understand it better after we review."

Rory stands on her tippy toes to kiss me and goes to collect her stuff from my bedroom.

∼

We take a cab to NYU, and I hold her hand the entire time. I feel like a kid in high school, and I know she feels the same way. I can't get it out of my head that while her peers were enjoying first kisses and fumbling encounters in the backs of cars, some twenty-something asshole had his way with her. It irks me to no end. He better hope I never see him.

When we arrive, I kiss her on the top of her head, telling her I'll see her at my apartment after six. We don't discuss if she's going to sleep over, I assume that she is. Class is boring, Financial Modeling and Analysis. It's not the professor who's boring; it's that I know this stuff cold, and I can probably ace this course without attending. The professor lectures on and on. I sit in the back, thinking of Rory. I'd love to text her, but I don't want to disturb her.

She must be thinking the same thing as me because she texts me. I'm glad I remembered to put my phone on silent.

I miss you. I want to be in your bed right now.

I feel my dick twitch at the mention of being in bed with her. The things I want to do to her.

I miss you too, but please stop torturing me by mentioning bed.

I'm trying not to laugh in class right now. I'll see you at six.

I'll be there waiting.

Rory's adorable, and I wish it were the weekend so I can spend time with her all day. This is totally unlike me to be hanging on a girl, but I can't help it.

Finally, the class is over, and the professor gives us some readings for next time. I'll skim the chapters at lunch while I'm in the office. I don't remember if he gives quizzes, but I might as well know the material before the next class.

I call my father on the way to Lawson. I don't want any surprises with the acquisition I'm working.

"Dad, how are things?"
 "Terrific. I think we're all set."
 "Do you need me when I get in?"
 "Are you on your way?"
 "I should be there in fifteen minutes."
 "I'll be leaving in five for a meeting downtown. I'm not sure when I'll be back."

I breathe a sigh of relief. I don't want to be bothered today, and hopefully, I can get some reading done if I'm not swamped with work.

 "I'll see you when I see you."
 "That might be tomorrow. I'll talk to you later."
 "Bye."

The office is quiet, and I stay in mine for most of the day and hear nothing from Rory. I know she has several classes today, and I let her alone. I want to make sure she passes everything so she can graduate. Then I realize, if she does, we'll be at the ceremony together. That will be fun.

At the end of the day, when I'm getting ready to leave, my father enters my office.

I'm surprised since he said I might not see him until tomorrow. "Dad, how was your meeting?"

"It went well, but we have an after-hours meeting tonight. I need you to stay." He frowns as his eyes scan my clothing. "Do you have a suit with you?"

 "I do. It's in the closet."
 "Get changed. The meeting is in half an hour."

He leaves my office, and I push out of my chair, undressing and putting on my blue pinstriped suit. Just when I thought I would escape unscathed. I'm not sure how long this meeting is going to take, but if it goes past six, then Rory might as well stay home.

She doesn't have a key to my apartment, and I'm not sure I want her there alone anyway. I guess it's strange to think that way since I'm in love with her, but really, I still don't know her well. Does that make sense? Can you be in love with someone you barely know?

I quickly text her and let her know I'm stuck, and we might not be able to get together tonight.

I'm sorry. My father roped me into an after-hours meeting. I'm not sure when I'll be home.

Rory sends me a bunch of sad faces, which makes me chuckle. She is refreshing to be around, and I hope I can see her tonight.

The meeting is short and sweet. The clients just wanted us to change some wording in their merger paperwork. I wish we didn't work with clients, but my father feels the company can expand our reach by handling other mergers and acquisitions not related to us. I have plenty of experience, and if it's going to help raise the bottom line, then I'm all for it. I text Rory to let her know that I'm on my way home.

I'm coming home now. I should be at my apartment by 6:30.

Bauer came by, and we went out to dinner.

. . .

I frown at this enough to cause my head to ache.

Why are you with him? He wants you.

He does not. He's just a good friend.

I don't want to argue with her, but if I've ever seen a guy that wants to get into her pants, it's Bauer. Rory led him on last week, and now she's out to dinner with him? The guy has it bad for her, and she's naïve about the situation. I'm not sure how to bring it up without causing a fight.

Are you coming by tonight?

I promised Bauer I'd go to a movie after dinner.

It sounds like a date to me.

Stop it. I told him we're together and he's fine with it.

Sure he is. I can almost bet he isn't fine with it, and I wish I could've seen her face when she told him that she was dating me. I'm sure he was all smiles, but then when she turned away, he had a sour face. Guys like him who exist in the friend's zone are always looking for a way in. I sigh as I type Rory a text.

. . .

Will I see you tonight or should you call me tomorrow?

Are you angry with me?

I wanted to see you tonight, but I can't stop you from spending time with friends. Have fun, and I'll talk to you tomorrow.

Are you mad? Please don't be.

Sweetheart, I'm not mad. Go have fun and call me tomorrow or tonight if you get home early enough.

I am mad. I feel like telling Bauer to back off, but I don't want to damage Rory's relationship with her friends. She can enjoy herself, and we'll discuss it tomorrow. I'm so annoyed I almost miss my subway stop, sliding out the doors just before they close.

CHAPTER 7

It's starting to get chilly out at night and soon I'll have to wear a coat. I hope that we get a warm snap as sometimes we do in mid-September. Technically it's still summertime. I seriously hate winter and usually take a week off to go to a warmer climate. Now that I have Rory in my life, I'm not sure I'll be able to do that. I don't want to be away from her too long, and I bet she'll be too busy to join me.

Once I get into my apartment and divest myself of my suit, dressing in a pair of lounge pants and a t-shirt, I look for something to eat. Of course, I end up with my favorite, a big bowl of Apple Jacks. I'm a creature of habit. I carry the bowl to the living room and click the television on with the remote. The Yankees are on and winning against the Toronto Blue Jays.

I scarf up my cereal and when I'm finished, lie back against the couch, closing my eyes for a brief moment. I must have fallen asleep because the buzzing of the intercom from the front desk wakes me. I hurry to answer it.

"Yes?"

"A Miss Barton is here to see you."

"Send her up, please."

The intercom squawks as the concierge clicks off. Rory probably told that idiot Bauer she couldn't go to the movies and headed right over here. I need to talk with her because I don't want to be one of those guys who doesn't let his girlfriend have a life outside of me. I want her to enjoy herself, and if that means taking a day off from each other, then so be it. Now that's the Hunter I know. Don't get too attached. But I have misgivings. I want her to be with me all the time. We'll have to compromise.

I leave the door open and wait until Rory walks out of the elevator. She steals my breath away each time I see her. Tonight, she's wearing a pair of dark blue jeans that hug her delicious curves and a peach-colored v-neck sweater with a hint of cleavage. I want to bury my face there and inhale her scent.

I lean against the doorjamb as she approaches. "You didn't have to end your date early."

"I wanted to. I wanted to be with you tonight."

I usher her in and close the door after us.

"Rory, let's get one thing straight; I don't want you to put your friends off for me. You need to have a life outside of us, just like I do."

She frowns at me, and her sapphire eyes darken. "You don't want to spend time with me?"

"No, I didn't say that. I said we need our own lives outside of each other."

Rory's eyebrows knit together. "Yes, so you don't want to spend time with me."

I sigh deeply. "NO! I mean, we can't spend every waking moment together. Come sit down so we can talk."

"Why?" she asks suspiciously.

"I want to tell you about the things that I do. I spend time with friends and other activities. I want to continue to do some of them, and I'm sure you have things you want to do with your friends. So tell me."

"We don't do anything. Not scheduled anyway. Every so often

on Sundays, Ellie and I and sometimes Veronica, that's the girl who had pizza with us, goes to breakfast. I love waffles."

"See, I didn't know that. We don't know things about each other. I like to play soccer on Saturdays in the park. Of course, now that it's getting cooler, I probably will stop that soon."

She giggled. "I like to have sleepovers and fill up on popcorn and jellybeans."

"Sleepovers with who?"

"Friends."

"Male friends?"

"No, silly. I told you I only slept with three men, and you're one of them. In high school, I used to have a few girlfriends sleepover, and we would stay up all night until my mom yelled at us to go to bed. We'd watch movies and eat pizza."

I smile because it's such a kid's thing to do. I'm sure she looked sexy in her little nightgown. I don't remember the last time I had a sleepover, but then again, do guys do that type of stuff as much as girls?

"I like root beer floats with whip cream on top," Rory said.

"You do? So do I. My grandfather used to make them for me."

I see her frown as if something hurts. "He died a few years ago. I miss him."

"I'm sorry. I know it's hard to lose someone."

I run my hands through her hair, and she crawls onto my lap. I can't resist, I have to kiss the creamy flesh just above her cleavage. She smells so good, and I keep my nose there, just inhaling her scent.

"Hunter, stop it."

"Oh? Is this a turn on for you?" I mumble into her skin.

"I like to feel your lips on me."

I smile because I love to feel her lips on me, too. I raise my head to press them against hers. She's wearing lip gloss, and this time, it tastes like strawberries. This makes me stir in my pants. I want her. We start making out, and by the time we come up for air, I'm at full staff. She straddles me and presses herself against my erection, bucking her hips against me.

"You're being very naughty," I say.

"I'm not the one with the erection."

"Really? This isn't arousing you."

"Not one bit," Rory says with a straight face.

I reach between us and start to unbutton her jeans, but she stops me.

"Not here, the bedroom," she whispers.

I give her a lopsided grin as she grips my hand. "I thought you weren't aroused?"

"Maybe just a little."

She climbs off my lap, and we head to my bedroom. I pull down the covers, and she starts to undress, but I stop her. This time I'm going slow. I want to take her clothes off one by one. I begin with her pants, unbuttoning, and unzipping them. Her sapphire eyes are shining as I slip my hand into her lacy panties. She's indeed wet and oh so aroused. Her little nub is swollen, and I swipe my fingers against it, which causes her to gasp.

I kneel and pull her jeans over her curves until they're at her ankles. Rory places her hands on my shoulders while she steps out of them. I'm facing her pussy, and I see she's wearing nothing more than a black scrap of cloth with a string. In fact, the scrap of cloth is see-through mesh. Can these even be termed panties?

I thrust my face against her pubic area and stick my tongue out to lick the apex between her thighs.

"Ohh," Rory says.

I do it again but press my tongue harder until I'm touching her clit. Her nails dig into the cloth at my shoulders as I continue to lick her.

"You're going to make me come," she moans.

"Come. I want you to come; it would be more pleasure for me than you."

"I doubt that," she pants.

I keep it up until she is gripping my shoulders so hard it feels like she's going to cut off the circulation. Rory howls loudly as her orgasm takes hold, and I see her legs shake as it rumbles through her body.

"Oh God, Hunter, that was so good."

I can see she's still a bit unsteady, so I stand and scoop her in my arms, placing her in bed. I hook my thumbs in her panties, she raises her hips, and I slide them down her legs until they're at her ankles. They're glistening with her arousal, and I seriously want to keep these for myself.

I once again kneel in front of Rory, pull her up, and remove her sweater. She's wearing a bra that matches the panties. What is the point of wearing a mesh bra? I'm not sure if I should be annoyed she wore this on her dinner date with Bauer. Her nipples are pressing against the thin fabric, and I lean in to suck them while unclasping the bra from the back. She runs her hand through my hair as I pull her bra away and toss it to the floor.

"Hunter," she murmurs.

My name sounds so sexy coming out of her mouth. Her breasts are full, and I cup them, thumbing her nipples. She's looking up at me with such innocence that I feel almost feel ashamed for what I'm about to do. I'm like a train charging down the tracks with no brakes; I can't stop.

I climb off the bed to release my aching cock from my pants, dropping them to the floor and following with my shirt. I practically pull the drawer out of the nightstand opening it to retrieve a condom.

"I want to do it," Rory whispers.

I hand her the condom more than happy to watch her sheath me. As she slowly rolls it down over me, I almost lose it. Her fingers deftly working over me is so hot to watch. When she's done, she gets up on her hands and knees in front of me.

"Are you sure you want it this way?" I ask.

"Yes, I love this position."

I don't want to tell her that I hate it but not because I hate the position. It's because I can't see her face. I want to see her eyes when I make love to her. But if she wants it this way, who am I to argue? I press myself against her slick opening, and Rory moves back against me, pushing my head inside her.

Rory is like a roaring fire on my dick as I enter. I need to control myself, or I'm going to thrust into her so hard she'll see stars. Instead, I move in slowly until I'm to my base, then I start working my hips, thrusting in and out. She meets my thrusts, and her ass keeps slapping against my hips, her perfectly round ass.

I place my hands on her back, running them over the smooth skin. She has flawless skin, not a blemish on it. I move my fingers to her hips and begin to speed my gyrations, pounding into her hard. I hear her breathing become ragged, as is mine. She keeps whispering my name.

"Hunter…"

Rory slams back against me, and I reach around to rub her clit. It's enough to send her over the edge; a few swipes over her swollen nub, and she is coming hard. I feel her clench around me, but I'm not quite there, and I continue to gyrate my hips, pushing in deep. She's patient and waits until I call her name as I explode inside her. I wish it were without this condom; I long to feel her against me with nothing in between.

Once I finish, I immediately pull out because I want to hold her. I unroll the condom and drop it into the garbage can near my dresser; then I climb on the bed next to her. She's lying on her back, and I nuzzle her breasts, flicking my tongue over her nipple. Rory's quiet, and I wonder if I hurt her.

"Sweetheart, was that good for you?"

Her voice is strained. "I came, didn't I?"

"That doesn't mean it was good. I want you to tell me what you want."

"All I want is you. I don't want you to be angry."

"I'm not angry. Is that why you cut your date short?"

"I thought you were."

"I want you to have friends outside of me. I told you that. I don't want to control you like some men do."

I wonder what the predator did to her. Did he control her? Tell her what to wear and when to wear it? What friends she could have? And the other man she had sex with, she hasn't mentioned who he was. Did she date him recently? I want to ask, but this isn't the right time.

"I know, but I want to be with you."

"And I'm not saying you can't. I'm just saying to enjoy yourself."

The pillow rustles as Rory nods, and the look on her face tells me she's not agreeable, but she says nothing. I wish she wouldn't be afraid to tell me things. We're going to have to work on that if we stay together. I snuggle up next to her and pull the covers over us.

~

The next thing I know, its morning. It wasn't that late when we went to bed, but the day wore me out. Rory is not next to me, but I hear the shower running in the bathroom. It's barely six, and I don't have to be in the office until 8:30, and I have no intention of getting up. I turn over and cuddle the pillow Rory slept on. It smells of her perfume and her.

When she comes out of the bathroom, I pop one eye open. She's wearing only a towel but still so sexy. She could wear a paper bag and still make it look elegant. Rory sees me watching and teases me by undoing the knot in the towel and flashing me. I'm becoming aroused, but what I want to do to her will take time, and she probably has to get to class.

"What time is your course today?" I ask.

"I have one at eight and then another at ten, twelve, and two."

I raise my eyebrows. "Wow, busy day for you."

"Well, I told you that I took a full course load. I want to graduate in December."

"Have you thought about what we talked about?"

"The internship?"

"Yes. You can work at Lawson, and it would set you up for a good career even if you went to work somewhere after the internship is over."

"I don't know. Wouldn't it be hard to work for you?"

"You'd make me hard working for me."

"Oh, so you want me to work for you so you can take advantage of the help?"

I smirk. "No one else but you."

"I'd get the job because we're dating?"

"No, I don't make the decisions on interns, but I can put in a good word for you."

"I would have to apply like everyone else?"

"Of course."

I'm not going to tell Rory that my say has plenty of clout. I want her to know she's getting it on her merits and not my referral. Most people would be thrilled to do an internship at Lawson after they graduate, but she's acting like it's a horrible thing.

"Can you get me an application?"

"I'll bring you one tonight. You need to work on it soon because it's due at the end of this month."

"That's only two weeks."

"I know, so you better get the essay, and the questionnaire finished quickly."

"I'm not sure I'm going to be able to do it. I have all my classes plus the project, and now this?"

"Rory, you'll do fine. I can handle most of the project."

"That means I would be riding your coattails instead of doing my own work."

"It's not a problem. It's a simple project. Did you read the syllabus? We have an even bigger one due at the end of the semester. I'm not sure if Professor Stanish will assign partners or it's for each student to complete."

"I hope partners and I hope you're my partner. I'll help you as much as I can, but I'm not sure how much time I'll have. I have another project due next week. The work is coming fast and furious."

"It always does. In a few short months, you'll be done unless you go for your MBA."

"I might. My father wants me to."

"Does Noah still live in the city?"

"No, he moved his business to Boston when he married my mother. He still comes here to serve clients, but mostly he sends his staff. Why do you ask?"

"I'm not sure how happy he'll be that we're together."

"Why?"

"Because we had a poker game one night where we talked about our exploits. He mentioned he would never let a daughter of his date me. Now you are."

Rory frowns and clenches her towel in her hands.

"I didn't know that."

"Well, now you do. I think you might smooth the way before we meet."

"You're not the same."

"But he doesn't know that, and he knows Lexi is my sister in law. That complicates our relationship a bit, not only on your side but mine."

"I'm not going to worry about it until we get together with my parents."

"I agree. We have other things to worry about."

I flip the covers back to reveal my semi-erection. Rory looks at it and smiles, but I shake my head.

"Why not?" she pouts.

"Tonight."

"I've meant to talk to you about tonight."

Fuck, here it comes.

"I'm not sure what time I'll be over. I have classes; then I need to go home and do laundry. After that, I have some research for my other project. I might not be able to come until ten."

"Stay home then."

I try not to sound disappointed, but I also don't want her traveling to me that late in the evening.

"Why?"

"I told you I don't like you traveling here that late."

"Then why don't you stay at my apartment?"

"Hmm, never thought of that. But won't Ellie mind?"

"She's been spending nights with Matty."

This is a development that I have not been made aware of. I'm going to have to call him to see what's going on. He's a notorious serial dater, and I guess he got over his last break up quickly if he took up with Ellie so fast.

"Oh, so you'll be alone?"

"More than likely."

"I'll come then. What time?"

"Seven, I guess. I can cut my research at the library short and do some on the internet when I get home."

I snort because I know if I'm there, we aren't studying unless it's each other's anatomy. Rory throws her towel at me and starts to get dressed. She brought underwear in her purse, but she put on the same clothing she wore when she came to see me last night.

"I have to stop at my apartment and change before class."

"We can leave for class later tomorrow since we'll be near NYU."

"Yes, that's true."

She's fully dressed, and I sit in bed, eyeing her ass as she applies some makeup in the mirror over my dresser.

"I see you watching me."

"Do you have a problem with that?"

"Not at all."

I'm starting to get aroused again, and by the time she comes to the bed, I'm fully hard. I hide it under the covers as she kisses me goodbye. As soon as she leaves, I throw the covers off to take a shower. I can't get the image of Rory naked out of my head, and I have to jerk off or take a cold shower. I prefer jerking off. Now I can start my day with Rory on my mind.

CHAPTER 8

The office is surprisingly quiet, and I don't hear from Rory all day. I assume it's because she has so many classes today — poor kid. I never had more than three classes in one day; she has four. My father is in one of his rare moods where he's bitching about the smallest thing.

I take most of the brunt of his complaining, but I know he's harmless. My mother always says that his bark is worse than his bite. He was always harder on JC, which is why my brother refuses to work for him. Of course, he had to sacrifice salary, and I get paid more than he does even though he holds a vice president position at his company.

I hang around late so I can stop at my apartment, grab my clothes and head to Rory's. I still haven't heard from her by six and send her a text. She doesn't reply, and I'm starting to get worried. What if something happened to her? I might as well head to my place and wait until she communicates with me. I don't want to be standing like an idiot in her lobby waiting.

At my apartment, I pack a small bag with some clothing and change into a worn pair of blue jeans and a white fisherman's sweater. I text Rory again, nothing. I call her, and it goes right to voicemail. What the fuck is going on? I decide to call Matty to see if Ellie knows where she is. He puts Ellie on the phone.

"I saw her around four when she got out of class. She had a meeting with Professor Callender. She's been having some issues with him."

"Who called the meeting?"

"Professor Callender."

"Thanks, I'm going to your apartment."

I hang up and wonder what happened. Professor Callender is one of the hardest instructors around. He gives complicated tests and expects excellence. I even had a hard time in his class. It was one of the few I studied for, but I still pulled out an A. With Rory's course load, she might be falling behind, and it's early in the semester.

I set up a ride with Uber, and it's the same freaking guy in the Mercedes I had a few days ago. What are the chances? I keep texting Rory on the way there but still get no answer. Now I'm beginning to panic. What could've happened to her?

In her building, the front desk phones her apartment, and I breathe a sigh of relief as they tell me to go up. It means she's there. I'm starting to get angry on the ride in the elevator. She could have had the decency to call or, at the very least, text me.

I expect her to be at the door when I come off the elevator, but she's not, so I knock. I hear shuffling in the apartment, and she opens the door. Her face is full of black tracks of mascara, and she's been crying.

The panicky feeling begins to rise in my chest again. "What's wrong?"

"My grandmother had a stroke this afternoon."

"Shit, I'm so sorry. Is she okay?"

"She's in the hospital. They gave her medication, and I'm waiting for news. They said she's paralyzed on her left side."

Rory begins to cry hard, and I pull her against me and kiss her head. I've never had to deal with the death of someone close to me. My grandparents were gone before I was born, so I don't know how she's feeling.

"Are you going home?"

"I want to, but with classes and our project, I shouldn't."

"Why don't you wait until tomorrow and then go? I can come if you'd like."

She pulls away and shakes her head. "My parents don't know about you, and I'm not sure I'm ready to tell them."

I feel hurt. Like I'm such a horrible person that she can't reveal we're dating? I know her father knew about me a few years ago, but I'm not going to be that person with her. I'm devoted to Rory and only her. I want to make this work.

"Okay, but I would come if you wanted me to."

Rory sniffles and dabs at her eyes with a tissue. "I appreciate that, but it's not necessary. I'm not even sure I'm going."

"Do you want me to stay? I don't want to bother you if you want to be alone."

"Stay. I need you."

We go to sit on the couch, and she crawls on my lap like a little girl. I cradle her in my arms, and Rory buries her head in my neck. I hug her like I don't want to let her go, and I really don't. Several minutes later, her phone rings, and she goes to her bedroom to speak to the caller. When she comes out, her face tells me it's not good news.

"They want to do surgery, and I should go home. I'm very close to my grandmother, and I want to be there. She and my grandfather took care of me a lot when I was younger. When he died, it was very hard, and I was away on a school trip. I don't want to be away from my grandmother if she dies."

"I understand. I'll take care of the project. Let me know how it's going. Are you flying up there?"

"It's the quickest way. I might be able to get a flight tonight."

Rory starts tapping into her phone and looks up at me after she finishes.

"I booked a flight from JFK, which leaves at ten."

I look at my watch, and it's 7:30, so she better get moving.

"Do you want me to go to the airport with you?"

"No, I'll catch a cab and be fine. You should go home so I can get things packed and ready."

All of a sudden, she's all business, and I'm bewildered by her attitude. She doesn't want comfort or my help. Maybe this is how she deals with crises in her life, so I prefer not to push it. I offer a kiss, and she offers me her cheek before I walk out the door. As I summon an Uber, hoping it's not the guy in the Mercedes again, I start wondering if I did something wrong.

∼

That night, I toss and turn, having a hard time falling asleep. The pillow she slept on still smells of her perfume, and I miss her. Geez, less than two weeks, and I've turned into a sap, just like Bauer. I must really be in love with Rory. I finally fall asleep around 3:00 AM, but it's not fitful.

I wake with my alarm set for 6:30 AM. The first thing I do is check my phone, and there is nothing. I guess I'm being selfish because she has a lot more to worry about than texting me. I go about my day and hope that eventually she'll let me know how things are with her grandmother. I have class today, and it's not going to be fun without Rory to look at. When I get there, I tell Professor Stanish that she's going to be out today for a family emergency. He nods and says she already notified him.

I go back to my seat, none too happy. She contacts him, but not me? I'm her boyfriend for Pete's sake. I spend most of the class daydreaming and not paying attention to anything the professor says. I'm bored here and wish I could just come in for tests, but that's not the way it works. I can only hope Rory will come back by next week. My attention turns to the professor as he discusses the project.

"I'd like to see rough drafts of your projects. I want to make sure you're all heading in the right direction."

Most of the class nods and a few partners look at each other. I wonder how many of them haven't started the project.

The class ends with the professor telling us he wants to see some rough drafts of our progress on our projects due in a couple of weeks. So I'll have to work on it over the weekend so that Tuesday, I have something to give him. It's not just my grade I have to worry about, but Rory's.

By the afternoon, I still haven't heard from her, and I can't concentrate on my work at all. Fortunately, I farmed the contract for the latest acquisition out to the legal team. Let them handle the language. I'd rather work on some financial graphs anyway.

My heart is heavy, and I decide to call Matty to find out if Ellie told him anything about Rory's grandmother. I could text her, but I don't want to bother her. She might be upset with what's going on, and I might add to it. I dial his number. He answers right away.

"What's shaking, Hunter?"

"Do you know if Ellie has heard from Rory? She hasn't called me."

"As far as I know, nothing so far. We're supposed to have dinner tonight, so I'll ask her and get back to you."

"Thanks, I appreciate it. I'll talk to you later."

"Hunter, what's the deal with this girl? Are you in love with her?"

"Probably as close as I've ever been."

Matty chuckles. "I never thought I would see it. Someone finally tamed the huntsman."

"There is just something about her that's so appealing."

"She's young."

"Yeah, but so is Ellie, and that hasn't stopped you."

"I'm younger than you."

"By one year."

"And Ellie will be twenty-one in January."

"Whatever."

Matty laughs in my ear and has to hang up because he has a client coming to an open house he's holding. I'm bent. I don't know what to make of the situation, and I hope Rory's grandmother is doing alright.

～

I stay in the entire weekend. It's shitty and rainy, typical fall weather. I still haven't heard from Rory, and now I'm getting worried. Matty texted me that Ellie went to visit her mother in Boston, so if she found anything out, he would let me know.

I work on the project for Professor Stanish's class. I can't walk in there with nothing, so I practically finish the damn thing. The sooner I get it out of my hair, the better. I'll take it to work and let one of the secretaries enter it into the computer. I'm old school and like to write my rough drafts on paper. I need to do the graphs, and I'm good to go.

By Tuesday, it's been almost a week, and Matty never got back to me. I enter class with the rough draft even though in my desk at the office, I hold the completed version of the project. We have a quiz, and when I hand mine in, the TA tells me Professor Stanish wants me to stay after class. Fuck, what did I do now?

By the time the class ends, my stomach is tight with anxiety. I wait until all the students file out, then I head down to the podium. I need to wait for Professor Stanish to shuffle through some papers he hands to his TA.

"Mr. Lawson, I have some bad news for you."

"Sir?"

"Miss Barton notified me today that she's taken a leave of absence for a family emergency. She won't be back this semester. I'm afraid you'll have to finish the project on your own."

I need to reel my jaw back up from the floor because you

would think that as her boyfriend, she would let me know this information. It makes me think that she wasn't serious about loving me, and that was just a line. Who would treat someone they love like this? I need to find out you're dropping out of the semester from the fucking professor? I feel like a damn idiot. I must have spaced out for a minute or two.

"Mr. Lawson? Are you alright?"

My eyes swing up to meet his. "Uh, yeah, sure. I can handle the project on my own. Thank you."

"Good. I assume you don't need a little extra time because you're on your own?"

"No, sir. We did enough research for me to compile the project. Thank you."

I want to get out of there as fast as I can. I don't know what to do first. Call Rory or go to the nearest bar and get a good stiff drink. I stop into The Watering Hole, a bar right near NYU. It's barely 1:00 PM, but fuck it, I need a drink. The place has a few patrons, and I sit at the bar to order some whiskey.

While I'm sipping it, I call the office and tell them that I have the stomach flu, and I won't be in today. I don't care if my father is pissed. I feel blindsided and heartbroken. What was I thinking when I fell in love? This is the reason why I fuck with no strings attached. Emotional attachments suck, and this is how they end.

I sit in the bar for over two hours, drinking whiskey and feeling sorry for myself. By the time I walk out of there, it's before four in the afternoon, and I'm drunk. I can barely stumble out of the place and hail a cab.

"Mister, we're here. You need some help getting out?"

My eyes flutter open, and I wipe the drool from the corner of my mouth. "Nope. I think I can handle it," I say with slurred speech. I toss him some money through the Lucite window and almost fall as I step out of the cab.

I drag myself out and upstairs to my apartment. Two women who shared the elevator with me huddled into the corner like I would lunge at them or something worse. When I get into my door, I get a load of myself in the foyer mirror. I look like shit. My hair is disheveled, my clothing wrinkled, and I smell like the bottom of a liquor bottle. I just don't care.

While I'm trying to wrestle my shoes off, the urge to vomit takes over, and I hurry to the small bathroom near the foyer. I don't quite make it and spew all over the closed toilet seat.

"FUCK!" I scream.

I leave the mess and pull off my jacket, leaving it on the floor. I have trouble with the buttons of my oxford shirt and end up ripping it open, sending buttons flying everywhere. It too ends up on the floor along with my belt and t-shirt. I don't give a fuck.

I fall into my bed and lie on top of the covers. I don't know how long I was like that because I think I passed out. I wake to my sister in law, Lexi, stroking my back and calling my name.

"Hunter, are you okay?"

"Rory?"

"Who?"

"Rory?"

"Turn over; I can't hear you."

I turn on my back, and I'm greeted by the pretty face of my brother's wife. I love Lexi. She always takes care of me.

"Holy shit, Hunter. You smell like a brewery. Jonathan asked me to check on you. I guess you don't have the stomach flu."

"Fuck no. I have the biggest case of feeling sorry for myself."

I realize that I'm slightly slurring my words, which means I'm still drunk.

"Why, exactly, is that?"

"She left me. I don't know what I did, but I guess I deserve it for how I've treated women over the years."

"You must be drunk because you're making no sense. I'm going to leave you for a bit. You made a mess in the hall bath. Let me clean it up because the whole place stinks."

"No, please don't leave me."

I see concern cross her face, and she frowns.

"What's wrong?"

"I'm fucking heartbroken. The one time, I open myself up, and I get screwed over. How did it feel?"

"How did what feel?"

"When JC did it to you? I know what he did when you were dating. He didn't deserve you, but he changed. I thought I could make the change."

"It felt like shit, but JC has more than made up for years ago. He's a wonderful husband and father."

"I know. I see how much he adores you."

"Let me clean up, and we'll talk. I'll make you some tea, and you can tell me all about it."

She strokes my hair out of my face, just like a mother would, and leaves the room to clean up my mess. When she comes back, she has my clothes in her hand and three of the five buttons from my shirt when I ripped it open.

"I think your shirt is done. You tore the fabric pretty good."

"I don't care. Throw it out."

"Get changed. I put up the kettle for tea."

"I don't have tea in the kitchen."

"I have it. Ginger tea. It helps settle my stomach, and I carry it in my purse."

I remember that she's pregnant. Poor Lexi had to clean up my mess being pregnant. I'm such an ass — a drunken idiot. I hear her in the kitchen, getting cups and silverware out, so I drag myself off the bed and find a shirt to put on. When I come out, two steaming mugs of tea are on the counter, and she's putting honey in hers.

"Now, sit down and tell me what happened."

I'm hesitant to tell her I fell in love with Rory, the daughter of her ex-fiancé, Noah. JC warned me not to upset her.

"I fell for this girl, eh, woman, and she just dumped me."

"When did this happen? You never told us you were dating someone. This would be a first since I've known you."

I take a sip of tea. "Almost two weeks ago. I met her in my finance class."

I neglect to tell her I fucked Rory this summer in a one night stand.

"So, you met her and immediately started dating?"

"Sort of like that."

"What happened? It's such a short time."

"Her grandmother had a stroke. She went home to Boston, and I haven't heard from her since Thursday when I saw her last."

"Does this woman have a name?"

Oh boy, if I say her name, Lexi will know its Noah's daughter.

"Rory."

I can see the cogs in her brain turning, and then she purses her lips.

"Rory Barton? Aurora?"

"Yes," I say meekly.

"God Dammit, Hunter! That's Noah's daughter."

"I know. I'm sorry. I couldn't help it."

"Maybe you should stop thinking with your dick once in a while."

Lexi's pissed at me. I can hear the venom in her voice, something I rarely have to deal with from her direction.

"I didn't think with my dick. At least not when I met her in class."

"What's that supposed to mean."

I take a deep breath. "I slept with her this summer during July Fourth weekend. But in my defense, I didn't know she was Noah's daughter."

Lexi frowns. "Did you know what a bitch she was to me when Noah and I were together? She said some very hurtful things."

I almost slip and say JC told me, but if I do, the poor guy will be in the doghouse. So I keep it to myself.

"She told me, and she was very apologetic. It doesn't matter. I don't think we'll be seeing each other for a while."

Her face softens. "Explain to me what happened."

I tell her everything and wait for her to say something.

"I'm sorry. It seems like you cared for her."

"Does it show that much?"

"Yes, and I know how it hurts to lose someone you love."

"But it worked out for you and JC, eventually anyway."

"Yes, it did, but it was seven long years. I thought after Noah… well, you know the rest. It takes time to find the right girl. Maybe she wasn't for you. She is quite young."

"I think Rory was the right girl. It just was the wrong time. I thought she would at least offer me an explanation, but I got nothing."

I finish my tea and go to hug Lexi. She's always been a wonderful friend, and I could have kicked my brother for treating her so poorly. I'm glad he came to his senses and asked her to marry him again.

"When are we going to see your smiling face at our home? Your nephew keeps asking where Uncle Unter is."

I laugh because my two-year-old nephew, Johnny, can't say my name, so he calls me Uncle Unter. I love that little guy.

"I'll try to make it over this week."

"Would you be interested in babysitting for him? JC and I could use an evening out."

"Lexi, I'm not the type of babysitting guy. I don't know if I can handle all the diapers and bottle things. You'd be safer asking Megan."

"I did, but she's busy. We were hoping to go to a show on Saturday. You would be helping us out."

I think about it for a minute and agree. How hard could it be taking care of him? By the time I get over there, it will be his time to go to sleep for the night.

"Great. Get yourself together. It hurts, but it's not the end of the world. You'll find someone better suited for you."

I kiss her cheek, and she grabs her purse where she dropped it on my couch, then tells me goodbye as she walks out the door. Now I know the score. I'm stuck with the project, and I'm probably not going to see Rory again. I guess I learned my lesson, and this is exactly why I don't date. At least fucking holds no emotional attachments.

My head hurts, and I pop a couple of aspirin, spending the night watching television while reading a few chapters for my class tomorrow. My focus has to be finishing these courses, graduating, and my job. We have a few acquisitions I need to work on but nothing major. Usually, springtime is our busiest season, haven't figured out why.

CHAPTER 9

During the week, I have my assistant create a new cover page for my project, one that doesn't have Rory's name on it. I'm finished, and we still have another week to go before it's due.

This week has been hard not having Rory with me. It's like she fell off the face of the earth. I won't give her the satisfaction by chasing her. If she doesn't want to contact me, then fine. I can't worry about it even though my heart is broken.

On Friday, just as class is letting out, Bauer approaches me, asking if I've heard from Rory. I tell him no, not since over a week ago. He tells me neither has he, which means she just cut everyone off. I haven't spoken to Matty to see if Ellie told him anything about her. The whole thing is odd.

I told my father since work wasn't busy that I was taking the day off to spend some time researching my project. Since I'm finished, it's a lie, but I need a break. I want to relax and take it easy in my apartment for the rest of the day. Tomorrow I'm babysitting for Johnny, and I have no idea how that's going to be.

I decide to text Megan, Lexi's sister, to see if she wants to go out. Megan and I have history. We had sex a few times. She's a couple of years older than me, but who cares. She's hot and has the same attitude I have about dating. She dated Lexi's ex-fiancé's brother, Lucian, a few years ago. It didn't work out.

Hey, want to go out tonight? I'm bored.

Hell yeah. Where do you want to go?

Want to do a bar crawl or you up for a club?

Bar crawl sounds great. Not in the mood for dressing up unless you want me too.

Meet you at Steps at 7:00?

I'll be there. Don't start hitting the hard stuff until I get there.

Will do. See you later.

Okay, so now that I'm going out tonight, I'm taking a nap. But before I do, I'm getting rid of Rory's smell. Enough wallowing. If she doesn't want me, then the hell with her. We could have been good together.

I strip the bed, put on clean sheets, and open my nightstand to put my charger away. Inside is a torn wrapper from a condom that I used with her. Dammit, just what I don't want to see. But I'm glad I did because I have to remember to get more condoms. I'll do that tonight before I get Megan. You never know, I might get lucky.

After my two hour nap, I take a shower and throw a little gel into my hair. It's getting long, and I need to have it cut. As I'm walking out of the bathroom, I step on something that hurts my barefoot. It's a button from the shirt that I ripped open a few days ago. I toss it out — another reminder of my failed attempt at dating.

I have a huge bowl of Apple Jacks for dinner. I'm in no mood to cook as I'm usually not, and I have about ten boxes of cereal to choose from. I'll probably end up getting a late-night snack with Megan. The woman can put it away, and she doesn't seem to gain a pound. Her body is so hot. I know it's wrong to have naughty thoughts about your sister-in-law's sister, but I do, especially since I've seen her naked.

I select a pair of black jeans, a light green sweater, and my brown leather jacket. It's getting a bit chilly at night, so this will be perfect for me. I call an Uber, but the app estimate is wrong, and I get impatient, so I hail a cab. I don't care if they charge me.

When I arrive at the bar, Megan is already there and talking to some guy who looks like her ex, Jeremy. I kiss her, and she turns her face, so our lips meet. The guy stares at us and walks away.

"What was that about?"

"He wouldn't leave me alone even after I told him my boyfriend was on his way."

"That's because you look so hot."

She does. Megan is wearing a v-neck sweater, and her beautiful cleavage is so inviting. She's wearing jeans too, and they hug every curve. Her hair is in a long blonde French braid. I prefer when she wears it loose, but we aren't dating, so it's not my call. At the bar, I order a couple of beers and a shot of tequila for each of us. We down it quickly and find a spot near the pool tables.

Our conversation is kept light, and after a couple of beers, we're feeling good. We decide to head over to Flanagan's, which is a couple of blocks away. Megan holds my hand, and I practically swallow it up with my big paw. At the next bar, she treats me to a shot of whiskey. They have darts here, and we play a few games than watch the other people.

Next, we head to The Red Hot Poker. I love this bar because it's not only huge, but there always seems to be some beautiful women there. Not that I care about other women. I think the way the night is going; I wouldn't be surprised if I end up in bed with Megan. She's already a bit tipsy and hanging on me. I keep teasing her by sucking on her ear and neck.

"Do you want to get out of here?" she asks.

"Sure, where do you want to go next?"

"My place or yours?"

"Mine is closer."

I grab her hand, and we weave through the human traffic until we get outside. It's gotten sharply colder since we went inside, and a stiff wind is blowing. We have several blocks of walking so I grab a cab that just put its in-service sign on and let Megan get in first.

We makeout while the cab is driving to my apartment, and when the driver gets there, he has to ask three times for payment. I hand him more than the ride was worth. I think I gave him a ten-dollar tip. Both of us are a little wobbly, but we help each other into the elevator. I again start to kiss her, and her hand is rubbing my growing erection.

In a couple of minutes, we're in my place, and we shed clothing as we head to my bedroom. I'm glad I changed the sheets. Then I realize, I forgot to get condoms. I have one left, but if I know Megan, she's going to want it more than once. I'll worry about it later because right now, I want to fuck.

It's probably not the smartest thing to fuck your sister in-law's sister, but I want her so much that it's too late to stop. She's naked, on all fours on my bed, and begging for me to give it to her. I don't even have to give her foreplay, thank you alcohol for making her so horny.

I think we've been here for five minutes and as I roll the last condom over my cock. I position myself in front of her opening and thrust in hard. Megan pushes back against me, and I grab her hips, working myself hard into her. Since we've screwed before, I know she likes it a little rough. I love to watch my cock slide in and out of her, it's so erotic, and she's tight.

"Is this good?" I ask.

"Yes, but a little harder."

I oblige, and I'm practically ramming in and out of her. I push her legs apart more and thrust several times upward before she starts to moan loudly. She's practically screaming my name when she comes, and her orgasm squeezes me so tightly that I can't help but climax before she finishes. I continue to thrust into her until

I'm spent. Then I quickly pull out and get off the bed to dispose of the condom.

When I come back, she's lying on her side facing me. Her breasts are inviting, and I kneel by her to suck on her nipples.

"You want me to leave?"

She knows the drill, but this is Megan. I don't mind if she stays.

"No. Why the fuck would you ask that?"

"I know you like to get rid of your dates."

"Megan, you're not just any date. You know the score, and we both have the same views on sex."

She yawns and nods. She doesn't want any emotional entanglements, either.

"I'm thirsty. Do you have any bottled water?"

"Yeah, I'll get you some."

"I can get it. I didn't want to get up if you didn't have any."

"Megan, I said I'd get it."

She smacks my bare ass as I turn to leave the room. Why can't all women be like her? She's not clingy or annoying. When I come back, I see that she's sleeping. Megan is beautiful, but she's also Lexi's sister, and I don't think it's a good idea for us to be involved sleeping together too much.

I climb in next to her and resist the urge to pull her against me. Rory got me used to spooning, but this isn't her. I slip over to my side of the bed and pull the covers over both of us. Megan stirs and turns towards me, putting her hand on my chest. I like the contact and don't remove it.

In the morning, I wake to the sound of the shower. A glance at the clock startles me because it's almost 9:30. I never sleep this late on a Saturday. I'm usually up by eight and either working on stuff for the office or off to breakfast with one of my friends.

As soon as Megan comes out, wearing my bathrobe, I kiss her forehead.

"Thanks for last night," she says.

"No, thank you. I need to shower."

I head into the bathroom, which is already steamed up from Megan. While I'm washing, I think about last night. I fell right back into my old habits and with a woman practically related to me. Megan's dressed by the time I come out with a fluffy white towel around my waist. I don't want her to leave, but she has her own shit to do.

"Want to hang out later this week?" I ask.

"I'll text or call you. I have a big project I'm working on and might be getting out late the whole week. Maybe next Saturday?"

She looks at me expectantly, and I know what she's hinting at, another fuck session. I'm game.

"Possibly or Friday if you get out at a reasonable hour."

"If you promise to get me some hazelnut coffee pods."

"That can be arranged."

She strokes my damp chest with her nails and my dick twitches.

"You better get out of here before I take you back to bed."

Megan laughs and plants a soft kiss on my lips. God, she is sexy.

"Bye, Hunter. I'll call you."

I watch her saunter out of the room. She's definitely friends with benefits material, but I also need to tread lightly with her because she's family.

I don't have to be at JC and Lexi's to babysit until six, so I have a good chunk of the day to lie around and do nothing. I do exactly that. I sit in front of the television and watch college football all day. At five, I start getting ready. I was going to wear a cashmere sweater, but if Johnny slops it up, I'm not going to be happy. Instead, I pull on an NYU sweatshirt that's getting a bit threadbare and a pair of dark blue jeans.

It only takes me ten minutes to get to JC's by cab, so I have plenty of time. I pour a bowl of Captain Crunch in a bowl, add some milk and begin chowing down. When I'm finished, I pop the bowl in the sink and get my leather jacket on, pulling my NY Giants cap on my head.

I'm at JC's by 5:30. From inside, I hear Johnny screaming. I hope that this isn't going to be my night. I love the kid, but not when he's like that. Lexi opens the door holding a red-faced Johnny with tears streaming down his face. He sees me and stops for a second, then continues to wail.

"I'm sorry, Hunter. He's usually pretty good."

"Let me have him."

Lexi raises her eyebrows and hands, Johnny, to me. He looks puzzled, but that gets him to stop crying, and he grabs the bill of my cap. I kiss his little tearstained cheek, and Lexi smiles at me.

"Go, I got him," I said.

I took my cap off and put it on his head, causing him to laugh. Then I sit on the couch to play peek-a-boo. My nephew is a handsome kid. He has the same sandy-colored hair as JC. His eyes are sea blue like JC, and he has the Lawson cleft chin.

I bounce him on my knee, and he keeps laughing. JC comes out of the bedroom, smiling at me.

"He looks good on you brother. You should think about settling down."

In a flash, I think he realizes what he said and his face clouds. Lexi must have told him about Rory. It stings, and he looks up at me apologetically. I wave it away and continue to play with Johnny. He's calm now, and I hope I have an easy night with him. This will be my first time babysitting alone. Usually, it's with Megan or my parents.

Lexi comes out looking beautiful in a pretty short black dress and heels. I haven't seen her dressed up for a while. I guess with Johnny, a night out is hard to come by. I'm glad to give them a break since, by next year, they're going to have two little ones to watch after.

"Can you handle him?" she asks.

"Of course. I'll be fine."

"If you're not, call us."

"Lexi, leave him be. He's taken care of Johnny before," JC said.

He helps her with her coat, and he pats me on the shoulder.

"Call mom if you need help. She needs a break," he whispers.

"I heard that," Lexi says.

I start laughing because they are so perfect together.

"Go, I can handle this little slugger."

After they leave, I take Johnny to his room. Even though he's only a little over two, he has a big boy bed.

"So, what do you want to do?"

He looks at me, puzzled, and starts to suck on his finger. I sit on the floor and grab a container full of blocks that I dump out. He's fascinated as I start to stack them like a wall, and he joins me.

"Unter, like this," he says as he knocks the blocks down and places them in a row. I follow suit, and before I know it, we've been sitting there for over an hour. Johnny looks like he's falling asleep, and I tell him we should clean up.

"You want me to read you a book?"

He smiles and points to one sitting on his nightstand. I remember this when I was a kid, "Are You My Mother." My parents used to read it to me, and so did JC since he's several years older than me. I pull the bed guard out so I can sit down, and I get Johnny settled in bed. He's leaning against me, and I can smell his sweet little head. Suddenly I'm overwhelmed with love for my nephew.

I begin to read, and his eyes start to droop until he's asleep. I hold him for a few minutes, and I love feeling him against me. What would it be like to be a parent? Maybe it's time I settle down and have one just like him. I gently get up and pull him down a little until his head is on the pillow, then I cover him and push the bed guard back. I can't help but stand there watching him sleep for a few minutes.

I keep checking on him through the night, and when JC and

Lexi come home, it's almost midnight. I fell asleep on the couch, watching a football game.

"Hunter, wake up," JC says as he touches my arm.

"Hey."

"Johnny wore you out, didn't he?"

"Nope. We played blocks, and then I read him a story. He was the perfect little gentleman. No crying or fussing."

"You lucked out because he could have been a little terror."

"I'll watch him for you anytime."

Lexi and JC exchange glances. I bet they thought I was going to pull my hair out with him.

"We just might take you up on that again."

"Please do," I yawn.

Lexi heads to check on Johnny.

"Do you want to sleep over tonight?" JC asks.

"Nah, I'm going home. It's only a few blocks."

"You sure you're not going out?"

"Seriously, I'm not. I went out last night."

"With?"

"Megan. We did a bar crawl."

"And where did you two end up?"

I can't help but smirk. JC knows we've hooked up before.

My brother shakes his head. "Hunter, you have to stop doing that."

"I know, but neither one of us wants an attachment. It's just casual."

"Yeah, but she's family."

We stop talking as Lexi enters the room.

"What are you two girls talking about?"

"Nothing, sports. Want to join in?"

"Not really."

"I'm leaving anyway," I say.

I kiss Lexi and hug JC then head out the door. It's blustery, and I pull my leather coat tighter around me. Of course, no cabs in sight. I tap on my Uber app and wait, thinking it better not be the Mercedes guy. In three minutes, a white Toyota Camry comes by to pick me up.

At home, I get myself a beer and turn on the television. A bunch of reruns is on from the seventies, and I stay up until almost three watching them. This isn't like me, but I feel different since my breakup with Rory. I can't explain it, but I do.

CHAPTER 10

Christmas is finally here. I recently got my Finance Degree from NYU. I'm glad to be finished. The city is all decked out in lights. Megan, Matty, Olivia (Matty's sister) and I went to Rockefeller Center to see the tree lighting at the end of November; then we went to look at the decorated store windows on Fifth Avenue.

I picked up my tree two days ago just in the nick of time since the holiday will be here in four days. This is the first year I've decorated my apartment. Usually, I spend most of the holiday hanging out with friends, drinking, and having numerous one night stands.

In the past few months, I've only slept with three women, one of them being Megan. That stopped weeks ago since she started dating some guy named Craig. I'm just not into it anymore. I want a meaningful relationship, and now that I do, I'm only finding women that want to fuck, a one and done.

It's getting to the point where I think I'm going to start setting up profiles on the dating websites. The guys on my summer soccer team told me that they couldn't believe I want to settle down. Half of them are married, and the other half were, are, just like I was. Those are the guys that give me a hard time about the change in me.

As I decorate my tree, I'm getting excited about Christmas. I decided to sleep over JC and Lexi's because I want to see Johnny's face when he opens his gifts. They trust me with him now more than any other family member except my parents and Lexi's. I watch him a couple of times a month to give them a break. In a few months, Lexi will give birth to their second child, a little girl.

My father gave me a pretty great bonus this year because of all the extra work I've been doing. We expanded our intern program, and now each department gets two interns starting in December and May. We've been able to retain several new employees that way in the past.

The company has been expanding, and my father is looking to branch into other areas of business like real estate development. We certainly have the funds to do it. Now we need to think about the proper personnel to get that department off the ground. It's something we plan to discuss in the New Year.

Poor JC. Dad keeps trying to get him to come to work for us. We really could use a strong person in the sales and marketing department. The salary is enticing, but our father was overbearing when we were growing up, especially to JC. He doesn't want to be under his thumb, but it's getting hard to resist the money that our father is dangling in front of him.

He and Lexi could use a bigger apartment because they had to give up their office for the new baby's room. More money would mean a bigger place, and Lexi could work part-time or not at all. I know that JC has been going back and forth about this for a while. It would be great to work with him.

∼

As the time grows to Christmas Eve, Matty and I are shopping in Macy's for some last-minute stocking stuffers. We run into Ellie,

Rory's old roommate. Matty and she broke up a few months ago, but they occasionally hang out. I'm looking at a pair of women's leather gloves for my mom when she taps my shoulder.

"Rory is coming back to New York in January to finish her degree."

"That's nice," I say matter of factly and go back to looking at the gloves.

"Maybe we can get together for lunch or something."

I don't want to be an asshole because Ellie is nice, and I like her, but I need to end this now. I have nothing to say to Rory.

"Rory made it abundantly clear she doesn't want to have anything to do with me. If she did, she would've contacted me when she went to Boston."

Ellie's face tightens. "Hunter, there are some things you don't know about her. It's not my place to tell you either; it's hers. If you don't want to see her, that's your decision."

"It is, and I came to terms with it a long time ago. No use dredging up things that can't be changed."

I sift through the rest of the gloves looking for a size medium while Ellie talks to Matty for a few more minutes, then I move on to matching scarves. My mother probably has a million of these things, but I need to look like I'm busy. I don't want to talk about Rory anymore. After we say goodbye to Ellie, Matty questions me.

"You really are pissed at Rory, aren't you?"

"She dumped me without any explanation, and I don't want to discuss it. It's ages ago. I've moved on."

"You might run into her in the city. Don't you think you should talk to her when she gets back to New York? Maybe she can offer some insight as to why she did what she did."

"Matty, I don't care anymore. She had her chance, and she stepped all over it. I learned my lesson."

"If that's the case, why aren't you out there? When was the last time you slept with someone?"

"I don't remember, a few weeks ago."

"Why?"

"Because I don't feel like that anymore. I think I spent too much time fucking around, and now that I want to settle down, I don't know where to start. I keep running into these women who don't want relationships; they want sex."

Matty starts to laugh and tells me that I used to do the same thing. I did, and maybe I'm getting it back in spades. I punch him in the arm, and we head to the cashier to pay for the items we have. The line is long, and the young woman in front of me is loaded down with so much stuff she can barely hold it.

I have three items, gloves, a scarf, and slippers.

"Can I help you out," I say over her shoulder as she juggles her items.

She turns, and I'm struck by her. She's adorable. Not the painted nails and dressed to the nines women that I usually screw, but really cute. Her light brown bob slips into her eyes as she turns to me.

"You're a lifesaver," she says as she hands me some of the clothing she's holding, and we strike up a conversation. I glance at Matty, who's grinning like a Cheshire Cat.

"I'm Lily Carlyle."

"Hunter Lawson. I'd offer you my hand, but both of ours are full."

She smiles, and I know it's genuine. We continue to chit chat until it's her turn to be rung up by the cashier. I place her stuff on the counter, and she thanks me. Matty is smirking at me when her back turns to pay for her purchases. I know what he's thinking, but I have no plans to fuck her, not yet anyway. This is a woman I could get to know. After she's done at the counter, I push Matty ahead of me to pay for his items so that I can talk to her.

"Lily, would you like to go on a date?"

"Oh, I'm sorry, but I'm dating someone already. Maybe we could hang out, though."

"Sure. Let me have your phone number, and I'll call or text you."

She asks for my number first and then texts me. So now I have her number. I wish she weren't dating someone, but you have to start somewhere, and if friends are it, then fine. On the way home, Matty says I crashed and burned, but I don't see it that way. Maybe her relationship won't work out, and then I can date her. The possibility is there.

～

At home, I finish wrapping the few gifts I have left and pack them up to take to my brother's apartment. Everyone is coming over tomorrow, and Lexi is making a big spread along with my mother, her mother, Megan, and Lexi's other sister, Emma. Megan's boyfriend is going to join us since his family lives in Oregon, and he can't afford to fly home for the holiday. That should be awkward.

I decide not to bother with Uber and find a cab instead. I have two big suitcases filled with clothing and gifts. I hope everyone likes what I bought them. I can't wait to see Johnny's face when he opens the gifts I got him. This will be his first Christmas where he understands what the holiday is all about. I wanted to take him to look at the Fifth Avenue windows, but it's been incredibly cold out, and JC said no.

When I get to JC and Lexi's apartment, the whole place is aglow with Christmas lights from the tree, around the fireplace mantel, and the windows facing Central Park. Johnny is still up, dressed in feety pajamas with snowmen on them. He flings himself at me when I come in, almost knocking me over. I love this freaking kid.

"Unter, Santa coming," he screams.

"Yes, I know. I thought you would be in bed by now. He won't come to people's houses if they're still up."

His sweet face gets all serious, and he puts his index finger in his mouth and begins to chew on it. I pick him up and dislodge it, kissing his chubby cheek.

"Don't worry, I'm sure Santa will make it here, but you need to go to bed."

I see JC and Lexi watching me as he struggles for me to put him down, which I do. He holds his hand out, and I gently take it. Johnny pulls me into the bedroom and hands me a book that was sitting on the floor. It's the same one I read to him months ago, "Are You My Mother."

"Read Unter, read."

"Okay, get into bed, and I'll read you a story, but then you need to go to sleep."

He nods his head, and I move the bed guard so I can sit down. From the doorway, Lexi is watching me with amusement as I read to him. Halfway through the book, he's asleep, and I get up to cover him and put the guard back in place.

"We could not get him to sleep for anything. Then you come over, and he's out," Lexi whispers.

"What can I say, the kid loves me."

"He definitely does. I'm glad you came."

I go back to the living room and unpack the gifts I have for everyone, placing them under the tree.

"Hunter, you bought Johnny way too many things."

"He's my only nephew, and I want to spoil him."

"Yeah, you and his grandparents and his aunts. He is going to have so many gifts he won't play with them all for weeks."

"It will keep him busy."

After JC prepares some hot chocolate and tea for Lexi, we sit around the tree, talking and watching the colorful lights blink on and off. I really like this family thing. Soon I'm going to be twenty-seven, and I want this for myself: a wife and some children. I can more than afford to take care of a family, and I'm ready.

"Hunter? You okay?" JC asks.

I realize that I'm daydreaming.

"Yeah, fine. This is going to be a great Christmas."

My brother raises his eyebrows because, in the past, I've high tailed it out of family gatherings right after dinner. Now I can't wait.

"Where is my brother, and what have you done with him?"

I laugh because it's true. I've changed, but it's for the better. At least something good came out of me falling in love with Rory even if it was for a short time.

∽

The holiday turns out to be awesome. Johnny wakes up early, and I sit on the floor with him while he opens his gifts. I got him an activity toy with some plastic cars that he dropped his other toys for the minute he opened it. I'm thrilled that he loves it, and I beam as I play with him. I look up, and JC is just shaking his head in disbelief.

Later on, the rest of the family comes over with more gifts for us all to open. My mother, Jillian, loves the leather gloves, woven scarf, and Michael Kors bag I got her. Lexi's mom, Susan, and father, Brian, thank me for the crystal vase and knife set I gave them. I got Megan and Emma the same thing, gift certificates to Victoria's Secret. You can't go wrong with those.

I received a bunch of gift cards, a silver engraved flask, and a new pair of soccer cleats. It's a perfect day, and by the end of it, my face is hurting from smiling so much. Emma, Lexi's youngest sister, sits next to me. She looks more like Megan than Lexi with long blonde hair she likes to keep in a ponytail and green eyes. She's the most petite of the three sisters and very appealing, but also off-limits. I would never sleep with her for fear of Lexi cutting my balls off.

"Hey Hunter, surprised to see you here so late," Emma says.

"I'm enjoying myself, so why would I leave?"

"Usually, you have something to do."

I grin at her. "Not tonight. Tonight is for family."

"We should hang out sometime. I want to go to some clubs here in the city."

Oh boy, that could only lead to trouble if I take her out. I've already had a friends with benefits thing with Megan. I have a feeling that Emma wants more than that. I prefer not to get involved.

"You'd probably be better off going with Megan. I don't frequent the clubs much anymore," I said.

She pouts, "Neither does she now that she's with Craig."

"I wish I could help you, but I just don't go anymore."

"Maybe Matty would be interested?"

"You'd have to ask him."

"Is he dating anyone?"

"Not right now, but you should talk to Lexi since Matty is her best friend's brother."

"I don't need her permission."

"I didn't say you did. I'm just saying."

She gets up in a huff, and I'm glad I don't have to continue this conversation any longer. Johnny comes over to me and wants to sit in my lap. He's been my little shadow all day, and I love it.

"What do you have there, big man?"

He hands me a small red sports car that he had in his pants pocket. I start making vroom, vroom noises, and have his giggling. I think he's tired because he leans back against me and starts sucking his thumb. I stroke his hair and kiss the top of his head. In a matter of minutes, he's asleep. I wave to Lexi, and she comes to take him from me.

"He had a long exciting day. He's exhausted."

"You know, I can take him to bed. You have guests."

She doesn't blink an eye because she knows I'll take good care of him. Johnny continues to sleep as I rise with him in my arms and stays that way until I start to undress him for bed.

"Unter, not tired," he mumbles as he looks up at me with his eyelids drooping.

"Yes, you are. Santa is still watching you for next year, so you have to be a good boy."

He lets me dress him for bed and wants me to finish the story I was reading the night before, except he wants me to start from the beginning again. I do, and he falls asleep in my lap. I sit there smelling his clean hair and the unique scent of baby. When I come out of his bedroom, Lexi asks if he gave me a hard time. I tell her no, he just wanted me to read a story.

～

The rest of the holidays go well, and I almost forget about Lily until I see her in a Starbucks a couple of weeks into January.

"You never called me," she said.

"I'm sorry. Work has been crazy now that the holidays are past. We are dealing with some expansion issues."

"You can say you forgot. You don't need to explain."

She seems annoyed, which surprises me since she has a boyfriend. It's not like I promised to date her and never called. We were only supposed to be friends.

"Okay, I forgot. But I'm here now. Do you want to make time to get together? Lunch maybe if you and your boyfriend don't have plans."

Lily frowns. "We broke up just after Christmas. He was a jerk."

I should say he was. Who breaks up with their girlfriend after Christmas? Someone that wants gifts, that's who.

"That's horrible. Well, his loss is my gain. Would you like to go to dinner this Saturday?"

"Sure. We could split the bill."

"I won't hear of it. I'm buying for my gross lack of response."

She giggles at this, and I think that I'm going to like this woman.

"Are you free later?"

"Unfortunately not. I have to get to work for a conference. It's an all-day thing and then a working dinner. I seriously wish I didn't have to go, but I'm a presenter."

I want to find out more about her, but we both have to get to the office so I'll save it for later.

"Then Saturday, Lily Carlyle."

She laughs again, "Thank you, Mr. Lawson."

"I'll text you, and you can tell me where I'm picking you up."

"I will. Have a nice day."

She leaves the shop, and I wait for the Barista to finish my order. I'm glad I ran into her because I need to go on a date already. It's been far too long. I'm glad it's Thursday because I just asked her, and I'm anticipating Saturday already.

The next two days of work are mentally fatiguing. Getting the new development department off the ground is taking a lot of time. I'm not involved, but I am. My father wants me to be aware of all the nuances of the business so I can eventually take over. Because of it, most of the contractual duties for acquisitions and mergers have been farmed out to the legal department.

By the time I get home on Friday, I'm ready to spend the next ten hours in bed and watch the NHL channel all day Saturday. But I have a date, and I'm not even sure where to take Lily. I could go Italian or Japanese; maybe she would like Chinese or Indian. I should text her to find out.

What would you like to eat tomorrow?

Would you mind if we go to a French restaurant?

. . .

French is one thing I would never have thought. I know of a place in midtown, but I'm not sure if I can get reservations at this late date.

Let me see if I can get reservations for Fontaine.

Really? I've always wanted to go there.

Give me a minute.

I call them, and they're booked up for the night. I wonder if JC's friend from college, Paul Borrego, who coincidentally owns a restaurant named French's Steakhouse, can get me a reservation. I phone him.
"Hey, Paul. Could you do me a favor?"
"What kind of favor?"
"Do you have an in at Fontaine?"
"I might. What were you looking for?"
"Reservation for Saturday?"
Paul hisses into the phone. "Weekends are rough, but I'll see what I can do."
"Thanks."
"I'll give you a call back."
Paul hangs up, and I text Lily while I'm waiting.

Fontaine is in the works. Don't get your hopes up, though; weekends are tight.

. . .

You can't see me, but I'm smiling. I'm crossing my fingers.

Twenty long minutes later and I'm thrilled when Paul calls me back and says he got me a reservation at 7:45. I thank him and let him know if there is anything I can do, don't hesitate. I text Lily again.

We have a reservation at Fontaine for 7:45 on Saturday. Let me have your address, and I'll get you.

She texts me her address in Soho, and we're all set. I'm excited like a teenage boy going on his first date. What's wrong with me? I'm usually pretty at ease with women.

I spend the rest of the night and all day Saturday getting things ready for my date. Fontaine is a very expensive and very swanky place. I need to look sharp and decide on my blue pinstriped suit with a crisp white shirt and light blue tie. I shine up my black shoes until I can see my reflection.

At 7:00, I head out and see that it's flurrying. I hate winter and can't wait for the warmer weather. My doorman hails a cab for me, and I give the driver Lily's address. When I'm on the way, I text her to let her know I'm coming. She's waiting at the door, and I can't see what she's wearing because it's covered by her thick blue wool coat. Her long thick brown hair is styled to frame her face, and her smoky eye shadow accentuates the soft gray of her irises.

"Thank you for asking me to dinner. I can't believe I'm going to Fontaine."

"I had to promise the moon for these reservations."

She turns to me with a frown on her face, "I didn't want you to

ADDICTED BY LOVE

go to any trouble. We could have had burgers, and I would have been fine with it."

"I could ask the driver to turn around, and we can go to a burger place."

"Are you serious? We can, if you want."

"Hell no. I want to show you a nice time and so Fontaine's it is."

She pats my arm, and I wrap my hand around her tiny one. Lily doesn't pull away, and I like the feel of her hand in mine.

Fontaine's is as beautiful and elegant as I have heard. Crystal chandeliers hang over each round white linen-covered table. The wallpaper is striped gold, and the carpets a mix of mustard yellow and rust. The service is fantastic, and so is the food. We share a bottle of wine and great conversation during dinner.

Lily tells me that she works for a software company and handles the sales of their educational products. On the weekend, she volunteers for a food bank and visits nursing homes to play the piano for the residents. She seems like a very giving person. Before we know it, it's almost 11:00 PM, and the place is closing in a half hour. I summon the waiter for the bill, and Lily reaches for it, but I pull it away.

"I invited you, and I'm going to pay, but thank you for the offer."

Besides the bill, I hand the waiter a couple of hundreds for the great service then I escort Lily to get our coats. On the way to her apartment in the cab, she asks me if I want to come up to her place. I want to very much, but I don't want to seem too forward, so I decline. She looks disappointed, and I use my thumb to push a lock of hair off her cheek.

"I had a wonderful time tonight, and I hope you'll do me the honor of letting me take you out again."

"You want to go out again?"

"Of course. What gave you the idea that I didn't?"

"I thought because you didn't want to come up to my apartment."

"Nonsense. I like you, and I think we should go out again. How about brunch tomorrow, say noon?"

She smiles, and I can see how straight her teeth are perfect and white.

"I'd like that very much except for one thing."

"What's that?"

"I'm paying."

I want to argue, but it doesn't matter now. I'll discuss it with her tomorrow. When the cab pulls up to her apartment, I get out and take her hand to help her out. Before she goes in, I softly kiss her lips and give her a gentle hug.

"Until tomorrow, sweet Lily."

She's perfect; I think on the way home and thus starts our dating life together.

CHAPTER 11

"It's our four-month anniversary Hunter. I can't believe we've been together that long already."

I smile because our relationship is so easy. "I know. We should celebrate."

I'm getting dressed in my closet while Lily combs her hair in the mirror over my dresser. She's been wonderful, and I'm in love with her. I hesitated to say the words for weeks because of what happened with Rory. With her, I said it too soon and got burned. Lily told me after a month; she was in love with me. She was patient and let me reciprocate on my terms.

I finally told her about Rory and what happened. She also knows all about my life with women before her, and she didn't chastise me or seem repulsed. I've treated her like gold because she deserves it.

It's the third week of May, and Lily attends her annual software summit. She gets together with others in the business, and they talk shop. This year she's one of the speakers and has been preparing for the last two weeks for her speech. I'm in awe of how comfortable she feels speaking in front of people. I hate it, but sometimes, I need to do it at work.

"Remember, I'm leaving tomorrow morning for Dallas and won't be back until Tuesday," Lily said.

That's almost an entire week that we'll be away from each other, and I know I'm going to miss her. Our soccer league starts up soon, and some of the guys on my team want to practice now that the warm weather is here, so that will keep me occupied.

"I know. I'm going to miss you, but I've got things to keep me busy."

She raises her eyebrows. "Oh, I hope those things aren't getting into trouble and carousing until all hours of the night."

She got a taste of that when I attended a bachelor party here in the city about a month ago. I drunk dialed her at four in the morning. Lucky it was a Saturday. She good-naturedly laughed it off and told me to get my ass home. That's what I love about her; she doesn't judge. Lily knows that it's not a constant thing. I've limited myself to a drink here and there since we've been together.

"Nope. Just some practice and maybe a beer after. I have to keep sharp for work since tomorrow the new interns are coming in. I've been so busy I never got a chance to see who is assigned to my department."

Since the New Year, my father has brought in consultants to help get the real estate development department up and running. I've been taking the lead, and after four months, I have a pretty good handle on it. We have a couple of projects in the works with some buildings we purchased by the Hudson River. The plan is to build luxury apartments with garage space. We're working on the zoning for it right now.

"I hope that will mean you won't be coming home at eight each night anymore."

"I might still be late, but hopefully, after the contractors start construction, I can relax. Plus, a few interns can help lighten the load."

Lily embraces me, and I bend my head, pressing my lips to

hers. We deepen the kiss, and I back off when I feel a stirring below my waist. She's been the perfect girlfriend, more than I could ever want. She's sweet, kind, cooks great, and is compassionate. During the winter, I did some volunteer work at the food bank. I even pledged several thousand dollars in the name of Lawson Corp.

"I have to go. I need to speak with my assistant and the developer who's coming with me."

Lily smirks. "You're no fun."

"We'll spend some time tonight if you come home at a decent hour. I have to go home, though, so you might want to stay over at my place."

I nod, but I hate her place. She's been living there for five years, ever since she started in the software business. Her apartment is small and basically a studio. She can afford better but hasn't had the chance to look. At least it's in a decent neighborhood.

We go down in the elevator together, and I hold her against me. I feel sorry that she's going to be away for a week. We part on the sidewalk, and I hail a cab. Her office is across town, so we never travel together.

Today, I'm bogged down with one meeting after another. I barely have time to inhale a sandwich my assistant got for me. One of the building's zoning has come through, and we're deciding on bids for contractors that's been in the works for the past two months. I'll be glad to get this project off the ground.

It's well past eight when I leave the office, and I'm on my way to my apartment when I realize I need to go to Lily's. I give the driver the address and text her to let her know I'm on my way.

Don't come. It's too late. I have to go to bed in about an hour because I'm getting up at four for my 7:00 AM flight.

I want to come. I wanted to see her before she leaves, but it's my fault. I got involved with paperwork that I could have let sit until tomorrow. Before I knew it, it was after eight.

I'm sorry, I'm so late. I wanted to see you before you leave. Can I please come over? PLEASE!

You can come over, but you can't stay. If you stay, I'll never get any sleep!

Lily's right. I won't let her sleep, but we're so good together in bed that it's hard to resist. I guess I'll be well acquainted with my hand this week while she's gone.

By the time I get to Lily's apartment, she's already in her pajamas. Not the sexy kind that she wears at my place but simple cotton ones in a dark shade of blue. It's not a turn off because anything she wears is sexy because she wears it.

I look at her sheepishly. "I'm sorry. I had to see you."

"I'm glad you came." She grasps my hand and pulls me to the couch.

We sit on her couch and kiss for a little while. I want to hold her and get my fill of her in my arms.

She pushes at my chest. "You should go."

I nuzzle her cheek, looking into her eyes. "I just got here a few minutes ago."

I know the look on her face, it says she was getting heated by my kisses.

"But if you stay any longer, I'll be exhausted tomorrow."

I chuckle because I think a little more kissing, and we'll be in her bed soon.

"So, you want me to leave?"

"Want is not the word I would use. Have to leave is more like it, and you know why."

We rise from the couch as I plant a big wet kiss on her cheek, and Lily smiles.

"I'll miss you. Do good," I said.

"You know I always do."

I smirk. "My, how conceited you are."

"Is it conceited to be aware of how good you are at your job?"

"No, but sometimes it's better to let everyone else let you know."

"You're silly, Hunter. It gives me confidence knowing."

Lily pushes me out the door, and I stroke her cheek before I head for the elevators.

"I love you, Lily. Be careful."

"I love you too."

The doors close on the elevator, and down I go. I have to figure out what I'm going to do this weekend without her. I might take Johnny to the park and give Lexi a break from him. She's ready to pop and will probably give birth soon.

∾

That night, I find it hard to sleep. Over the past few months, very rarely have I slept in bed alone. Lily doesn't go to events often, and this is the first time since we're together that she has. I keep to my side but toss and turn through the night. We normally sleep with our legs or arms entwined, and it's weird not to tonight.

When I wake up at six to workout, I'm exhausted, but I trudge on. Taking a day off will only lead to bad habits. I want to maintain my physique and push myself hard on the treadmill, then upper body training. When I'm finished, I'm soaked with sweat. My building has a full-service gym, and at that hour, it's usually not busy.

Today is the day we meet the new interns. I wonder if we will find that diamond in the rough. There is always one in each group that is quite impressive. We get students and recent graduates from area colleges, NYU, Columbia, CUNY, and even a few from out of state. In the past, we've had several interns from Harvard, Yale, Dartmouth, and Cornell. Lawson is such a large corporation with a great reputation; that we get many applicants.

There is a meet and greet in the conference room at 9:00 AM, where the interns will get their assignments and meet the senior staff. Because I'm a Vice President, I have to be there even though I have a ton of stuff to do. When I walk in, I see the twenty-two interns that were invited to Lawson. I scan their faces, and I freeze when I see one…Rory.

What the fuck is she doing here? After what she did, I can't believe she would have the balls to apply for our internship program. There are a hundred other companies she could have applied to, why ours? My father comes into the room, and I lean against the back wall listening to him while he makes introductions.

Rory's face fixes on mine when he introduces me, and I give her an icy stare. I'm rattled by her presence and almost trip over my tongue when I say hello to our newest staff. The Human Resources Director hands out assignments to each one of the interns, and I practically snatch the master sheet out of her hand as she passes.

Quickly I scan the sheet and find Rory's name. I could scream. She's been assigned to my department, along with three others. My first question is, why? She was a Finance major, so why is she working in Real Estate Development? I'm sure the Accounting Department could use someone like her.

After my father dismisses everyone, I hurry over to Rory and grasp her elbow. She whirls around at my touch, almost knocking me off balance.

"I want to see you in my office, now," I hiss.

"Of course, Mr. Lawson."

ADDICTED BY LOVE

I walk ahead and hold the door for her, so she goes first. She's dressed very businesslike in a charcoal gray suit. The skirt hugs her ass and hips. My stomach tightens, and a lump forms in my throat. Why is she having this effect on me? When we get to my office, I open the door and gently push her in ahead of me, then close the door.

"Sit down. We need to talk," I say sternly.

She sits, and I go around my desk, sliding a mountain of folders to the side so I can see her.

"I'm not going to mince words. What the fuck are you doing here?"

"I beg your pardon?"

"I can't believe you would even have the gall to apply for an internship after what you did. Didn't you think you would see me here?"

"I did, but out of all the places I applied, Lawson had the best opportunity for me to learn and grow my career."

"Really? Out of all the companies? You're from Boston, doesn't your father's family own buildings? Why didn't you work for them?"

I can't help spitting out the words with venom attached to them. I'm so angry that she would disrupt me at my company, in my department no less.

"I didn't want any special favors. I just graduated, and this company has a growing development department. I thought maybe I could score a job after I'm finished. I plan on staying in New York."

"You can't work for me."

"Why?"

I place my arms on the desk and lean towards her.

"I loved you, and you just blew me off like it meant nothing."

She nervously smoothes her hair off her face, and then I see it, a large emerald cut engagement ring on her finger. It just makes me angrier. She notices me staring at it and puts her hand in her lap.

"You don't know the full story. I had some issues I needed to work out. My grandmother was sick. It was for the best."

"For who? You? You tore my heart out. I see you moved on pretty quickly. Congratulations. You sucked some poor bastard in, and he asked you to marry him?"

"That's not fair."

I see her lower lip quivering, and I want her to hurt like she hurt me.

"What's not fair is you coming here to work. It's like thumbing your nose at me. I'm asking Human Resources to transfer you to another department."

"You can't do that. I want to work here in this department."

"Too bad. As long as I'm the head of it, you will not work for me. You can go."

She gets up and walks to the door with her head down, then turns to me.

"Hunter, for what it's worth, I loved you, but things got in the way."

Rory walks out the door, and my heart clenches. It's unlike me to do what I did. I would never speak to a woman that way, but she destroyed me. Thank God for Lily. She brought me back and taught me that not all women are like Aurora Barton.

After I cool down, I head to Human Resources. The interns are in orientation for the rest of the day, so I have time to get Rory transferred. Only the joke is on me. All the interns have been assigned based on their qualifications. Rory worked for her family's company, which means she has real estate experience. HR has two choices, she stays put, or she gets dismissed.

I'm not so mean spirited that I would have her dismissed, but I'm not going to make her life easy. She will get the shittiest, most labor-intensive, mind fatiguing assignments. Maybe she'll quit. I know that's being petty, but can I be blamed for how I feel?

I'm not sure how to proceed for the day. My emotions are shot, and I spend most of it going over the same report more than once. Nothing is sinking in, and what's more alarming is that my mind keeps drifting to Rory's naked body. Every time I try to shake the memory out of my head, it comes back. I come to my senses when Lily texts me to tell me she's okay and very busy preparing for her speech.

I don't see Rory or any of the other interns for the rest of the day. I need to figure out what I will have them doing starting tomorrow. I plan on having Rory run errands to the zoning board. That will keep her busy for the entire day, and I won't have to speak to her.

At home, I down a couple of shots of whiskey and think about the lucky bastard that gets to marry her. How fast she forgot me. Did she go home and take up with some guy right away? Or was this the one man that she never told me about?

Again, I can't sleep, and it's not because Lily is not beside me. It's because I have no clue what I'm going to do about Rory. I want to know what happened, what was she referring to when she said she had some issues to work out? Did they have anything to do with me?

What's more, I can't deny my lingering attraction to her. I'm her boss now, and I need to remain professional, or she can bring me up on sexual harassment charges. The only ones in my family that know I had a relationship with her are JC and Lexi. My father has no clue, and if he found out, he would probably let Rory go or move her. Is it twisted to want the ex-girlfriend who broke your heart to work for yo
u?

The next morning, I wake up to several texts from Lily. They were sent to me about 2:00 AM, which means she was up at midnight.

Normally, she's in bed before me, which is around ten, unless we make love.

I had an awesome speech.

They were eating out of the palm of my hand. I made an impression.

Lots of great comments. Now I can breathe and enjoy the rest of the conference.

I wish you could've seen me. I wish you were here.

I wish I were there too. I've turned into a huge mush over the past few months. I'm happy for her and decide not to tell her about Rory until she gets back. I get up, rubbing at my considerable erection.

I'm horny as hell and will end up with aching balls all day if I don't jerk off.

I set the hot water and stroke my cock before I step into the shower, trying to keep Lily in my thoughts, but Rory pushes her face away. I can't stop my brain or my memories. I feel guilty after I come, I shouldn't be thinking about anyone but Lily unless it's a fantasy about a movie star.

I dress in a dark blue suit with a light blue shirt and red tie. I want to look commanding now that I have interns who are in my charge. I haven't met the other ones, but I know their two men and another woman. I hope Rory is ready to work her ass off because she's going to hate me when the three months are up.

The office is quiet because I came in earlier than usual. I want to try to knock off some of the smaller details before I get started with our new employees. I'm engrossed in my work when I hear a knock on my door. I glance at my watch and realize it's past 9:00 AM, and I need to sit with my interns to delegate work. I can't wait.

"Come in," I said as I leaned back in my office chair.

They're all eager-eyed as they file in, but my focus is on Rory, who's wearing a tight black skirt and silky gray blouse. I shake my gaze from her because I'm an attached man, and she's an attached woman. There should be nothing intimate between us.

When all four of them are sitting in my office, I hand out assignments. I smile at Rory as I hand her the info I need her to retrieve from the zoning department. She doesn't bat an eyelash. The other three interns, Joe, Rick, and Paula, are all assigned smaller items to do in the office.

After they leave, I settle down to work on the items I was dealing with before I was interrupted. My mind drifts to Rory. She fixed on me with those beautiful sapphires when I handed her the zoning paperwork; it made my cock twitch. I can't help but remember looking into those eyes when I was fucking her.

I'm starting to feel guilty about making her go to the zoning office, but I shouldn't. She had to know that working for me wasn't going to be easy after what happened between us.

The other interns are in and out of my office over a few hours, but I don't see Rory until well after three in the afternoon. She comes back and hands me the information I requested, and I look it over, nodding as I review it. She heads to the door and closes it, then sits in the tweed chair in front of my desk.

Her eyebrows are knitted together, and her grip on the arm of the chair has her knuckles turning white. "Is this how it's going to be?"

"Excuse me?" I said.

"You're going to assign me the hard stuff while the others get silly sorting and filing jobs?"

I focus my eyes on hers. "You wanted to work here, and this is what it's all about. You aren't going to get anything easy just because we fucked."

Rory pouts her bottom lip. "Is that what you call it?"

"It apparently didn't mean anything to you, so it was just fucking."

"That's not true. It meant a lot more to me than just sex."

I drop the paperwork I'm holding and give her a hard stare.

"Rory, why did you do what you did then? If it meant more to you than just sex, if I meant more to you, then why?"

"I was dealing with a lot. School was a disaster, my grandmother, and then you."

Now it's my turn to grip the arm of my chair, digging my nails into the soft leather. "What me? You were in love with me, were you not?"

"Yes, I was."

"Are you still?"

"Are you?"

"Don't you know it's impolite to answer a question with a question?"

"I just want to know."

"I wasn't going to wait for you. When someone ignores you and doesn't have the decency to let you know what is going on, they don't care. I didn't have to date to know that. I wasn't going to chase you. Did you know I had to find out from Professor Stanish that you dropped class?"

"I'm sorry about that. I asked Ellie to tell you since she was still dating Matty."

"Why couldn't you tell me?"

"I didn't know what to say."

"You didn't know how to say that you weren't coming back to

school for a semester? I would have been fine with a long-distance relationship."

Rory raises her eyebrows and grits her teeth. "Would you? With all your fucking around. I bet after a few weeks; you would have fucked some other woman behind my back."

I deflate. I'm shocked that she would think so little of me that I would cheat on her. I run my hand through my hair and look at the ceiling. It's obvious there is sexual tension between us. I'm not sure if she is aware, but I am.

I soften my voice, trying to keep myself in check. "Rory, I would not have cheated on you. You never took a chance to find out. Who's this guy you're engaged to?"

I really don't want to know, but I do. Who snapped her up the minute we were apart?

"His name is Derek. He works for my grandparents at Wilton Properties."

"So you went home, and in a few short months, you're engaged?"

"I dated Derek when I was in high school. He was a junior in college when I was a senior."

I calculate in my head how much older that makes him than her. She graduated early when she was sixteen, almost seventeen. So this guy must be about three to four years older. She's going to be twenty-one soon, so he must be twenty-four.

"Is this the third guy?"

"What third guy?"

"You told me you slept with three men. Me, the predator and someone else."

"Yes, I slept with him."

"You were sixteen, so he's a predator too."

"Don't say that about him. What does that make you?"

"Not a predator. I slept with you when you were twenty."

"And you were twenty-six, so that's a bigger age difference than Derek and me, big deal."

I realize we have this trivial argument that means nothing. It's not going to change that she's engaged or that I'm heartbroken, still. I thought I was over her, but I'm not. I feel bad for Lily. Here I thought I was giving her my heart and I wasn't because it belongs to Rory, only I can't have her.

As she talks, I focus on her red plump, kissable lips. I want to press mine to them and kiss her until she's breathless, but I can't. This isn't September, and I'm her boss. I need to push her out of my mind and treat her like any other intern.

I sigh. "Does any of this matter?"

"Not really. We aren't together."

I hand her some folders I need to be filed, and she holds the stack in her arms as she heads for the door.

"Uh, Rory?"

She turns to me, and I ask. "You never answered my question. Are you?"

"And you never answered mine."

My eyes travel down her body as she opens the door and slips through. The way I feel, if I had something to throw, I would, preferably a nice vase so it would shatter in a million pieces like my heart is doing right now. Now I have a problem. I love Lily, but I also love Rory. If it were between the two, I would choose Rory even though Lily is much sweeter, and we get along great. I'm not sure what the answer is or that I can make it so easily.

CHAPTER 12

Throughout the next few days, I try to avoid being alone with Rory. My emotions are a mess, and I don't want to snap at her. Lily has had limited communication with me, and I'm missing her. Often, she's my voice of reason. I need to tell her that Rory works for me, but I refuse to do it over the phone.

The end to Friday finally rolls around, and I'm thrilled. Several of the interns are going to The Slide, a bar close to the office. They ask me, but I decline, especially when I find out that Rory is going. I'm afraid that a couple of beers in me might open the flood gates. I'm curious to know about her fiancé and why he didn't date her before her senior year in college? Why did they break up in the first place?

All these things are curious, but it's not my place to question. The size of the rock on her finger tells me he's got money. Maybe the Wilton's pay him quite well, better than my father does me, though I doubt it. I don't want to open up Pandora's box, so I prefer to go home and relax. Lexi invited me to have pizza since Johnny has been asking for me. I'd rather see my family than spend time in a bar.

As I change into jeans and a sweater, I stare at my bed. The same bed that I made love to Rory. I start to harden, and I grow angry at myself. I have to stop obsessing over her. It's not only that she's engaged to someone else but other issues. Lexi dislikes Rory, and her father, Noah, is a former fiancé. That isn't the biggest problem. I have Lily, and I don't want to hurt her. I love her, and she deserves better.

The evenings are getting warmer out, and I have no idea why I chose a sweater. I'm uncomfortable wearing it, but I can't take it off since I didn't put on a t-shirt underneath. Walking the several blocks to JC's place has me sweating, and I pull my sleeves up. By the time I get there, I'm ready to pull my sweater off in the lobby, but I wait until I get in the elevator.

∽

"Well, this is some greeting," Lexi says as she opens the door to my bare chest.

"I made the wrong shirt choice. I'm all sweaty and will need to borrow a t-shirt from JC."

"He went to pick up the pizza, but help yourself."

I go into their bedroom and find a t-shirt in one of my brother's dresser drawers. A picture of JC, Lexi, and Johnny at a park is sitting on the dresser. I pick it up and run my thumb over the glass. I want this. I want a family, a son I can spend time with and teach things. Speaking of which, Johnny comes in and hangs on the back pocket of my jeans, yelling, "Unter." I put down the picture, pull on the t-shirt, and grab him, giving kisses over his chubby cheeks until he tries to push away.

"No, Unter, no," he screams.

Lexi comes into the bedroom to see what the racket is and grabs her stomach, her face going pale.

I put Johnny down, going to her. "What is it?"

"I think I'm going into labor, but it's early. I'm not due for almost two weeks."

I freeze, not sure of what to do, breathing a sigh of relief when I hear the door to the apartment open, and JC calls out.

"We have a situation, brother," I yell.

He rushes to the bedroom and sees Lexi holding her stomach. She smiles weakly at him, and he nods.

"Time to go?" he said.

"I can probably wait, but let's not tempt the fates."

"You're on deck, Hunter. I need you to stay here and take care of Johnny. Call mom and dad and the Stanfords."

I kiss Lexi and clap my brother on the back. In a few hours, I'll have a new niece. I feel a pang of envy because I want children. I fish my phone out of my pocket to call my parents and the Stanfords to let them know Lexi has gone into labor. After I'm done, I put Johnny in his booster seat, and we have pizza that JC left sitting on the counter.

I'm the perfect babysitter and bathe my nephew, blow dry his hair, put him in his pajamas, and read him a story until he falls asleep. I've never sat for Johnny overnight, but I can handle it. As I'm passing by the office, now a nursery painted in soft light green, I turn on the light and go in. The whole room is prepared and waiting for the baby to come home.

Lexi and JC put up a border with alphabet blocks on it. The crib is decked out with a small yellow blanket and a mobile with monkeys, elephants, and giraffes hang over it. I twist the crank and watch as it gently spins. The changing table in the corner is stocked full of baby wipes, powder, and tiny diapers. The mobile stops turning, and I shut the light out, then sit on the couch to watch a baseball game.

I must have fallen asleep on the couch because the ringing of my phone wakes me. It's past three in the morning, and the television is still on. I groggily answer it.

"Hunter, congratulations, you're an uncle again," JC says.

I'm wide awake now and smiling from ear to ear.

"What did you name her?"

"Arabella Jillian Lawson."

"You gave her mom's name for her middle?"

"Sure, why not. I know mom will love it."

"When can I see her?"

"This morning, but Johnny can't come in, so we'll need to take turns watching him. We can take him by the maternity ward to see her. Besides, he'll be sick of her in a few weeks."

I laugh and wonder if JC was sick of me. We're over six years apart, and he always complained that I was a pest.

"I'll bring him later this morning. Get some sleep and tell Lexi I'm proud of her."

"I will. See you later."

I'm smiling ear to ear when I fall back to sleep. I'm an uncle again to a beautiful little niece. I can't wait to see her.

∽

A few hours later, I'm ushering Johnny into the hospital maternity ward. Arabella is peacefully sleeping her crib. I can't see her hair because she's wearing one of those cute pink caps on her head. The nurse comes to the window, and I point to the crib marked Lawson. She lifts my niece out and cradles her, bringing her to the window, and I lift Johnny so he can see his baby sister.

"Mine, Unter."

"Yes, that's your sister. You treat her well and take care of her. Little girls are special."

"Big girls are too."

I turn to see JC. He looks a bit worse for wear with a day's worth of stubble, but he's happy. He takes Johnny from my arms and hugs him.

"Daddy missed you."

"Daddy, mine," Johnny says as he points to Arabella.

"Yes, she's yours."

"Mommy?"

"Come, let's see Mommy before they bring in your sister."

~

He takes Johnny, and I'm left to stare at my beautiful little niece.

The rest of the morning and part of the afternoon is filled with relatives and friends stopping by to see little Arabella. Megan comes with Olivia, and I kiss them hello, two gorgeous women, one with dark hair and the other light. Olivia is Lexi's best friend, and she's excited to see everyone since she was away on a business trip, just getting back this morning.

I'm exhausted and ready to fall asleep by mid-afternoon. Luckily, my mom offers to take Johnny for the night so that I can get some rest. I'm grateful though I would have toughed it out because I love the little guy. I kiss everyone goodbye and head home to my apartment. It's drizzling, and now I could use the sweater I left at JC and Lexi's place.

I take a long shower, forgoing the need to jerk off because I'm tired. It's only 3:00 PM, but I decide to take a nap, and about a minute after I slip under the covers, I'm asleep. When I wake up several hours later, the light outside has dimmed, and the rain is no longer falling.

I check my phone and JC has sent a bunch of pictures of my niece. I plan to get some prints of them so I can put one in my wallet to join the few I have of Johnny and the rest of my family. I feel happy, but I also have this gnawing feeling. Lily hadn't contacted me since 2:00 AM yesterday. That's unlike her. I shoot her a quick text to let her know that Lexi gave birth; her reply is immediate.

Congratulations to everyone! Do you have a picture of her? What did they name her?

. . .

Yes, I'll send them to you. She's a beauty. Arabella Jillian Lawson.

I send her a couple of pictures and wait for her reply.

She is gorgeous. Makes you want to go right out and have a few.

Whoa lady, a few?

I'm kidding. I want to be married first. I'm sorry I haven't been in contact. I've been off to one seminar or another. I met some old coworkers from my last job. I miss you.

I miss you, too. Go, enjoy your friends. I'll talk to you soon. Love you, Lily.

I hear nothing back, but I don't let it bother me. I'm wiped and order some Chinese food from Ming's. The front desk doesn't let delivery places come upstairs, and I'm in no mood to get dressed and go down. So I bribe one of the guys at the desk with a twenty-dollar bill to bring it up.

When I'm done gorging myself on spare ribs and General Tso's chicken, I turn on the hockey playoffs. I end up going to bed around 9:45 PM and sleeping late on Sunday. I wake feeling uneasy. I remember dreaming about Rory. I smelled her perfume. My subconscious has turned against me.

Sunday, I feel like doing nothing. I miss Lily, and it's raining again. I know I should go to the hospital to see Lexi, but she should be home this afternoon if she feels okay. Mom is staying with them for a few days to help her with Johnny and the baby. JC took off two weeks from his job. I'm sure that his boss must be going crazy because Lexi is home on maternity leave for the next four months.

I can't wait until the kids get older. There is so much I want to show them. I want to take them to concerts and teach them to play soccer. Maybe take them to some New York Rangers and Yankees games. A year ago you couldn't get me to babysit, now I love it, and I'm good at it too.

Tomorrow is Monday, and the zoning should be complete for the second building that we want to develop. This will also have luxury apartments but no subterranean garage like the first building. I'm debating whether to send Rory out on errands again. She did a good job last time, but I don't want her to feel that I'm picking on her. If she does, she knows why.

I couldn't resist jerking off to the image of her when I was in the shower. I hope when Lily gets back that this need for Rory will stop. I feel like I'm cheating on her even though I'm not. You can't stop someone from fantasizing. I know plenty of guys who jerk off to women they see around the city. My married soccer buddy does it to his babysitter, who's totally hot. I know he loves his wife, so there is no harm.

CHAPTER 13

We're in one of those shitty weather patterns where it rains for three days. Today, when I left for work, it was drizzling, and when I got out of the cab, it was pouring so hard that my head got drenched. I'm glad I wore my raincoat and keep extra shoes and socks in the office, or else I would be squishing around all day.

Two of my interns are here, and I assign them some research work on a few buildings we're interested in purchasing. Rory is late, and I hope that I didn't scare her off with my behavior last week. Though I'm angry with her, I don't want her to quit on account of me. Eventually, we need to discuss what happened. I still want an answer to my question.

She and the other intern, Joe, come in at the same time. Her hair is up in a ponytail, and I immediately want to kiss her exposed neck when I see her. They sit down in front of my desk, and I assign Joe some work, asking him to close the door when he leaves. Rory gives me a look, and I'm not sure if she's scared or annoyed.

I hear her sigh loudly. "Please, let's not get into this again."

I shake my head. "What? I'm not interested in arguing."

She swipes a strand of hair out of her face, and I see her engagement ring sparkling in the overhead lights.

"That's good to hear."

"Not so fast. I do expect you to give me an explanation, eventually."

Rory purses her lips. "I will when I'm ready. I need to work some things out in my head. What I have to tell you isn't easy."

She's piqued my interest, and I want to know what was so bad that she couldn't tell me. What could she have possibly done?

"I don't want to push you, but I do want to know. Was it something I did?"

"No, it wasn't anything you did. It just happened. I don't want to discuss it right now."

I can see her face start to flush, and I realize I've upset her. Whatever the reason, it's not easy for her to get out. I need to let this alone.

"I have some work for you to do."

"It's pouring, lucky I wore my raincoat with the hood."

I'm puzzled by what she means. "Why would that matter?"

"I'm sure you want me to run some errand. To the zoning office again?"

"No, not at all. I need you to research these buildings in the folder. See who owns them and the tax rate. It's all outlined in the notes."

"Fine."

I hand her the folder, and she goes to walk out. I decide to play the little game we seem to have established.

"Rory, are you?"

She turns to me with a smile. "Are you?"

She's out the door before I can reply. I'm glad we've established a more comfortable rapport together. I don't want there to be tension between us besides sexual, but even that is wrong. We're both attached to other people.

I don't see Rory for most of the day until the end of it when she brings me back the folder with all the research she did. I look it over, and I'm impressed. She did more than the other two interns I also asked to do research.

I close the folder and look up at Rory. "You did a great job. I might have more for you tomorrow."

She smiles, and it's like the sun just rose. "Works for me. As long as I don't have to go to the zoning office again."

"You didn't like to get out in the warm weather?"

"No, it's not that. There were several contractors at the office who were leering at me. It made me uncomfortable."

I chuckle, and Rory scowls at me.

"I'm sorry. It's just that I don't blame them. I think you would be used to all the male attention you attract."

"I am used to it since I was about eleven. But it still makes me uncomfortable, especially when these men are more than twice my age."

I have to bite my tongue, not to mention the predator that stole her virginity.

"For you, it's a fact of life. You're beautiful, and men notice."

Her face turns bright red, and she looks down at her lap — wrong thing to say, especially since she's not mine.

I immediately feel guilt wash over me. "I shouldn't have said that. Please forgive me."

"Can I go?"

"Sure, it's nearly five."

I debate continuing the game we play, but I decide it's not the right time.

"Goodnight, Hunter."

I shiver as my name rolls off her tongue.

"Goodnight, Rory."

And she's gone. It's then that I realize I'm semi-erect. I sit at my desk until it subsides, thinking I can't wait for Lily to get back. Tomorrow she will be back in my arms and my bed.

∽

I get home, change, and I'm munching on leftover Chinese food when my cell rings. It's Lily, and I quickly swallow my food and answer it.

"Hello there, stranger."

"I'm sorry I haven't been communicating. It was so busy at the conference."

"I can't wait to see you tomorrow."

"You can see me tonight."

"You're home?"

"Yes. I got home a couple of hours ago. I thought I would surprise you. My side meetings were over, so I figured I would catch an earlier flight. You can only do so much networking."

"Do you want to come here, or should I come over?"

"I'll be over in a little while."

Lily hangs up, and I'm happy that I'll see her soon. I didn't realize how much I missed her until she called. I have knots in my stomach, anticipating seeing her, like a middle school boy on his first date. It really is silly since we've been together for a while.

In a half-hour, Lily's walking through my door, and there's something different about her, but I can't put my finger on it. We hug, and she pulls me down by my shirt collar to claim my mouth as she pushes me in the door. Lily is not aggressive like this, so it sort of shocks me.

"I need you," she whispers into my mouth.

I'm more than happy to oblige since we haven't had sex in a week. Our lips remain locked as we move toward the bedroom. Whatever happened to her in Dallas, I like it. I've always wanted her to be more dominant in bed. Not all the time, but once in a while is a real turn on.

She pulls at my shirt, and I break the kiss to pull it off. Her nails rake across my chest, leaving marks and causing me to shudder. She cups my balls through my shorts, and my cock immediately hardens to full staff. She runs her fingers over the length, and with a tug, I'm naked as everything pools at my ankles.

Lily does something that is an infrequent activity for her. She pushes me back to sit on the bed and drops to her knees. Her hands wrap around my cock, and she licks at the bead of dew that has pooled on the head. I'm not sure if I should question her behavior, but I like it, no, I love it.

I run my hands through her thick brown locks as she greedily laps at my precum. When she takes me fully into her mouth, I have to control myself from exploding. I want this to last. Stroking her cheek as she takes me deeper, I begin to moan her name. Lily is bringing me closer to release, and I can barely stutter the words that I'm going to come. She ignores me and keeps me deep in her mouth.

When I start coming, she fondles my balls and gives them a gentle squeeze as if pushing all the cum I have in them. I'm breathing hard by the time I finish, and she's releasing me from her mouth. I'm very surprised at her behavior because it's not like her.

"You, that. What came over you?"

She smirks. "I just wanted to do it. I haven't done that to you in a long time."

I put my fingers under her chin and tip her face up to softly kiss her lips. Her gray eyes are shining as I pull back.

"I want to return the favor."

"I'd rather you make love to me."

"I need a little recovery time, and I thought I could get you nice and wet."

"I'm already nice and wet."

Though I came a few minutes ago, my dick twitches, what do they put in the water in Dallas? My sweet, demure girlfriend who rarely talks dirty is talking dirty. Not only that, but she's doing things she rarely does. I don't want to break the mood by questioning, so I stand up and kick away my shorts and boxers pooled around my ankles.

I pull her up and move her ponytail away from her neck to suck at her pulse. She runs her hands through my hair, tugging at the sides, then caressing my ears with her fingers. I unbutton her blouse, and I pull the tails from her jeans. Her skin is smooth and smells faintly of vanilla, her favorite scent, which I inhale deeply.

I work my fingers under the cups of her bra and roll her nipples between my thumb and index. She moans against my shoulder, and I hear her breathing hitch. My cock is growing, and since she's been so agreeable tonight, I want to try a position I love. I pull her blouse off and pop the clasp of her bra, then pull it off her arms, dropping it to the floor.

Lily has already started working on the button of her jeans, and I take over. Quickly unzipping them, I pull them down to reveal a thong I've never seen before. It's barely there panties and all-black lace except for the waistband which hardly exists, just a thin string of elastic. I raise one eyebrow because this is not my Lily, at least the one that left me a week ago.

"Are you surprised?"

"This whole night has been a surprise."

I turn her to look at her backside, and It's sexy. I grasp the band of her thong and tug, pulling it down to the floor. She steps out of it, and I place the thong on my nightstand. I want this for a souvenir. I hope this is a permanent change, but if it's not, I'll still be happy. Before I can speak, she does.

"Do you want a certain position?"

"You know what I want."

Lily never told me why she dislikes doggy style, but it could be someone who was too aggressive with her. I plan to be gentle because I know she likes that. She gets on the bed on all fours, ass in the air. It's all I can do not to blow my load right there.

We've both been tested, and Lily is on the pill, so I don't need to put on a condom. She's the first woman who I haven't had to wear one.

I position myself in back of her and tease her with my fingers. She's soaked, and I can't wait to slip inside her. I hear her whimpering as I pull my fingers away, and I replace them with the head of my cock, thrusting gently as I enter her. Lily pulses around me as I begin to move, then she says something that amazes me.

"Harder."

"Are you sure?"

She doesn't answer me, and I grasp her hips, digging my fingers into her soft flesh as I pump hard. Sweat is forming on my upper lip as I speed my rhythm up. Lily is pushing back against me to meet my motion. This is the best sex I've had with her since we've been together.

I reach around her and rub her swollen nub. She's moaning my name, and just before she releases, I thought I hear her say something else. Maybe I didn't listen closely, but it sounded like Scott. I ignore it, concentrating on my own impending orgasm, which comes shortly after hers. It's hard, and I thrust until I finish my climax.

Lily feels so good, and I don't want to pull out yet. I bend over her and kiss along her back, a light layer of sweat covers it, and I taste salt and skin cream. She stretches forward to lie on her stomach, and I slip out. I realize that I feel worn out. Maybe it's the lack of sleep over the past few nights or the fact that I haven't fucked anyone that hard in a long time.

I lie on my back next to her, stroking her shoulder and hair. I'm still wondering about what she said, but it just could be my imagination.

"I love you, Lily."

I get no response, and when I look over, she's asleep. She traveled a good amount of the day, and I'm sure she's exhausted. I pull the sheet over us and turn to my side to grasp her hand that's on the pillow near her face. Lily looks angelic, and I reach over to tuck her hair around her ear before I fade to sleep.

The next morning, I wake up alone. I know that Lily has off today, and I expected her to sleep until I got up. It's not even six yet. I usually get up at 6:30. She must still be here, though, because the pleasant aroma of coffee wafts into the bedroom.

"Lil?" I call out.

"I'm here."

She's standing in the doorway of the bedroom with a steaming mug of coffee wearing my t-shirt from last night.

"You got up early."

"I couldn't sleep."

"I enjoyed last night."

She looks down at her coffee and takes a sip. It's as if an hour goes by before she replies.

"I did too. I have to go. I still need to unpack."

"I could've stayed at your place."

"It's a mess with suitcases and papers. It's better I stayed here."

"Are you taking a shower?"

"No, I'll take one at home."

"I should go work out."

I slip out of bed and head to the closet to get some workout gear. When I come back, Lily is no longer in the doorway. I find her in the kitchen staring at the wall.

"Lil, is there something wrong?"

She looks up at me. "No, why would you think that?"

"You're different."

"I'm not. I just was a little wild last night. Didn't you like it?"

"More than you know."

I bend to kiss her, and she offers her cheek, which I kiss, then wrap my arms around her. She seems stiff to me and not responsive. I'm bewildered, but I don't question her, not yet anyway. I let go.

"I'll see you later," I said before I head to the building gym on the main floor. I do an hour of cardio, pounding the treadmill. Sweat drenches my clothes by the time I finish.

When I come back, Lily's gone, and I really am confused by her. Last night was fantastic, but this morning, she's cold. I wonder if anything happened at the conference and she is having a hard time telling me.

I have no time to worry about it now. I have a meeting with my father at nine in the conference room and need to get moving so I get there before him. One thing you don't do is keep Jonathan Lawson waiting. I arrive at 8:45, just enough time to discuss with my assistant what I want the interns to do.

My father and two attorneys are in the conference room when I get there. They need to go over some other properties that we're interested in purchasing. I think we have enough on our plate with the two buildings we already purchased, but my father wants to get the paperwork started on plans and zoning. It means we're going to be busy for the entire year and beyond with projects.

∽

Work keeps me busy throughout the week, and I don't see much of Lily due to my hours being long at the office. She seems distant from me, and I don't know why. We had great sex on Monday, and here it is Friday afternoon, and it's been four days.

This weekend is the annual Lawson Corp. picnic for Memorial Day. We usually hold it in Randall's Island Park each year. A good majority of people come since it's on the Saturday before the holiday. I hope Lily can make it because I heard that Rory is bringing her fiancé. I want to size him up and see what she traded me for, but I also want to show that I'm happy in my relationship, and I'm not pining away for her. I text Lily because I mentioned the picnic a couple of weeks ago and hope she hasn't forgotten.

. . .

Are you coming with me to the picnic tomorrow?

Oh, shit. Thank you for reminding me. I've been so busy I almost forgot.

Is there something wrong? Did I do something?

She doesn't reply to my text but rather calls me several minutes later. I get up to shut my door while I answer the phone.

"Why would you think something is wrong?"

"Lily, we had incredible sex on Monday night, and I feel like your pulling away from me. We haven't been together since then. I sleep better with you next to me."

"I'm sorry. I didn't realize it. You're not the only one that's been busy. We pulled in quite a few new customers at the conference, and I've been working on packages for them."

"I wasn't aware."

"You should be. My job is very important to me," she snaps.

Seriously, Lily has never talked to me like this before. She was always sweet and kind. Have I just been too selfish to notice that she has needs too?

"I know. I apologize. I should've been paying better attention."

My desk phone buzzes. "Can you hold on a second, please?"

Her voice is deadpan, with no emotion. "Yeah."

When I come back to my cell, she's no longer holding. I begin to feel sick. I know something is wrong between us, and I need to get to the bottom of it. I still haven't told her about Rory, and if I don't do it tonight, it's going to be ugly tomorrow.

I call Lily back, but her phone goes right to voicemail. Rather than leave a message, I find a florist and order roses for delivery to her office. I want her to know that I love and appreciate her. A couple of hours later, I hear nothing from her even though I got a text that the flowers have been delivered. Maybe it's better she doesn't come tomorrow, there is too much tension between us.

At five, all my interns come in and say goodbye. Joe asks if I want to come to The Slide to have a drink, but I decline. I want to go home and be miserable. Rory lingers until the others have left, then shuts the door to my office and sits on one of the chairs in front of my desk. I can smell her perfume from where she's sitting.

She looks lovely today with her hair in a French braid and a body-hugging emerald green dress. The top is cut just low enough to see a hint of cleavage and the beautiful ivory flesh of her upper chest.

"Something you need?"

"I'm bringing Derek tomorrow, and I want to ask you a favor."

"And that is?"

"Please be nice to him. He doesn't know about us."

"He doesn't know that you fucked your boss?"

"You weren't my boss when we were fucking."

I grin. "True, but you really should tell him that I've seen you naked."

She huffs. "This is what I mean. Please don't make snide comments."

"Then answer my question. Are you?"

She stares at her hands in her lap. "I'm not playing this game."

"Rory, look at me."

Her sapphire eyes fix on my brown ones, and I see a hint of sadness.

"I promise not to say anything, but before your internship is up, I want an answer."

"You haven't given me your answer, but you expect me to reveal mine."

"Yes."

"Yes, what?"

"You want to know my answer. Yes."

Her jaw drops. "Excuse me."

"I'm still in love with you. I can't shake it. Maybe it's because I never had closure."

"I'm not."

Her answer makes me sad, but somehow I feel it's also a lie. During the short time we've worked together, I frequently notice Rory staring at me. When I look up, she looks away. She feels something for me.

"I don't believe you."

"You asked for my answer, and I gave it to you. Now I expect you to be respectful to Derek tomorrow. Give me your promise."

I reluctantly promise, but I'd rather take her over my desk and fuck her until she screams. Of course, my conscious mind would never allow it, but I can dream. After Rory leaves, I shut down my laptop and pack it to take home. I have a few things to do tonight, and since Lily hasn't answered me, I guess she's still pissed. I thought tomorrow she would come, but now that seems in doubt.

CHAPTER 14

The next day, Lily calls me just before I'm leaving for Randall's Island Park. She says she'll meet me there and we have to talk. Great, just what I don't want

to do at a picnic, especially with Rory there, is have a serious talk. I want to put on a show that my relationship is just as strong as hers. Although is it, since I'm still in love with Rory?

I grab a few things, including a couple of soccer balls, and head out to the park. It's still early, but the catering company we hired is there setting up an overhead tent and some tables. My father goes all out with cold and hot foods since it would be too complicated to barbecue for this amount of people.

Lily meets me at eleven, which is an hour before the picnic is scheduled to begin. This is a family picnic, and everyone has been requested to bring their significant others and children. We have a prime spot near one of the soccer fields with plenty of activities.

"Hunter, we should get this over with now," Lily said.

I follow her over to some benches, out of earshot of my parents and other coworkers who came early to help set up. After we sit down, I turn to her.

"Are you breaking up with me?"

"It's more complicated than that."

I look at my hands in my lap, afraid to look in Lily's eyes. "Just be straight with me."

"I have to end this because it's not fair to you."

My heart sinks. She says the words I didn't want to hear.

"What's not fair," I said so she doesn't hear the distress in my voice.

"I love someone else."

My head shoots up to stare at her. "So, you've been cheating on me?"

"No. I'm trying to end it before something happens."

"I don't understand."

"I met an old boyfriend at the conference last week. He lives in the city now, and we spent some time together."

"Did you fuck him?"

"Hunter, I said nothing happened."

"Who is this guy?"

"His name is Scott. We dated three years ago, and he was moving to Georgia for his career. I didn't want a long-distance relationship, so we broke up. It was a mistake because I never got over him."

I start to think back to Monday when I thought I heard her say his name when we were having sex. I wasn't hearing things. She did say it.

"So, Monday night was the big fuck off. You were giving me the last of us."

"I wanted to see if I could overcome it with you, but I can't."

"And this is the big fuck off?"

"Hunter, I want to be friends. I don't want to hurt you."

"It's too late for that. I'm hurt. I thought I meant something to you."

"You did, you do but not as lovers. I'm trying to make this easy."

I bite my lip. "It's not. It's painful."

"I'm sorry. Do you want me to stay?"

"It's better you don't."

Lily stands up and leans in to kiss my cheek before she walks away. I sit there looking at my feet until JC, who just arrived, comes over to me. Lexi's mother is helping watch Arabella so that JC could bring Johnny for a little while.

"What's wrong," JC says as she sits down.

"It's over with Lily. She has someone else."

"She cheated on you?"

"No, but she wants to end it before she does. It's an old boyfriend."

"How do you feel?"

"Like I've been punched in the gut. I need to go back to just fucking women. I can't take this relationship bullshit."

JC pats my shoulder. "You'll find someone. Keep trying."

"You found someone the first shot."

"Yeah, but it took me years to realize it. I was lucky Lexi didn't marry Noah."

"That reminds me, Rory is coming today with her fiancé."

"Why would she come here?"

I forgot to mention to JC that Rory now works for us as an intern. So I explain to him that not only does she work for Lawson, but me. He watches my face as I tell the story then whistles after I finish.

"It's fucked up, and because I don't want to mess with her career, I left well enough alone. She works for me, and I need just to let it be. It's only for another couple of months."

"Does Dad know?"

"No. He would've said we should let her go. He probably would worry about a lawsuit if we kept her on. I don't want to get involved with that."

"How are you handling it?"

"Not good. I'm still in love with her. I thought I wasn't, but seeing her brought it all to the forefront."

"Does she know you are?"

"Yes, but there is nothing that can be done. I need to sit on the sidelines and watch her day after day, knowing I can't have her."

My mother comes over with Johnny, and we end the conversation. I stand up to kiss her and take my nephew in my arms.

"Unter, ball."

Johnny points to the soccer balls I dropped on the lawn.

"You want to kick?"

He nods, and I take him by the hand as we head towards them. It's nearing noontime, and some of the employees have arrived. The food is set out, and everyone can start to eat or play games. Whatever they want. After a half-hour, Johnny has lost interest in the soccer ball and wants to eat.

I'm not sure where JC or my mother is, so I make him up a plate of chicken nuggets and French fries. We're sitting at one of the tables when I spy Rory coming in with her fiancé. She looks hot in white Capri pants and a peach polo shirt that is practically buttoned up to her neck, which is peculiar. At the office, she wears much lower necklines than even a fully unbuttoned polo shirt would allow.

Her fiancé is tall with a blonde crew cut that makes him look like he belongs on the battlefield rather than an office. He's wearing aviator sunglasses and a gray Ralph Lauren polo shirt with a black sweater tied around his neck. He looks preppy in his khaki shorts and Topsiders with no socks. I decide he's a tool.

Behind my sunglasses, I follow her with my eyes until Johnny is finished with his meal. JC comes by and picks him up.

"I can take him home if you want to run some errands," I said.

"Thanks, bro, but this little guy needs a nap. By the time we get home, he's going to be asleep."

I hug my brother and give Johnny a big sloppy kiss on his cheek that he rubs at with his hand as he tells me no. After they leave, I find a few of my coworkers and sit down to play a game of cards. I'm not concentrating and lose several hands before I concede defeat and give up. I'm still paying attention to Rory and her fiancé.

The interaction between them seems strained. She unbuttoned her polo shirt, and I watch as he grabs her wrist and talks to her. When he finishes, she buttons up her shirt again. WTF, is he bullying and trying to control her? I feel my blood begin to boil. They're in the food line, and I decide to join them. I'm a couple of people behind, and when Rory takes a scoop of macaroni salad, her fiancé comments that she needs to watch her weight.

I think she has a rocking body, and what kind of guy is going to tell the woman he supposedly loves that she's fat and needs to watch herself? I would never do that. They finish going through the line, and I see she barely has anything on her plate while Derek's is stacked high. The table they sit at is only occupied by one other couple, and I go over to sit down.

"Rory. Is this Derek?" I say as I slide into a chair.

He speaks up before she can. "Hey man, Derek Folsom."

"Nice to meet you. I'm Hunter. Rory has told me a little about you."

She shoots me a look and looks fearful.

"Oh yeah? Like what?"

"She told me you work for the Wilton's. I know her father."

"Rory didn't mention it to me.

You're her boss?"

"I guess you could say that."

Rory gets up to get something to drink, and Derek tells her to get him a soda. When she's out of earshot, he leans into me.

"You keep your hands off the merchandise."

I'm taken aback. "Excuse me?"

"You heard me. I know guys look at her, but she's mine. The ring on her finger says so."

I frown. "I'm her boss, and that would be inappropriate. I have no desire to do what you're suggesting."

"Things happen. You're working late one night, and she comes into your office looking all hot. I know what happens in those situations."

"You might do those things, but I do not, and I'm offended you would even elude so such a thing."

I pick my plate up and rise just as Rory comes to the table.

"Where are you going?" she asks.

"I just lost my appetite. Thank you, and I'll see you on Monday."

The other couple on the opposite end of the table looks at us as I walk away, the fucking nerve of that guy. He talks about Rory like she's an object and not a person. It took all I had not to kick his ass. How did she get involved with Derek in the first place? He's all wrong for her. I throw the rest of my food in the garbage; I have no desire to finish it. Then I go to find my father and let him know that I'm leaving.

"Hunter, is something wrong?"

"No, Dad, I'm not in the mood for this right now."

"I'm sorry."

"About what."

"JC told me about Lily."

"He shouldn't have."

"He cares about your wellbeing, and so do I and your mother."

"I know, and I appreciate it. I want to be alone right now."

He claps me on the back, and I nod at him as I leave the park. I glance at Rory, who's looking at me while Derek scarfs the rest of his food. I'm not sure if I'm more upset about Lily breaking up with me or the fact that Rory is in danger with this guy. I'm afraid he's going to hurt her.

∽

I moped around most of the weekend, and even though I was invited on a boat trip for Memorial Day, I declined. Matty had rented the boat and was going fishing with some guys from our soccer club. I was just in no mood.

On Tuesday morning, I was the first one in the office. I even beat my father in. I couldn't sleep, and after an early morning workout, I decided that sitting around after my shower was no good. I needed to keep my mind busy and put it to good use on some of the outstanding work that I left on Friday.

One by one, my interns came in, and I assigned them something but no Rory. 9:00 AM came and went without her calling or coming into the office. I was starting to get worried. The way Derek treated her on Saturday, I wonder if he assaulted her in a jealous rage. I kept thinking the worst until 10:45 AM when I got a knock at my door.

"Come in."

There was Rory, and she looked horrible like she'd been crying. I rose to meet her as she came in the door.

"I'm sorry I'm late, it's been a bad morning."

"You've been crying. What happened?"

"It's nothing."

I shut the door and lead Rory by her arm to one of the chairs in front of my desk, then sat next to her.

"What's nothing?"

"I don't want to discuss it."

"Rory, you don't have to be afraid to tell me things. I'm not going to judge you."

"I saw the look you gave me on Saturday. You disapprove of Derek."

"I'm just going to come right out and say it. He's abusive, and I don't like it."

"He's not abusive. He wants things perfect between us."

"Oh, you mean like you not gaining weight?"

"You heard that?"

"Yes, I did. What kind of asshole says that to a woman he loves?"

"He just wants me to be healthy."

"He wants to control you. I won't even tell you what he said to me when you were getting him a soda."

"Derek told me what you said. How could you?"

I'm shocked, and my mouth drops open. "How could I? I defended you."

"He told me you said you would love to get me alone."

I look at her incredulously and vigorously shake my head.

"That's not what I said. He's a fucking liar. Do you want to know what he said?"

She looks at me, and before she has a chance to speak, I tell her.

"He told me, hands-off. He knows what happens when you work in an office alone with no one else around. Derek said you were his. How would he know what happens in an office late at night? Does he do it? Did he do it to you?"

"No. I started working at my grandparent's office, and I met him again. We started dating. He's good to me."

"Rory, if by controlling and being abusive is good, I prefer not to be."

She begins to cry, and I'm not sure what I should do, so I pull her against my chest. She seems so small and vulnerable in my arms. I want to comfort her until she feels better.

"What happened that you're so upset?"

"Derek wants me to move back to Boston. He said I should quit and come to work for my grandparents where he can watch me."

"Sweetheart, he's all wrong for you. You need to end it with him."

"You're saying that because you want me."

"I do. I want you body and soul, but I would never push you. You have to make that decision yourself."

"I can't. I love Derek."

I push her off my chest and look into her bloodshot eyes.

"Do you really, or are you looking to escape?"

"What do you mean?"

"You told me you came to New York to get out from under your parents. So you get engaged so you can marry and get out of their house when you go back."

"I'm not going back to Boston. I want to stay here, but Derek doesn't want to move to New York. He gave me an ultimatum. Move back to Boston, or he'll get me and drag me back."

"Rory, you need to end it with him. He's an asshole."

"And then what? Date you?"

"Preferably."

"Hunter, there are things you don't know. When I tell you them, you're going to hate me."

"I could never hate you. I love you."

"You won't after I tell you."

"Then, just tell me already. I'm bursting to know."

"I was going to wait until the end of my internship. I couldn't bear to see the look on your face day after day."

"How bad could it be?"

"I should have told you right away."

I stroke her hair. "Tell me. I'm not letting you leave this office until you do."

"I was pregnant when I went home to Boston to see my grandmother in September."

My hand freezes, and I withdraw. I can't believe what she's telling me. She was pregnant. How could that be?

"You were on the pill, and I used condoms. How were you pregnant?"

"I kept forgetting to take my pills, and with everything going on, I think I skipped a couple of days at least. As for your condoms, I have no idea why they failed."

My mind wanders back to when I bought them, and I remembered that I had them in a bag with my brush and razors. They were from the summer when I went on weekend trips. I wonder if either of the items pierced a hole in them.

"We only had sex a few times. Are you sure it was mine?"

She scowls. "Are you saying I was sleeping around? I told you I only slept with three men. I didn't have sex in a while, so it had to be yours."

"But you're not pregnant, and there isn't a little one running around, so what happened?"

"When I realized, I didn't know what to do. I walked around for two weeks before I made a decision."

"You had an abortion?"

"No. I was going to do it but kept going back and forth. I didn't know if I could do it. I wanted to tell you, but I didn't know-how. I was a month into my pregnancy and had a miscarriage."

"And when did you realize you were pregnant?"

Rory won't look at me. "The two days after I got home. I was feeling sick for several days in the morning, and I threw up a lot. My mother had some pregnancy tests in the linen closet. I took one, and it came up positive."

I feel sick to my stomach. "You should have told me. How could you not? I had a right to know."

I think about the what-could-have-beens. I could have a child of my own, one that would be almost the same age as Arabella. I wanted that so much.

"I went round and round, thinking that I needed to tell you, but when I miscarried, it made no sense. We weren't together anymore."

I backed away from her, with my shoulders slumped. "You broke up with me. You went home and cut off all communication from me like I didn't matter. Like I was nothing. Now you come to me with this?"

The past few days were more than I could stand. First, Lily breaks up with me; then, I see that Rory's fiancé is an A1 dickhead, and now the fact that she was pregnant and didn't tell me.

"Maybe you should go back to Boston."

"You mean that?"

I'm not sure what I mean. I still love her, but she held back, telling me something that she should have.

"I don't know."

We stay silent, and I go around to my desk to get some tissues for her. I have so many emotions bubbling in me that I'm afraid to speak. I want to go home, which is a childish response to the situation, but I'm having trouble handling what Rory just told me.

"I should go. I hope you don't hate me. I'm sorry."

Rory gets up to leave, and the sleeve covering her forearm rides up. I notice an angry bruise, and she quickly pulls the cloth back down. I'm up in a flash before she can escape out the door. I jump in front of her to stop her from leaving.

"I want to see it," I growl.

"It's nothing."

"You're not leaving this office until you show it to me. I don't care if you scream bloody murder. Pull it up."

Rory slowly pulls her sleeve up, and I can see a large purple bruise on her arm the size of my palm. I gently grasp her hand and rotate her limb until I see the other side. That bruise is in the shape of fingers. I look up, and I can see the tears welling in her sapphire eyes.

"You have to leave him before he kills you."

"It was a misunderstanding. I should have done what he wanted."

"Rory, there is no excuse for this. I'm going to drive to Boston to kick that preppy bastard's ass."

"He's my fiancé."

"Sweetheart, he wants to own you, not to love you. You're a possession to him."

"He does love me," she insists.

"Does anyone else know he's doing this to you?"

"Maybe, Ellie."

"What do you think she would say if you discussed it with you?"

"I don't know. We haven't been talking much lately. She doesn't like Derek much."

"I wonder why."

I swipe my thumbs underneath her eyes to push the tears away, then put my forehead against hers. I'm so close to kissing her. I want to kiss her. Right now, my compassion outweighs any anger I have toward her.

"You can talk to me anytime. I love you despite what you've done."

She pulls her head away from mine and heads to the door.

"Rory, are you leaving? Don't run from me."

"I have to get to work."

I laugh because I'm her boss. Who's going to yell at her for not working other than me?

"You find this funny?"

"I'm your boss. I can request that you sit here in my office and do nothing all day if I like."

"I think I should go home."

Panic starts to hit me because I don't want her to leave. I'm afraid I'll never see her again if I let her walk out the door.

"I think you should stay and talk to me."

"I've said all I have to. There is nothing left to say."

"Go then," the anger comes back full force, and it's noticeable in my voice.

Rory gives me a sad look, and I immediately want to take her in my arms, but I don't. This is not something that's going to work itself out in a day.

I pretend to engross myself in work as she heads out the door, but I'm sick with fear. If she doesn't want to be with me, at least I want her to be safe, and with Derek, she won't be.

After she leaves, I pace the office. I can't help but worry about her. I have to be careful because my interest in her is dangerous to us both. Rory can report me to the HR department for sexual harassment. I doubt she would do such a thing, but someone else might. If that happened and her fiancé found out, he could hurt her.

I debate whether I should call Noah Wilton, her father. He still has a security firm, and I can easily find his number. But I'm not sure that would be the right course of action. I think she would hate me for revealing what is going on with her and Derek.

Every time I think about that smug bastard, I want to drive to Boston and fuck up his perfect nose. Knock his straight white teeth down his throat and mark his face. It would serve him right for what he's doing to Rory. He deserves a taste of his own medicine.

CHAPTER 15

In the afternoon, I hunt the office and find my three other interns sitting in the conference room, compiling information for me. I nonchalantly ask if they've seen Rory, and they tell me that they haven't since they came in this morning. I want to know she's alright and I assume she went home. I text her when I get back to my office.

Where are you? Are you okay?

I hear a knock at my door.
"Come in."
It's Rory, and I feel a rush of relief come over me that she's okay and hasn't run away.
"I'm fine. I was in the filing room. There is so much to put away. When was the last time you did this?"
"I don't do this. This is for my assistant to do. We are so busy that we need interns. Play your cards right, and you might get to be one of my assistants after your internship is over."

"That's not going to happen. I made up my mind, and after I'm done here, I'm going back to Boston. Derek needs me, and I can work at my Wilton."

My face drops. "I thought you wanted to stay in New York?"

"I do, but if my fiancé isn't going to move, then I need to compromise."

"But you're the only one that's compromising. What is he doing?"

I shut the door and gesture for her to sit in the chair in front of my desk.

"Hunter, there is no use discussing this. I'm marrying Derek, and that's final. He loves me. He isn't always like this."

I throw my hands up in disgust. "Rory, would you listen to yourself? If there's nothing wrong with what he's doing, then why don't you tell your parents?"

"They wouldn't understand. They love him, and he helped me through my grandmother's stroke."

"Does he make you do things you don't want to?"

Rory sighs. "We all do things we don't want to, but we do them because we love that person."

"I'm not asking about basic stuff. I'm asking about sex. Does he make you do things you are uncomfortable with?"

"That's none of your business. It's personal," she said, raising her voice.

"Please. I can't deal with knowing he's hurting you."

"You have a girlfriend. Why are you so worried about me?"

I debate whether to tell her that Lily broke up with me. I'm afraid she'll run if she knows that I have no attachments standing in between us.

"I don't have a girlfriend."

"You do. I heard you mention her before."

"We broke up the day of the picnic."

"Is that why you care so much? You think you can get me in bed now that you're free?"

"No. I always cared. It breaks my heart that he's hurting you. Let me protect you."

"You can't. I'm marrying him."

I want to grab Rory and shake some sense into her. Derek is going to hurt her far worse than he's already done, can't she see that?

"Fine. Go live your life. It's time to leave for the night. I'll talk to you tomorrow."

I go to the door and hold it open for her.

"Goodnight, Hunter."

"Goodbye, Rory."

After she leaves, I shut the door and sit at my desk with my head in my hands. I feel sick. I stay in my office for another hour, contemplating what I should do about Rory. I love her, but she doesn't want me. It's a hard pill to swallow. I know we're perfect for each other.

∼

The interactions I have with Rory for the rest of the week are icy at best. She barely looks me in the eye, and I don't try to engage her in conversation like I do the other interns. On Friday, I overhear her telling one of her coworkers that Derek is coming down to visit, and Ellie is leaving for Boston to see her mother. That means Rory's going to be alone with him.

My gut clenches, and I'm full of worry for the rest of the day. I want to steal her away and keep her safe in my apartment for the weekend. Joe once again asks if I want to join him and a few other interns for a drink. This time I agree. I need a drink after the emotional rollercoaster that's been my week at the office.

The Slide is a bar that is frequented by the suit and dress crowd after work. Fridays, the atmosphere is more casual, though still a lot of suits and dresses. I feel old next to the interns, even though most of them are no more than three or four years younger than me. I end up having a conversation with Joe and another intern from the accounting department named Ben. We're talking about the stock market when Rory comes in with Derek.

I raise my eyebrows because I'm surprised that Derek would even let her come to a bar. But I guess it's because he's with her, so it's alright. He approaches me and gives me a handshake, and that fucking fake smile I want to slap off his face. He hands Rory a twenty.

"Why don't you be a good girl and get me a beer and a whiskey shot?" He gives her a gentle push toward the bar.

I feel the words "Fucking Prick" poised on my tongue and give him my fakest smile. What I want to do is rip his throat out.

When Rory comes back, he downs the shot and hands her the glass and sips on his beer. He proceeds to ignore her while he focuses on one of the other pretty interns from the acquisitions department. Her name is Julie, and she's been the interest of several of the male interns. Her figure is perfect, and she has long brown hair practically to her ass. I heard that she used to model while she attended college in New Jersey.

I glance over at Rory, and she has a slight frown on her face as she watches Derek engage Julie. I can see why it's so easy for women to get sucked into his bullshit. He's charming and polite besides handsome. I ease over to Rory to talk to her.

"Still think he's marriage material?" I say, just loud enough for her to hear.

"He's friendly. Is that a crime?"

"I think that if you weren't here, he would be taking Julie to bed soon."

"Fuck you, Hunter," she hisses.

"I wish you would. Oh, how I wish."

"Keep wishing. I don't love you, and I'm never sleeping with you again. If Derek weren't here I would slap you for saying that."

I'm done. She can't see that this asshole wants to control,

possess, and abuse her while he fucks around with other women. I can't change her mind. I announce that I'm leaving. I want to get out of here before I go off on the guy. I bid everyone goodnight and give my fakest smile to Rory, and I'm out the door.

It's hot out in the early June weather, and I take off my suit jacket as I walk. It's many blocks to my apartment, but I need the walk to cool off. I'm angry at Rory for not seeing what I see. After twelve blocks, I'm sweating my balls off, and I hail a cab. Traffic moves at a snail's pace because it's rush hour on a Friday.

When I get home, I strip off my suit and take a long shower while I jerk off to Rory's face. She can't control what I have in my mind. I want her so badly that it hurts, but I don't think that will ever be a possibility. I could use some of JC's wisdom right about now. Maybe I can join them for dinner. I would love to see Arabella and Johnny. I decide to call him as I sit on the corner of my bed wearing a towel.

"Hey brother, what's shaking? I thought you would be out tonight since it's Friday, and you're a free man."

"I'm not ready. Did you guys eat dinner yet?"

"Mom just went home. We're deciding on what to have."

"You mind if I come over? I'd love to see the kids, and I need to talk to you about something."

"Sure. Maybe you could give me a break and pick up some pizza on the way over?"

"Yeah, sure. How about Antonio's?"

"Fine. I'll see you in a little while."

I place the order and head over to Antonio's to pick up a couple of pies. I'm starving, and the walk to JC's has my mouth-watering. When I arrive, I hear the children screaming in the background. Arabella sure had strong lungs for a two-week-old baby.

JC comes to the door looking harried with Johnny right behind him, crying his eyes out. I hand my brother the pies and pick up my nephew in my arms. He immediately stops crying, and I see JC breathe a sigh of relief.

"What was the problem with him?"

"His favorite shirt is dirty, and he kept taking it out of the hamper. I put it in, and he started to cry."

"Can I talk to him?"

"Give it a shot. I need to help Lexi with Arabella."

I take Johnny to the couch and talk to him about the shirt. I know it's the one with a big soccer ball on the front.

"Buddy, I know that's your favorite shirt, but it smells, and it needs to be cleaned. You can't wear it all the time."

"No, Unter, want it."

"Yes, I know, but it needs to be clean. You don't want to be known as the smelly little boy, do you?"

He looks at me with the same sea blue eyes that he shares with JC, and shakes his head no.

"Okay, then. You need to let mommy and daddy wash it. Then you can wear it after it's clean. Deal?"

He nods his head, yes.

"Okay, let's get you some pizza."

I set the table with plates, and a few minutes later, Lexi and JC come out of the nursery with Arabella in Lexi's arms. The baby is quiet now, and she gets placed in the bassinet by the table so she can be watched while we eat.

"Thank you for taking care of Johnny," JC said.

"We talked, and he promises to let the shirt get clean before he wears it next. Right, Johnny?"

Johnny nods his head, and I smile at him. We eat dinner, and I give JC and Lexi a break by bathing Johnny and putting him to bed. By the time I finish, Arabella is tucked into her crib and fast asleep. My poor brother and sister in law look exhausted, and I'm glad I can help.

"Thank you so much for helping with Johnny. He's been impossible all day. We need to take him back to daycare so he can get worn out."

"I can take him off your hands tomorrow if you like. Maybe a visit to the park? They have a soccer clinic for the little ones."

"If you could do that, it would be great. Mom can't come by tomorrow, and Lexi's mom is working."

"I can get him at ten if that works."

"That's fine. I appreciate it, Hunter."

"That's what brothers are for."

I want to talk to him, but I'm not sure if I want to include Lexi in the conversation. When I glance over, she's fast asleep, so I'm free to talk to JC.

"I need your advice."

"Shoot."

"Rory's being abused by her fiancé. What should I do?"

"You mean that dick I saw her with at the picnic?"

"How is it that you know he's a dick?"

"When dessert was served, I overheard him telling her to have a piece of fruit because he said she was fat. If I told Lexi that, she would punch me in the mouth."

"But you wouldn't, and neither would I. I heard something similar when I was getting some food and was behind them. She has a terrible bruise on her arm. It looks like he grabbed her."

JC inhales deeply. "Have you talked to her about this?"

"Yes, and she's in deep denial. I'm afraid he's going to hurt her severely or worse."

"You have it bad for her."

"I can't stop thinking about her. I want to call Noah, but is it my place? She told me that her parents think he's great."

"Of course they do. He acts one way in front of them and another in private."

"Why can't she see he's a piece of shit? Another thing, we went to The Slide tonight for drinks with some of the other interns. Her fiancé, Derek, is visiting, and he zoomed right on Julie, one of our pretty interns, while he made Rory get him some drinks. I think he cheats on her."

"Isn't she twenty?"

"Yes, but she has a fake ID. I bet he fucks other women while she's away and then acts all perfect around her parents and grandparents. He also works for Wilton Properties, so they think he's wonderful. It's so fucked up."

"Hunter, you can't save her from herself. If she's in denial, there isn't a lot you can do. If he hurts her and someone else sees it, they can report it. But if she doesn't want to report it or drops the charges, I'm not sure how much can be done. You have to hope she comes to her senses before something serious happens."

We talk for a little while longer, and I start to yawn. I'm tired because I haven't been sleeping so well since Lily broke up with me. Now I have Rory to worry about, and I'm sure I'm not going to get any sleep this weekend.

"Thanks, JC. I appreciate you discussing this with me. I'll be here tomorrow at 9:30 to get Johnny."

He walks me to the door, and we hug. The weather is still pretty warm, and I decide to walk home. There are a lot of people on the street, and I don't feel like going home yet, even though I'm tired. I stop into a deli on Columbus Avenue to buy a large hazelnut coffee and spy condoms on the display rack at the register. I take two-three packs of ribbed, lubricated ones. Since I'm single, I might as well get back in the game.

I take them out of the box and shove them in my pocket, handing the empty boxes to the clerk to throw away. He's practically a kid and gives me a shit-eating grin as he takes them. Dumbass. I slowly walk home because I don't want to be alone. My apartment is not cozy or comforting to me any longer. I should think about moving to someplace smaller.

CHAPTER 16

Twenty-three little ones attend the soccer clinic that my buddies, Claude and Henri throw in Central Park. They're from France and have been playing soccer since they were the same age as some of these children. But they both have kids of their own, so they know how to interact with little ones.

I assist them since I'm pretty good at soccer, but some of the children are hard to control and don't want to do what we say. At least a few are paying attention. After an hour, I'm exhausted. I barely slept last night. I was worried about Rory. To top it off, I didn't have coffee, so I'm a bit grouchy without my caffeine.

When the time is up, we stay for a little while and play with Johnny, Claude's two daughters, Madeleine and Cecelia, and Henri's son, Jacque. By noon, I'm done, but I want to give JC and Lexi some free time, and I text them to let them know I'm taking Johnny to have lunch. They rain praise on me, but I can't help it that I love the little guy so much.

Johnny is extra good because I promise him we will go back to the park and get some ice cream, which we do. I clean him up with some napkins and water from the fountain; then it's off to home. He starts whining halfway there that he's tired and I pick him up. He must be tired because he falls asleep against my shoulder, and I carry him right to his bed when JC lets me in.

Now I'm free for the rest of the day. What the hell am I going to do? It's only 1:45 PM, and I have nothing going on. I guess I'll take a shower and maybe call Matty to see if he wants to go out tonight. Some dinner before we go would be good; then we can hit the bars. But my plans are derailed when I walk into my lobby, and I see a blonde woman sitting there. It looks like Rory, and I say her name. She looks up at me through her hair, and I know something is very wrong.

"Rory, what's the matter?"

"Take me upstairs."

In the elevator, I put my fingers on her chin, and she pulls away.

"let me see."

She holds still, and I move her hair off her face. She has a bruise under her eye, and I can see blood caked under one of her nostrils.

"I'm going to kill that motherfucker! Where is he?"

"No, Hunter, please just help me."

When the elevator gets to my floor, I take her by the hand and lead her to my door, gently pushing her in after I unlock it. I say nothing as I take her to my bathroom, get a washcloth, and clean the blood from under her nose. The bruise is swollen and turning black.

Still not saying anything, I take her to the kitchen, sit her on one of the stools in my kitchen and get some ice. I grab the dishtowel from the stove and wrap the ice in it, then hand it to her. It's then that I speak.

"When did this happen?"

She begins to cry, and my heart shatters. This delicate, fragile woman is falling apart before my very eyes. I take her in my arms, something I've wanted to do for the last week and kiss her forehead.

"Don't cry, sweetheart. It's going to be okay. Tell me what happened."

"He got drunk last night, and this morning when he woke up, he complained he had a bad headache. I told him that if he didn't drink so much, he would be okay. He got angry and backhanded me. That's how my nose got bloody. Then he told me I was acting like a whore last night talking to you. I'm his, and he shouldn't be embarrassed by my behavior. I told him he embarrassed me by hitting on Julie, and that's when he punched me."

As Rory's telling me the story, my nails are digging into my palms so tightly that it hurts. I want to run out of the apartment, find Derek and beat him to a bloody pulp. He put his hands on her and caused the injury for something so silly.

"Where is he now?"

"He left. He grabbed his bag and walked out the door. Derek didn't even care that my nose was bleeding, he just said what a slut I was, and if I want to be his wife, I better learn how to act properly."

"Sweetheart, you did act properly. No man should put his hands on a woman."

"I shouldn't challenge him. I know how he is."

I looked at her incredulously. Was she blaming herself for Derek's actions? I would never put my hands on her, and neither should Derek.

"And no matter what you said to him, he shouldn't touch you. You have to tell someone."

"I am, you."

"No, I mean your parents or grandparents."

"That would only lead to problems. They love him like a son. He's been working for my grandparents since he was twenty. They think he's great."

"And what would they think if they knew he was abusing their granddaughter?"

"They might not believe me."

"Rory, stop making excuses. You need someone to protect you."

"I'll apologize, and it will be fine. It's what I always do."

"He's done this before?"

"Yes, but usually he doesn't hit me in the face. I egg him one."

"I can't believe what I'm hearing. You're making excuses for his behavior?"

"He has a bad temper."

"Sweetheart, no matter what type of temper he has or what you say or do, he shouldn't touch you. It hurts me so much to see you hurt. It makes me angry, and I want to hurt him."

I'm trying to keep my voice even, but I want to yell at Rory. How can she think this is her fault? Her phone rings and she excuses herself to answer it. I can hear part of the conversation, and I think it's that asshole Derek that she's talking to. When she comes back, she has a weak smile on her face.

"He's waiting for me at my apartment. He wants me to come home so we can talk."

I shake my head. "I don't think it's a good idea."

"Hunter, he's my fiancé. If I want this to work, then we need to talk."

"Do you want this to work?"

"Yes. I want to marry him."

"And what about me?"

"What about you?" She says with annoyance in her voice.

"I love you. I want you to be with me."

"But I don't love you."

The look on her face tells me she's lying. I know she does.

"Then kiss me. If you feel nothing, then I'll forget you and move on. You can marry Derek and have a dozen babies."

"I can't do that. I'm engaged, and I will not cheat on him."

ADDICTED BY LOVE

"Rory, you think he's faithful to you? Based on what I saw last night, he's not. If he can do that in front of you, then he's doing it when you're here, and he's there. Don't be foolish."

Rory grits her teeth. "I'm leaving. I don't need a lecture from you. Thanks for the ice. She holds out the dishtowel, and when I don't take it, she places it on the counter."

I can't believe the conversation I just had with her. I watch as she heads for the door without looking back at me, and then she's gone. Now I need a drink, and I rummage through the cabinet until I find a bottle of twelve-year-old scotch. I need a good amount to calm my nerves.

I overindulge because the knowledge that Rory isn't leaving Derek weighs on me. I thought she would surely realize he's no good for her. I'm drunk by the time 6:00 PM rolls around. The scotch bottle is half empty, and I'm dizzy, so I lie down on the couch to sleep it off.

I'm awakened sometime after midnight by the ringing of my phone. I'm grouchy, and I ignore it to drag myself off the couch and go to bed. I'm still considerably drunk and not in the mood for conversation. I hear the blasted cell keep going off, and that's the last thing I hear before I fall asleep.

∽

The next morning, drums beat in my head, and my mouth tastes like I was sucking on an old shoe. Why did I drink so much? Coffee, I need coffee and aspirin. I sit up in bed looking for my cell, then realize I left it on the table in the living room. Getting out of bed takes great effort, and I realize I'm still wearing the shorts and t-shirt I put on yesterday morning.

I head into the living room to retrieve my phone while I rub my temples with my fingers. It really hurts. I have six voicemails, and I punch in my access code to listen to them.

Fuck, I scream. It's Ellie. Rory's in the hospital. She claims she fell a flight of stairs. How could that be since she takes the elevator up and down? I run to the kitchen, grab some aspirin from the cabinet, slug it down with a swig of orange juice, and I'm off.

I hail a cab and tell him to take me to NYU Langone Medical Center. I'm having a hard time controlling myself, and my pounding head is not helping matters. When we get to the medical center, I hand the driver some money, and he yells at me that I get change. I tell him to keep it. The front desk gives me Rory's room, and I tap my foot as I wait for the elevator.

Ellie is in the waiting room when I get there, and so is someone who I assume is her mother. She has a strong resemblance to Rory. I sit down with Ellie, and she introduces me to Vivian. The woman is gorgeous, and I can see why Lexi was so insecure about her being around Noah.

"You're Hunter?" Vivian asked.

"Yes, I went to school with Rory. She works with me at Lawson."

She frowns at my last name.

"She's mentioned you a few times."

The nurse comes in and summons Vivian leaving Ellie and me to talk about Rory's injuries.

"What do you think happened, Ellie?"

"I know exactly what happened. That asshole hurt her."

"She came to me yesterday afternoon with a bloody nose and a bruise under her eye. He hit her, and she thinks it was her fault."

"Rory told me that you went home to Boston. How did you know she got hurt?"

"I went to my father's. I can't deal with that dickhead and didn't want to hurt Rory's feelings, so I told her I was going to Boston to visit my mother. I forgot my laptop, and when I went back to get it, all hell had broken loose."

"He pushed her down the stairs, I bet."

"I don't think he did. I think he hit her or grabbed her arm and broke it."

My mouth drops open. "She has a broken arm?"

"Well, her wrist. I went to the apartment, hoping they were asleep. When I got there, she was hysterical, and Derek was saying he was sorry."

"Where is that piece of shit?"

"He left right after we brought her to the hospital."

"I bet he'll be running back to Boston and come up with some bullshit excuse. I'm going to kill that fucker."

"I told her he was bad for her. She rebounded from you with him."

"Ellie, she broke up with me. I got no communication from her at all after she left when her grandmother was sick."

"Her grandmother was fine after she went to the hospital. They administered medication, and it broke up the clot. She had no paralysis or anything. What did she tell you?"

I gape at her like an idiot. She told me that her grandmother was sick for a while. I feel like a fool and very confused. Why would Rory lie to me?

"She said her grandmother required care, which is why she quit for the semester."

"That's not true. A couple of weeks after, I went home to see my mom, and her grandmother was fine. She was walking around and everything."

"Ellie, did she tell you anything else? Did she tell you why she wanted to stay in Boston for the semester?"

"She told me she didn't feel well. She was overwhelmed since you broke up with her."

"I never did. I wanted her to be with me."

"Why would she tell me differently?"

"I can't tell you why. She had something going on, and I think it screwed up her head."

"Tell me."

"It's not for me to tell. Rory has to be the one to do it," I said.

"We haven't spoken a lot. I don't like how Derek treats her, and we've argued about it. She can't see my side. He's hurting her, and she thinks it's always her fault."

"I told her the same thing. She thinks I have ulterior motives."

Ellie stares at me. "Do you?"

"I'm in love with her. I never stopped. She fell out of love with me."

"I don't think that's true. Derek is familiar, and when he came around when she was home, she went with him. Of course, that asshole charmed her with flowers and nights out. Vivian and Noah love him, not to mention her grandparents. They think he's so wonderful."

"I wonder how much they would love him if they knew what he was doing to her."

Ellie starts to say something when Vivian comes back into the waiting room.

"Hunter, Rory wants to see you. She was surprised you're here."

"We're friends. I thought she would need me."

"Well, go, she's waiting."

I nod and head to Rory's room. She has a private room with a door, and it's ajar when I get there. I step in quietly, and her eyes are closed. When she hears the door click, they flutter open. She looks like shit. The bruise under her eye is now darker than it was the day before. Her left forearm is in a dark pink cast. She smiles weakly at me, and I go to her.

"I'm sorry, Hunter. You were right."

She begins to cry, and I lean down to kiss her forehead.

"Rory, it's okay. This is the worst of it, and it's going to get better. When are you going to end it with him?"

"I don't know how to do it. He told me he wouldn't let me go."

"You're going to do it. You need to do it because this is only the beginning. Next is full beatings, and it might even escalate to him, killing you. Do you know what that would do to me?"

"But this doesn't mean anything for us. We're not dating."

As disappointed as I am to hear her say those words, it's her choice.

"I understand that, but just knowing that you're here and alive is all that matters to me. I want to be friends, at least. Don't take that away from me."

"We can be friends, but nothing else."

I know it's going to be hard, especially when I know that she's free to date, but she won't date me. I have no idea why she denies her feelings for me even after Ellie confirmed she's still in love with me.

"Fine. I'll take what I can get. How are you feeling?"

"My arm hurts a little."

"Do you want to tell me the story?"

"What story?"

"I know it didn't happen when you fell down the stairs. So how did it happen?"

She looks around me to make sure the door is closed.

"I got home, and Derek had come back. We argued and I was going into the bedroom. He grabbed my arm, and I tried to pull away. He started to twist my hand, and I felt a sharp pain. I knew he broke it. Ellie came in a little while after it happened. I was crying, and she pushed him away from me and told him to get out of our apartment."

"You should have told him that. He needs to realize you're not his toy. You were his fiancée, but now that's over."

Rory turns her head away to look out the window, and I'm wondering if she's going to break it off with him. I knew a woman like her named Sandy. She worked for Lawson in the legal department as a paralegal.

I would often see her coming in with bruises on her arm, wearing long-sleeved shirts in the summer. She even had a black eye and said she ran into the refrigerator door. My father offered her help, but instead, she moved across the country to get away from her boyfriend. I heard he followed and almost killed her by strangulation. Her neighbor got him off her, and now he's in jail.

I shiver a little to think of Derek doing that to Rory. How would I feel if she was no more? I don't know if I could handle it, and it's when I realize how much in love with her I am. I can't lose her. It will take time for me to get her back in my arms, but I'm up for the challenge.

"Rory, look at me?"

She keeps her head turned away, so I go around to the other side of the bed. Tears are dripping down her cheek, and I take a tissue to gently wipe at them.

"I'm afraid."

"Then you need to tell your parents. I don't care about that dickhead and his reputation. He's typical, he wants to look perfect on the outside, but behind closed doors, he's a monster."

"If I say something, he'll get fired."

"Are you debating this?"

I carefully pick up her casted arm. "This is your future if you don't get out."

The nurse comes in, and I put her arm down on her bed, kiss her forehead, and leave the room. I'm going home because even with the aspirin, my head is pounding like a hammer. I need some sleep. I pass the waiting room, and when Vivian sees me, she gets up.

"Does she want to see me again?"

"The nurse came in, so I left. I guess you can go back in."

She heads down the hall, and I see that Ellie is still sitting there.

"She needs a push to dump Derek. She's afraid he'll lose his job."

"Fuck him. He deserves it. He doesn't even need to work there. His parents gave him a trust fund. Derek loves to shower Rory with gifts, so she'll keep her mouth shut. He's always buying her flowers and talks about her like she's his possession."

"So why does he work there?"

"Something to do, I guess. He's a supervisor and only because he's worked there for a few years. What they pay him is pocket change. If he were decent he would donate his salary to some homeless shelter. I mean, the fucking guy drives a Porsche to work."

"I'm leaving. Do you want to come with me?"

"Yes, wait for me. I want to say goodbye to Rory."

I sit down and wait, playing a game on my cell until Ellie comes back. We share a cab to my place and talk about a few things, including Matty. They see each other on and off. It doesn't surprise me. Ellie is cute, and Matty loves being in a relationship.

When we arrive at my building, I pay the driver for both of us since Ellie has a lunch date with Matty, and he lives several blocks up. She plants a kiss on my cheek and tells me she'll keep tabs on the Derek situation.

I get upstairs into my apartment, and my head hurts so badly that I want to throw up. I haven't had anything to drink but a small sip of orange juice. I take out a bottle of water and suck it down, then take another and do the same. Maybe a nice hot shower will help and a nap. After I finish and I'm settled back in bed, my cell buzzes. What now?

Hunter, I'm sorry that I worried you. I'll be at work on Monday.

I'm thankful that Rory's okay but pissed off that she has to debate whether she should dump Derek or tell her parents what is going on. He doesn't deserve her, and it's too bad if the trust fund baby is going to lose his job. A guy like him should be doing volunteer work at a battered women's shelter so he can see the aftermath of what a shit like him does.

I fade into sleep thinking about how pathetic Rory looked yesterday and this morning lying in the hospital bed. I wanted to take her in my arms, and cradle her, protect her, love her.

CHAPTER 17

I became an introvert, staying in my apartment most of my off-hours. I even stopped going to my Saturday morning soccer games. They only thing that cheered me up was my niece and nephew. Arabella and Johnny made me feel alive, but it was only temporary. Once I was away from them, the gloom sank into me. The only other thing that would pull me out was to see Rory again.

She had moved out of the apartment she shared with Ellie. All her clothing and personal items removed and taken back to Boston. Ellie told me she was still with Derek, and he was on his best behavior. But Rory was in denial, and I'm sure he was abusing her in some way, even if it was just emotional. Guys like him can't help themselves.

In mid-June, I took a trip up to Boston to see an old schoolmate. I left Manhattan early in the morning in a rental. I found the address for Rory's parents and sat in the car down the street until I saw her come out. She was dressed in tennis whites and carried a racquet in her uncasted hand. Derek was picking her up for a game. I ducked down as they passed by so they wouldn't see me.

She looked as beautiful as ever. Her body was so sexy in the short skirt of her tennis outfit. I wanted to jump out of the car and whisk her away. Derek didn't deserve her.

I spent the weekend moping around my buddy, Charles' place until he got annoyed and dragged me out to a beachside bar. We met a few women there, but I was in no mood to get involved. I talked to one very pretty blonde who kept going on and on about her poodle. I was hoping Charles would save me, but he was talking to two women and got their numbers.

Sunday, I ended up leaving early and sitting in front of Rory's house again, but she didn't come out. I did see her father, Noah, come out and leave. I didn't bother to duck down because I doubted he would remember me from a few years ago. As I drove home, Lexi called me and asked if I could come over for dinner that night. I told her I could.

Even my appearance had taken a toll, and I wasn't my usual dapper self. I didn't care, and it reflected. Who was I out to impress? I showed up at Lexi and JC's in a pair of frayed shorts and a stained t-shirt.

"Hunter, how are you?" Lexi said as she opened the door.

"Shitty, and you?" I said as I slipped past her.

"I'm fine. JC isn't here; he took the kids for a walk before dinner."

"I would have done that."

"I told him to go. I wanted to speak to you."

I follow her into the kitchen. "So what is this, an ambush?"

Lexi yanks open the refrigerator, extracting two bottles of water. "No. It's a reality check. What the hell is wrong with you?"

"Nothing," I said as I took the bottle of water she offered.

"Bullshit. Don't you lie to me."

"Seriously, I'm fine. Just have a lot on my mind."

"So, this has nothing to do with Rory?"

I stare at her and begin playing with the frayed seam of my pocket.

"How did you know about her?"

"Olivia told me. Matty's girlfriend, Ellie, told her the whole story."

"So, you know about her fiancé?"

"Yes, and I think you should've told Noah or at the least, Vivian."

I hear the venom in her voice when she speaks the woman's name.

"It's not my place to tell. Rory isn't a child. She has to make her own decisions."

"She's been brainwashed in a sense. Her fiancé has got her so afraid that she's not going to tell on him. Rory thinks what he does to her is the norm. You should've said something."

"She's not my concern."

"She is because you're in love with her."

"Who told you that?"

"I know, Hunter. I can tell when you were with her how happy you were. She was your first girlfriend, and now that light that she lit in you is out. You're not the Hunter I know. You're grouchy, and the only thing that makes you happy is my children."

"I miss her. I have no desire to sleep with anyone other than her. I'm not the same; she changed me. I saw her yesterday. I went to Boston to visit Charles, and I sat down the street from her house. She came out, and my heart fluttered. I can't get her out of my head."

"Does she know?"

"Yes, but she told me she doesn't love me. She can't give me what I want."

"Then you need to forget her. You're young, and you can't go pining away for someone that doesn't love you back. Are you going to Montauk this year?"

"Matty rented the house and asked me. I haven't given my decision, but I already put in for the week at work. My father said good; maybe I'll come back in a better frame of mind."

"Then go, enjoy yourself, and find someone to fuck."

I raise my eyebrows because usually, Lexi doesn't talk like that.

"Thanks, Lexi, I can always count on you for an emotional boost."

JC comes back just as we finish talking. He smiles at me and hugs me, well aware of what's going on with me. I need my family now, not just the kids. I haul Johnny up and swing him high in the air. He giggles, and I put him on my shoulders. Arabella is cute as a button, and Lexi takes her out of the carriage, which allows me to plant a soft kiss on her sweet-scented forehead. What a little beauty, just like her mama.

Dinner perks me up, and I leave feeling in much better spirits than I came. I've decided that if Rory doesn't want me, then I'm going to find someone who will. I'm probably just deluding myself into believing I can forget her so easily, but I have to. She'll be married soon, and there is nothing I can do.

~

The next two weeks leading up to the July Fourth holiday take their toll on me. My father purchased a third building, and with two others in progress, it's added to my workload. My head is filled with zoning, renovations, violations, plans, and complaining contractors. I can't wait to get out of Manhattan for a week, and I'm looking forward to Montauk.

It's been pretty hot this summer, and since the holiday is on a Friday, I'm heading up there on Sunday, the last day in June. I'm acutely aware that the next day is Rory's twenty-first birthday, and I wonder if I should send her a text. I decide it's not a good idea since that jerk Derek might get upset if he sees it. Better to leave it alone.

The drive out there with Matty and our friends, Jamie and Dario, is a good time. We filled half the back of the SUV we rented with cases of liquor and the other half with beer. We had to stack our suitcases on the third-row seating, or we wouldn't be able to take our clothes.

Since Matty is driving, we pop open a bottle of tequila and start taking shots. By the time we hit Long Island, we're feeling a good buzz except for Matty, of course. I'm feeling a bit queasy, so I stop drinking before we have to pull over so I can throw up.

Dario drops a bomb and says that he invited a few girls over to the house. We're going to make garbage punch, which is a disgusting way to use expensive liquor. I'd rather drink it from a glass than mix a good majority of it with beer and fruit punch in a clean garbage can. But it's a party, so I'll go along. It's about time I enjoy myself since it's been way too long.

Jamie and I fall asleep, and we pay for it since Matty and Dario shoot us with water guns after they pull into the driveway of the house. We jump out and chase them, and when we do, we get a glimpse of the house next door. It has a large pool, and there are several young women around it. Jackpot. I might get lucky tonight.

The women see us and wave. Dario goes over to invite them to our garbage punch party. After we unload everything, Matty and Jamie leave to get food and a clean garbage can. The weather is hot, and the water is calm. I'd love to go for a swim, but we have work to do.

By seven, we have everything in place. Garbage punch is mixed, and we have a ton of leftover liquor. Chips are in bowls along with dip and crudite. I bet no one will end up eating the vegetables. We have some cool tunes going and strung some lights around the massive deck overlooking the ocean. Now, all we need are guests.

We order a few pizzas and scarf them down before the guests arrive. If we don't eat, we're going to get drunk faster. An hour and a half later, the party is in full swing. More gal to guy ratio is great, and I talk to a few women that I might want to take to bed later. But I'm going to leave my options open since this is the new and improved Hunter, well new and improved from the one moping around.

People keep pouring into the house until we're spilling out onto the deck. There's a lovely warm breeze blowing off the ocean, and people are sitting on the built-in benches. I'm having a great time until I see her, a young woman standing in the kitchen with blonde hair wearing a dark green bikini top and khaki-colored shorts. I can only see her profile, but I know.

I walk closer to the open French doors, and she turns so I can see her full face, it's Rory, and my heart begins to pound. Two seconds ago, my mind was fuzzy from too many cups of garbage punch, but now it's clear. All at once, I feel anger wash over me. What is she doing here? She must have noticed Matty, and wherever he goes, I go.

I enter the kitchen and slowly move around people, so she doesn't see me until I'm practically on top of her. She's still wearing the pink cast, and I assume she has a few more weeks before she gets it taken off. I lean into her ear so she can hear me over the music. Rory is still not aware I'm behind her.

"I want to talk to you."

She wheels around, spilling the drink that she holds in her hand. Her eyes fly open wide in surprise as she focuses on me.

"Hunter."

"The one and only," I say as I brush off droplets of garbage punch from my shirt.

"I'm busy."

"No, you're not," I take the half-empty cup out of her hand, put it on the counter and take her by the arm. My bedroom is in the back down a long hallway on the first floor, and I lead her to it, gently pushing her in before I close the door.

"What do you want from me?"

"An explanation. What are you doing here?"

"I'm renting the house next door with some girlfriends."

I put my hands on my hips. "And you didn't happen to notice Matty here?"

"I did, but I didn't know he was renting this house."

"We're."

"We're what?"

"We're renting this house. Not just Matty."

"I didn't know. I can leave."

I step in front of the door. "You're not going anywhere. Where is your fiancé?"

It's then that I notice her finger is bare. The engagement ring is gone.

"We broke up. I mean, I broke up with him."

"Why?"

"Does it matter?"

"Did he hit you again?"

"No. He hasn't hit me since," her voice trails off.

"So, what was it this time?"

"I caught him cheating on me."

I smirk, and though it's cruel, I can't contain myself and start laughing.

She frowns. "You're an asshole. Why are you laughing?"

"Because I knew he was cheating on you. The way he went after Julie right in front of you should have given you a clue."

"When I found out, he wanted me to join them for a threesome. He wanted me to fool around with the girl in front of him. He demanded it."

"And what did you say?"

"I told him it was over, and I threw my ring at his head. He chased me and had a hold of my arm. I thought he was going to hit me, so I kneed him in the balls, and when he was bent over, I slapped his face. He screamed at me, and I ran to my car and drove away."

"When did this happen?"

"A week and a half ago."

That would account for why I saw them acting so lovey-dovey two weeks ago. The demise of their relationship hadn't happened yet. I'm glad she came to her senses, but that doesn't solve my problem.

"So, what are you going to do now?"

"I want to come back to New York. I still hold part of the lease on the apartment I rented with Ellie."

"Does she know you want to move back?"

"No, but I'm sure it won't be a problem. Anyway, it's none of your business."

"It is my business."

"I don't work for you any longer. We don't share a bed or a class project. Why is it your concern?"

I grab her and pull her against me, looking her square in the eye, "Because I love you. I'm in love with you, and I have been for months. You know this."

"Let me go, Hunter."

I refuse and put my other arm around her then start kissing her hair, forehead, and cheek. She smells wonderful. It's a mix of the ocean, suntan lotion, her perfume, and Rory. It's intoxicating, and I can't help myself even though she's struggling a bit to get out of my arms.

By the time I reach her lips, she's not fighting me so hard, and as soon as I press them hard against hers, she practically goes limp in my arms. I gently push my tongue into her mouth, and Rory sucks on it. I want to undress and take her to my bed, but I'm sure that's not going to happen. I'll take what I can get.

I'm not sure how long we're locked together, but during, my hands travel along her soft, silky tanned skin. The noise outside the door disappears, and there is only she and I. I want her so badly that I ache, but she has to be the one to make that decision. I'm sure she wants me too, especially when she moans my name into my mouth.

My body is humming, and my heart is pounding. I can feel

hers thumping as I move my mouth from her lips to her neck. Her pulse is rapid, and I gently suck the flesh just above it. Rory runs her hands through my hair and tugs on the curls at the nape of my neck. I feel overwhelming love for this woman.

"Are you?" I whisper into her neck. And then I hear the words I've wanted to hear for so long, the words that will make me whole again and bring me out of my melancholy.

"I am."

I reluctantly remove my lips from her neck so I can look into her sapphire eyes. They're dark with desire, the same desire I feel, but I want to make sure that I have it straight.

"Say the words, Rory."

She stares at me, and without batting her pretty long eyelashes, she says that phrase.

"I love you, Hunter. I always have. I was so stupid to deny my feelings."

At that moment, I'm not sure if I want to throttle her for the denial or take her in my arms and bring her to my bed. Instead, I take her hand, and we sit on the padded gray window seat that overlooks the ocean.

"Why did you then. I would have been good to you. I would have treated you like a princess."

"I was scared. You acted like the man who took my virginity. He treated me kindly, but it was a very physical relationship. Then it became dark, and he was demanding."

"I would never demand of you. I just wanted you to be with me."

"When I found out I was pregnant, it scared me. What if I told you and you didn't want me? You said you never had a girlfriend before. So, the first one you have, and she gets pregnant."

"You should've told me then. I would never have forced you to do anything you didn't want to do. It was your decision, and I would have stood by you."

"Even if I decided to have it?"

"Of course. It was mine, and I would take care of it and you."

"Would you have married me?"

"Rory, I love you, and if that's what it would have taken, then yes."

"I'm sorry I ran away."

"Do you know how devastating it was for me to lose you? Then you come back, and you're engaged. To see you day after day and then to meet that scumbag. To find out he was abusing you? It tore me apart."

"I was confused. When Derek came to me, it was a few days after I miscarried. I wasn't sure what I should do. He was sweet and brought me flowers. Then he took me on a date a few nights later. It wasn't always bad."

"But when he started to abuse you, you should have ended it."

"I know, but I had no one to talk to. I couldn't tell my parents. They love Derek."

"He's a wolf in sheep's clothing. He's lucky I didn't punch his lights out when I heard him say that you couldn't eat something because he didn't want you to gain weight. Who the fuck says that to someone they love?"

"He was always like that. He wanted me to be very skinny. Derek likes skinny girls."

"Then why didn't he leave you alone?"

"I don't know. I guess because I was familiar."

Looking at Rory, I can't resist but to touch her. I stroke her face, and she leans into my hand while closing her eyes.

"So, where do we go from here?"

"I want to come back to Manhattan, but my parents want me to stay in Boston. They said I could work for my grandparents. I don't want to be around Derek now that we're broken up."

"He still works for your grandparents? What did you tell them about your break up?"

"I said we just weren't compatible. We have different needs.

They told me I should work out it with him. I couldn't tell them the real reason."

"Maybe they should know that he's a cheater and an abuser."

"I didn't want to go there. It would bring up too many questions. My parents see his socially. I can imagine the discussion around the dinner table."

"Why do you care so much about what anyone thinks? They should know that their son is an asshole who treats women like shit."

I look out the window and see that a fire has been lit on the beach. Several of the party-goers are out there.

"Do you want to go to the beach?"

"No, I'd rather stay here with you. I don't want to be around other people."

"Sweetheart, we can do anything you like as long as it's with me. Are you tired? We can lie in bed. I'm not sure how much sleep we'll get with all the music."

Rory looks at me and laughs, "Do you think if I lie in bed with you, we're going to get any sleep?"

"Rory, I don't want to take you to bed. I want to lie with you. You need to make the decision when you're ready."

"I've been ready for a while. Derek couldn't hold a candle to you in bed."

I smile widely and kiss the tip of her nose, then press a soft kiss to her lips.

"So?"

"So what?"

"Do you want me to make love to you?"

"Very much."

From the kitchen, we hear something breaking and screaming. I grab her hand, and we run out to see what happened. Two of the men are fighting; they knocked over some wine glasses. Dario and Matty are trying to pry them apart, and I rush over to help them. We escort the men out of the house and tell them that they aren't welcome back. When we get back into the house, Rory is cleaning up the mess with one of her roommates.

"Sweetheart, don't touch the glass. I'll do it."

I take the dustpan and broom from her as Matty crooks his eyebrow at me. I shrug my shoulders and finish cleaning up the broken glass. Rory has wandered off into the house somewhere, and Matty takes me aside.

"Want to explain that to me?"

"Did you know she was here?"

"I didn't. I wasn't paying attention until I just saw her."

"She broke up with that asshole."

"And now you're going to pick up right where you left off? You think that's a good idea?"

"Matty, I love her. I don't want to be with anyone else, and I'm miserable without her."

"I just think she's too young for you."

"That didn't stop you from dating Ellie. You're my age, and she's Rory's."

"No, Ellie is twenty-two. How old is Rory, twenty? Not even old enough to legally drink."

"She's going to be twenty-one tomorrow."

"You do what you want, but if she breaks your heart again, don't say I told you so."

"I can't believe you would say that to me. You're supposed to be supporting me as a friend."

"I do support you, but I don't want you to be hurt. You were a mess, and when you realize you should be fucking other women after a long hiatus, she comes back. Just be careful."

"Thank you for your advice."

I'm pissed off as I walk away. Matty is my best friend, and he's supposed to be happy for me. I can understand that he's worried, but I don't need a babysitter or a lecture. I love Rory, and it's either going to work out, or it's not.

I look around, and I can't find her anywhere in the house.

Most of the people have gravitated toward the beach and the fire that Jamie and Dario started. Many couples are sitting around it and listening to someone who brought a guitar. It's romantic. I find Rory sitting in my bedroom at the window seat. She cracked open one of the windows and is listening to the waves.

"Are you okay?"

"This is happening quickly again."

My heart drops. "If you don't want it to, say the words. I'm not going to push you."

"I want it to happen. I should have been straight with you and let you know I was pregnant. Can you forgive me?"

I sit next to her. "I've forgiven you already. I want you to know that you can always come to me with anything. I'm not Derek. I would never hurt you. Not all men are like him and the other guy."

She pulls her knees up to her chest and wraps her arms around them. I want to take her on my lap and kiss her until she begs me to stop. She looks so vulnerable and fragile. I can imagine how it must have been for her to get up the courage to break up with Derek. He didn't deserve her, but do I? Can I make her happy?

CHAPTER 18

We don't know each other well, and most of our relationship was physical. Maybe we have nothing in common, and after we fuck, there will be not a shred of anything to talk about. I have doubts too, but I don't make them known to Rory.

"Would you like to go for a walk?"

"Not really. I'd like you to hold me."

I hold out my arms, and she unwraps her arms from her legs and moves onto my lap. I cradle her like I would Johnny with her head on my shoulder, stroking her back with my fingers. I keep running my hand over the tie of her bathing suit top, and I have the urge to pull the strings. But I want her to trust me. I want her to know it's not about just sex with her.

As much as I try not to, I'm hardening under her. She's gently rocking back and forth, which is arousing me. I try to think of something off-putting, but it doesn't help. I can't stop myself or will my erection away. I'm sure she can feel it, but she says nothing. We sit there, locked together, listening to the ocean pound the beach and the guitar music filtering in through the window.

I glance at the clock on the nightstand, which reads 12:04 AM. Rory is now twenty-one, and I want to be the first to wish her a happy birthday. I move my mouth to her ear, her eyes are closed, but I know she can feel my warm breath against her.

"Happy birthday, baby. No more fake ID for you."

Her head pops up. "You remembered?"

"Of course. It was when I met you a year ago, though I didn't know it. We should celebrate. I could take you out to dinner tonight."

"I have plans with my girlfriends. We're going to a club."

"Can I join you? I want to buy you your first drink."

"I've already had many drinks bought for me."

"But, I'll be buying the first drink now that you're legal age."

"I guess you can come. Maybe you could bring Matty, Jamie, and Dario. I'm sure my friends would like that."

"Then it's a date. Are you going home tonight?"

"I'd like to stay here with you if that's okay."

"I want that very much."

Though the party is still in full swing, I want Rory to myself. I don't want to share her with anyone. I start removing my clothes.

"What are you doing?"

"Do you want me to sleep in my clothing?"

"No, I guess not."

"Do you mind if I lock the door? I prefer that we don't get intruded on."

"Hunter, are you misreading this? I don't want to have sex."

"And I'm not inviting you to stay with me for that. I don't want to be bothered while I'm with you."

I lock the door, shut the windows, and pull down all the shades. I remove my clothes down to my boxers and watch Rory's eyes as she eye fucks me. A smile blooms on her face, and she reaches out to run her fingers over the ridges of my abs.

"Behave, or we won't be sleeping."

"Do you have something I can wear?"

I rummage around in my suitcase for a dark blue t-shirt. I would rather she wear a white or light blue one that would show her beautiful nipples, but she might think I have ulterior motives. I hand it to her to change into.

"Can you turn around?"

"Sweetheart, I've already seen you naked."

"Just do it," she says in an annoyed tone.

I turn around and hear the rustle of clothing. What she doesn't know is that I can see her in the mirror over the dresser. My breath hitches as she removes her bikini top. I forgot how wonderful her breasts are, perfectly shaped and topped with a dusky rose nipple. When she's finished changing, she tells me to turn back around.

"Ready to get in bed?"

"Yes. You promised."

"Rory, I'm not going to make you do anything you don't want to. Just know that I love and respect you."

We slide under the sheets, and she lies on her back while I turn onto my side to gaze at her. Slivers of light from the moon peek in from around the shades, and I lean over to kiss her.

"You promised," she murmurs.

"Relax. I want nothing but having you allow me to love you."

"I love you back."

I put my head down on her stomach, and she begins to stroke my hair. Her heart is beating loudly against my ear, and I hear its rhythm pick up as I tuck my hand under her back.

Even with the music, we manage to fall asleep, and when I wake up, it's still going but much lower. The clock now reads 2:23 AM. I've been asleep for a couple of hours, and Rory is still here, under my head, her even breathing indicating she's asleep.

The hand I tucked under her back is numb, and I pull it out, gently shaking it to give it feeling. When I can feel it again, I stroke Rory's leg, and she stirs, mumbling something which sounds like my name. I do it again, and she wakes up.

"That tickles. What are you doing?"

"Nothing."

"Well, nothing woke me up."

I have a wicked idea, but I promised no sex. However, this is for her gratification and pleasure, not mine.

"I want to give you a birthday present."

"Now?"

"Yes, now."

"What is it?" she asks suspiciously.

"I want to taste you."

"That's sex, and you promised."

"It is sex, but it's for your pleasure, not mine."

I can almost hear her thinking in the dark, and I wait for her answer.

"Alright, but that's all."

"Rory, I'm not going to do anything you don't want me to do. You can say no or stop at any time."

I sit up and push the sheet off us, then hook my fingers in her panties, which feel silky against my hands. She raises her hips, and I pull them off, dropping them on the floor. My face is so close, and her scent is making my mouth water. I move between her legs, and she instinctively pulls her knees up.

Even in the moonlight, her arousal is apparent; she's glistening. I place my hand on her mound, then slide my finger over her slickness. She's soaked, and I put my fingers to my mouth to sample her.

"You taste so good. I hope you're ready for this."

Rory says nothing, and I position myself so that I can lick her. I circle my tongue around her clit, and she shifts her hips. I do it again, and this time, she arches her back. Then I go to work by opening her slick folds with my fingers so I can tongue fuck her. She moans, and I have to shush her. People are still in the house. Not that I care, but I don't want her to be embarrassed.

"Fuck, Hunter, that's…wonderful."

I lap at her, not able to get enough of her nectar. The taste is incredible. I don't remember her tasting this good. By now, she's whimpering loudly. I swirl my tongue inside her, rubbing her swollen nub with my finger. I wish I could fuck her with more than my tongue, but I promised. My cock is so hard that it hurts pressed between my stomach and the mattress.

Rory's clenching her ass, and I slide two fingers inside her, sucking hard at her clit. She's close because I feel her tighten and call my name. Then she does something she never did before, Rory presses my head against her as she begins to orgasm. I keep working her clit with my tongue as she continues with her climax. When she finishes, my face is drenched with her juices as her hand goes limp.

I use the sheet to wipe my lips and cheeks then move next to her. Her eyes are closed, and she's breathing heavily as if she just ran a mile. I'm smiling from ear to ear like an idiot, and that's what she sees when she focuses on me.

"I haven't come like that in forever."

I want to laugh because I bet Derek sucked in bed, and he certainly never gave her the pleasure I just did. Or he was just too selfish to realize that ladies come first, literally.

"Since when?"

"Since you," she whispers.

I pull her t-shirt down and slip the sheet over us.

"What about you?"

"What about me? I told you this was for your pleasure, not mine."

I don't want to tell her how much I enjoyed doing it, because I did. Nothing pleases me more than making the woman that I love come.

"So we're done?"

"We're done. Now go to sleep."

She turns on her side, and I pull her against me, tucking my head against her shoulder. The scent of her is on my face, and I fall asleep dreaming of Rory.

The next morning, I wake up to the realization that Rory is no longer in my bed. *FUCK, she left me again.* Then I hear the toilet in the en suite flush and breathe a sigh of relief. She comes out still wearing the t-shirt I gave her, and I notice her panties are still on the floor.

"Good morning," she says.

"It is since you're still here. What are your plans for the day?"

She looks down at the floor when she tells me that her girlfriends are taking her out today. I'm disappointed but I don't want to smother her the way Derek did. I'll see her tonight when we go clubbing.

"Rory, it's fine. I'll see you tonight. Go have fun with your friends. I forgot to ask you how long you're going to be here."

"We have the house rented for two weeks."

"Oh, I'm only here until next weekend," I said.

"Then we can have the whole week together."

"And what about when I go home? What then? Is this just this week?"

"No. I told you I love you. I want to be with you. I have some discussions to have with my parents and grandparents. I know they weren't happy that I broke up with Derek. They thought we should talk out our problems. I didn't tell them the truth about why I broke it off."

"You should. He's a disgusting jerk. He had you, and he was finding other women. It just doesn't make sense."

"He wasn't always like he is. I don't understand why our relationship turned ugly."

"Think. I'm sure he was controlling you from the get-go but in the disguise of love. He told you things and bought you things; then he began to become physical, am I right?"

"Yes. For the first couple of months, he was very kind. Always a gentleman, and he wasn't pressuring me to have sex. There were times he would be late or get a call from someone and not tell me who it was. I guess these were the times he was cheating on me."

"He never stopped cheating on you. He wanted you on his arm, but he wanted girls on the side. Do you think this was the first time he did it to a girlfriend? It's a pattern with his type. They keep doing it, and even after they get caught, they can't stop."

"I was foolish when he started to abuse me. At first, it was just little things like telling me I can't have ice cream or a burger. He would insist when we went out that I order fish or a salad while he had a huge dinner and dessert. I sat there like a dummy watching him."

"Were you gaining weight?"

"No. I was losing it. He liked skinny girls, but why would he date me if he wanted someone like that. I'm curvy but not fat."

"He knew he could control you, and you looked good with him. Stop blaming yourself. You made a mistake, but you fixed it by getting away from him. God forbid you figured it out after you married him. Then what?"

"I don't know."

"Come here."

Rory comes to the bed and sits next to me. I tangle my fingers in her hair and pull her to me for a kiss. It turns passionate as she spears my mouth with her tongue. I want her, and I'm beginning to harden. Luckily, the sheet is over me since I don't want her to get the wrong idea.

"Do you want to shower with me?"

She raises her eyebrows. "Just shower?"

"I told you that I wouldn't touch you until you gave me the word."

"You requested something last night, and I allowed it."

"It wasn't last night, it was this morning, and that was for your pleasure. You could have said no, I told you that. You don't have to shower with me."

"I've decided that I want to, but I need a bag for my cast."

"I'll be right back."

No one is up in the house; I hunt around for a plastic grocery bag and some rubber bands, which I luckily found in a drawer in the kitchen. When I return, I must be grinning like a fool because she pretends to slap me in the face. I help her secure the bag around her cast, then back away.

She rises from the bed and pulls off the t-shirt she's wearing, throwing it at me. Rory has a beautiful body, and my mind starts to wander about what I'd like to do to her. I'm hard as a rock, and I can't shower like that, so I tell her to go and turn the water on, and I'll be right in. After she goes into the bathroom, I think horrible ugly thoughts, so I lose my erection. Of course, there is no guarantee that it will stay down once I'm next to her.

I head to the stall, and she's under the hot spray with her eyes closed until she hears the bang of the glass doors. She steps out from the water and wipes it out of her eyes. Even wet with her makeup washed off, Rory looks hot. I'd love to take her against the tiled wall, but I'm not going to be that forward.

She pushes me under the showerhead so I can wash my hair. After I finish, we switch, but I tell her I want to wash her hair since her hand is bagged. Again, she gives me a raised eyebrow, but I tell her it's sensual, and she'll love it. I keep forgetting she's young and has had less experience than I.

I squeeze a dollop of shampoo on my hand and work it into her scalp. Rory is facing me and closes her eyes as I work it in. I take the opportunity to look down at her body and notice her nipples are hard despite the hot water cascading over them. It's obvious what I'm doing to her is arousing.

"Are you enjoying this," I softly say.

"Mmm."

"I'm glad. I want every experience you have with me to be enjoyable. Let's get your hair washed out."

We switch positions, and I scrub at her hair with my fingers as the water washes it clean. Try as I might, I'm sporting a semi-erection through the entire thing. I can't help it where she's concerned.

"Can I wash your back?" she says.

There is nothing more I want than to have her hands on my body. I give her the body wash, and I hear her squirt some out of the bottle. Then her hands are on me, and she's washing my shoulders, my lower back and finally my ass. Unexpectedly, I feel her soapy fingers on my dick.

"Rory, what are you doing?"

"Nothing you don't want me to."

"You don't have to,"

I say it, but I do want her to.

She's stroking me, and in a minute, I'm rock hard. I feel her body press against mine with her cheek against my soapy back. I look down, and her hand wrapped around my length is so erotic. I can't stop looking, and I can't help moaning.

"Oh, baby, that's it. Make me come."

She begins working me harder. This pushes me over the edge, and I begin to release in big spurts. Rory continues to pump my cock until I've spent my entire load onto the shower floor.

I wrap my hand around hers to stop her, and she lets me go. My breath is coming in giant heaves, and I'm not sure if it's because I just orgasmed, or I can't believe she made me. I turn to her.

"You didn't have to do that."

"I wanted to. You made me feel so good last night that I think you deserved something for your efforts."

I laugh. "Thank you, madam."

We finish washing, and I step out first, wrapping myself in a towel, then holding one out for Rory step into. I cuddle her in my arms, not wanting to let go. I hope she'll change her mind about spending the day with her friends, but I won't say it.

"Maybe we can have lunch later," she says.

My heart leaps. "I don't want you to ditch your friends."

"I think we're going to spend most of the day on the beach, but I'd like some alone time with you."

"You're going to have a tan line on your forearm from your cast. When are you supposed to get it off?"

"In three weeks. I hate this thing, and it's itchy inside. I almost lost a pen down there."

"Hopefully, this will be the last cast you have to ever wear."

I kiss the tip of her nose, and we finish drying off. She holds out her cast so I can take the bag off. Fortunately, no water has gotten in, and the cast is still dry.

"What do you do when you're by yourself?"

"I manage, or I have my mother put it on for me."

"Rory, did you tell your parents about us?"

She looks at me, squarely. "No, I never said anything. My mother thinks you were just a good friend. She asked about it when you visited me at the hospital."

I'm hurt, and my face must show that hurt because she puts her hand up to stroke my face.

"We were only dating for a short time. I didn't think it necessary to mention it, especially since you know my father and your brother married Lexi."

I scowl. "Is it different now? Do I get to be part of your life, or are you going to hide me?"

"I told you I need to discuss it with my family. I want them to know what Derek did, and I want them to know you're my boyfriend."

I brighten when she says the word boyfriend. I want to be more than her boyfriend, but it's still early in our relationship, and she's young. There will be plenty of time for us to take things to the next level. I really want that. My mind starts wandering, and she taps me to bring me back.

"Hey, you got lost there for a minute."

"I was thinking about something."

We walk out to the bedroom in our towels, and she drops hers so she can dress. I move to the bed, and when she isn't looking, I swipe her panties and put them under the sheet. I want to keep these as a reminder of our renewed love.

She scans the floor then looks up at me. "Hunter, do you know where my panties are? I thought I saw them by the bed this morning when I got up."

I get off the bed and look under it as if I'm trying to find them.

"Not here. Are you sure you saw them this morning?"

"Yes. Where did you throw them last night?"

"Just by the bed, and I didn't throw them. I dropped them."

"Then why aren't they right here?"

"Does it matter? You're going right across the way. Slip on your shorts, and you'll be fine unless you want to wear a pair of my boxers."

Rory frowns. "No, thanks. Help me tie my bikini top. It's a little complicated with this cast."

I get up, and the towel around my waist falls to the floor. I see her looking at my penis, but it's not stirring.

"You're much bigger than Derek."

"I'm delighted to hear that though it's not the size but what you can do with it. I'm sure I'm a better lover than he was."

"You are," she whispers.

"Rory, I'm always going to put your needs first. Don't ever doubt that."

"I don't. It's just something that I need to get used to."

She finishes dressing, and we kiss before I walk her out. I watch as she heads over to the house next door, making sure she gets inside before I go back to my bedroom. I feel like a schoolboy who just got his first kiss from his crush. Rory is finally going to be mine.

CHAPTER 19

Even though I slept for several hours, I'm still tired. I have no idea when Dario, Matty, and Jamie will be awake. Instead of going back to sleep, I clean up around the house. After, I get dressed and leave them a note to let them know I took the SUV. I want to get Rory a few things for her birthday.

The first stop is the florist for a huge bouquet of red roses, not a dozen, not two dozen but exactly twenty-one. I stop by the bakery and choose a large round cake with vanilla frosting and pink piping. I ask if they can put *Happy Twenty-First Birthday, Rory,* on it in green. I'm not sure of her favorite color, but she seems to like green.

Next, I wrack my brain, trying to figure out what she would like as a birthday gift. I have no idea and walk around the shops until I find one that has jewelry. I'm not sure she's keen on jewelry, but I'll have to take a chance. The store has some pretty bracelets, and I see one where you can add charms.

It's fourteen-carat gold, and I decide to start her off with three charms. One is a small sailboat, a heart, and the last is a book. I might have to explain these to Rory, but I think she'll like them.

The clerk charges my credit card and wraps the bracelet up in a pretty white box complete with a small red bow.

The last thing I need to do is get her a card. There are several small gift shops, and I find exactly what I'm looking for in the second place. It's a simple card with a small black and white photograph of Manhattan. Inside, it says, let's paint the town for your birthday and below it is a photograph of the city in color. I wanted to go mushy and romantic, but I wasn't sure how she would take it. So as a backup, I get a card that speaks romance. I can give both to her.

I'm finished, and my last stop is the bagel shop for some breakfast for the guys: bagels, cream cheese, juice, coffee, and fruit salad. The last one is for me because I love it. Not sure if the guys would want to eat fruit. When I arrive home, Matty is sitting in the kitchen looking horrible, like a shade of puke green.

"What's up? You look like crap."

"I feel like crap. I think I drank way too much of that garbage punch. That shit sneaks up on you."

"How many cups did you have?"

"I lost count after midnight. I woke up with some girl in my bed. I think she's Rory's roommate."

"Was she naked?"

"No, we were both dressed in last night's clothes. I think we passed out on my bed. I do remember kissing her at some point during the night. Speaking of Rory, did you do the deed?"

I shake my head as I sip my coffee. "No, I did not. I'm trying to be respectful."

"Geez, Hunter. Are you serious? You've been pining for this girl for months, and you didn't fuck her?"

"Watch it, Matty," I growl.

He scrubs at his face. "You are in love with her, aren't you? What's in the bag?" he points to the white bakery bags I plunked on the counter.

"Bagels, cream cheese, juice, and fruit salad. I also have a box of coffee in the car; you know like Dunkin' Donuts has. I got some things for Rory's birthday. I bought some roses and a cake. I better go get it before it melts in this heat."

He gives me a look as I rush out the door. When I come back in, he's putting cream cheese on an onion bagel.

"I thought you felt horrible?"

"I do, but I'm starving."

He takes a huge bite of the bagel as I move stuff around in the refrigerator to fit the cake. By the time I get the roses and coffee, Jamie and Dario are up looking as bad as Matty.

"Who are the roses for? You know they shorted you three," Jamie said.

"Rory. Today is her twenty-first birthday. I'm taking her to lunch later. They did not short me. I asked them to give me twenty-one."

"So, are you the next in line to get married like Henri and Claude?" Jamie asked.

"No, far from it, but it's a start. Rory is a little young, and after Lily, I want to take it slow."

"That bitch burned you. She was all wrong for you, anyway."

"Jamie shut the fuck up. My head is killing me," Matty said.

I leave them arguing among themselves. I'll wait until they leave the kitchen so I can have some coffee and fruit salad in peace. After, I lay on my bed and place my head on the pillow that Rory occupied a couple of hours ago. It smells like her, and I wish she were here. As if she is reading my mind, my phone chimes.

I miss you. What are you doing? Did you fall back to sleep?

No, I did not. I had some covert ops to take care of this morning.

Oh God, now you sound like my father. Did it have anything to do with my birthday?

That is for me to know and you to find out later. Enjoy your fun with your girlfriends. When should I expect you here for me to take to lunch?

I guess about one or so. We just had breakfast. They made Mimosas.

DO NOT GET DRUNK! I want you sober for our lunch. You can drink tonight

I sent the message and realize that it sounds like I'm controlling her. It's too late because I already sent it, so I wait and hope she doesn't get upset.

Yes, sir. I promise not to get drunk. I only had one. They were yummy.

Good girl. I'll see you at 1:00, my sexy little birthday girl.

You're silly. I'll talk to you later.

I yawn and turn on my side. I think I'll take a nap. It's already 10:00 AM, so I have three hours before we go to lunch. I have no idea where to take her, but I'll figure it out before we go. In the kitchen, I hear Matty bitching about his head hurting before I fade off to sleep.

~

I wake up just after noontime. I don't hear anyone in the house, and when I get up, I look out the window and see the guys on the beach. I also see the girls from next door, but no Rory. I figure she went inside to change since she is meeting me for lunch in a little while.

I'm not dressed for lunch in my faded red tank top and basketball shorts, so I need to change. I put on a pair of navy blue Levi Dockers shorts and a white polo shirt. It's not even twelve-thirty when I hear a knock on the door. It's Rory in a cute little peach-colored sundress and sandals. I look down at her white-painted toenails. Even her feet are sexy.

"There's the birthday girl," I said as I place a kiss on her cheek.

I notice she smells like the beach with a hint of the perfume I love so much. Her hair is pulled back in a ponytail. The only thing that ruins her look is the clunky pink cast on her arm. But soon enough, it will be gone.

"So, where would you like to eat?"

"I'm not sure."

"We can decide when we get into town. I'm sure there are a million places we can go. What do you feel like eating?"

"I'm not good at making these decisions."

"Rory, we can go wherever you want. Don't be afraid to tell me."

"Can we go to Tartan's?"

"Sure. Craving a gourmet burger?"

"I want the Belgian Frites."

"Done. I have something for you. Wait here."

"You didn't have to get me anything," she calls after me.

I get the roses that I bought. Fortunately, they have these little plastic attachments for each stem that has water in them, so they didn't wilt. I also grab the box with her charm bracelet. When I come out, her eyes twinkle when she sees the flowers and box in my hands.

"These are for you. There are twenty-one roses for each year of your life. And I got you this."

I hand her the gift and hold the roses while she opens it. Rory is so careful. She gently pulls at the ribbon and folds it after it slips away from the box then places it on the counter to remove the top.

"Oh, this is so beautiful," she says as she holds the bracelet up.

She doesn't have to tell me she likes the bracelet. Her face says it all. I watch as she touches each charm with her white nail painted fingers.

"I understand about the book and heart, but I'm confused by the sailboat."

"The sailboat is because of when I first met you. Do you remember on the beach, there was a sailboat out on the water? I pointed to it."

A flicker of memory crosses her face, and she smiles, "I know what you're talking about. The lights were lit, and you said it's much better to sail in the daytime."

"Yes, that's exactly what I said. I want to add to the charms as our relationship goes."

From the confines of her purse, we hear her cell ringing. She excuses herself to answer it and heads onto the deck. Through the door, I can hear a heated argument which concerns me. When she comes back in, her face is red, and she looks like she's about to cry.

"What is it? Who was that?" I ask worriedly.

"Derek."

I grind my teeth, clenching my fists. "What did that bastard want?"

"He called to wish me a happy birthday and said now that I'd had time to cool off, we should talk. I told him there is nothing to talk about. He can't give me what I need, and I'm not marrying him."

"Did he say anything else?"

"Nothing of importance."

"Are you sure? You look very upset."

"I just want to enjoy this day."

I'm sure there is more to the discussion, but it's not my intention to further upset Rory on her birthday. There will be plenty of time to talk after we get back from Montauk.

"Then let's. On to Tartan's. Do you want to put the roses in your house before we leave?"

"Yes, and I need you to put the bracelet on me. I'm not going to take it off."

We exit the house, and while I'm cooling the blast furnace that is the SUV, Rory runs over to her house to put the roses in a vase. The vehicle is cool by the time she gets in. I curl my hand around hers as we head into town.

Since it's a Monday, Tartan's is not that crowded. We are immediately seated in a comfortable booth toward the back. The booth is small, and we're sitting near each other. Now near, I notice how incredible her scent is. A total turn on, and my mind wanders back to the night before and this morning. She touches my arm, so I come back into focus.

"What are you getting?"

"The Kobe beef burger with gruyere and Belgian Frites. I might get a side of the beer-battered onion rings, and you? What do you want? You can have anything."

"I was going to have the Mediterranean salad with a side of vinegar and oil."

I frown at her. I'm sure she wants more than that and I know it's probably because she's been so trained by that asshole Derek who told her she was fat.

"I thought you wanted Frites?"

"I did, but they aren't good for me."

"Come here."

She looks at me with a puzzled look on her face, and I ignore it to pull her close against me, wrapping my arm around her soft shoulders.

"Baby, you can have anything you want. Your body is sexy, enticing, and oh so appealing. I have a hard time controlling myself when I'm near you. I'll never speak badly of you even if you gained weight."

Rory ducks her head against my neck, and I smile. She feels so good in my arms, and I don't want to let go, but the waitress comes to take our order. I'm so happy when she decides to get the same thing as I do, and we'll share the onion rings. I want her to be comfortable around me.

We have a good conversation, and she tells me about how her semester went with Professor Stanish. She ended up getting a B+ in his class, which is pretty good.

"I graduated Cum Laude, but I did it in three and a half years, so I don't feel bad about not graduating with a higher GPA."

"It's commendable what you did. Don't ever feel you didn't accomplish, because you did."

"What did you graduate?"

"I graduated Magna Cum Laude. But you can't compare yourself to me. Things just come easy for me. I don't need to try hard. It's part of the reason why I picked up on the real estate development so quickly."

"How is that going?"

"We got two building projects for waterfront luxury apartments. They should be completed in another fifteen months. We recently purchased another building several blocks away. My father is not quite sure what he wants to do with it. We might build half residences and half commercial."

Rory tells me about all the projects that her grandparents have ongoing in Boston, New York, New Jersey, and Connecticut. Unlike Lawson, Wilton has been in the development game for years. We have a lot to catch up on before we get to their status in the business.

"I can get you a position at Lawson."

"As an intern?"

"No, all those spots are taken. As an employee."

"And how would that look that your girlfriend gets a cushy position because her boyfriend is the vice president."

"it's not about your relationship to me. It's about your capabilities. You're experienced, and I've already seen what you can do. I need someone like you. My assistant is leaving. She's pregnant and has decided to stay home full time. The position should be filled by someone who can handle a fast pace and has the knowledge I'm looking for. You fit the bill."

"I'm not sure it's a good idea we work together. I worked under Derek, and it got contentious at times."

"Rory, I'm not Derek. You've seen how I treat my employees. Do I snap at them? Do I treat them poorly?"

"Well, no, but this would be mixing business with personal."

"Suppose you worked there, and I asked you out? Then we started dating, would it be the same?"

"Yes, but different. What you are suggesting is that you get your girlfriend a job and have her work directly for you."

I lower my voice, "For heaven's sake, I'm not going to fuck you in my office. Of course, that is only if you don't want me to."

Rory gives me the hardest look, and I realize I went too far over the line. Should I start groveling or begging for forgiveness?

"Have you done that before?"

"No, I would never."

"Have you dated anyone in your office before?"

"Rory, I didn't date before you."

"Okay, have you fucked anyone from your office?"

"No, that would be inappropriate. I'm in a position of power. It could look like I was pushing them for sexual favors because of who I am."

She nervously laughs. "So, why would it be different with me?"

"Because we would already be dating, and I said I would never do that in the office. I much prefer making love in the comfort of home, yours or mine."

Rory lowers her voice. "Oh, so you think we're going to have sex?"

"That is entirely up to you. I'm patient, especially where you're concerned."

"I'm not, and I want to."

My stomach lurches at the prospect, but I want to get it right and not misconstrue what she's telling me.

"So, you're saying you want me to make love to you?"

"Isn't it obvious?"

"Rory, you're a multi-layered person and sometimes hard to read. Please tell me directly."

She grins. "For a Magna Cum Laude graduate, you're a bit slow."

"Humor me."

"I want you to make love to me," she whispers.

Now my stomach is in full-on turmoil. The meal I just ate is bouncing around. My balls tighten at the prospect of being with her physically. What's more, my palms begin to sweat, and my hands are shaking as I signal for the check. What's wrong with me?

I've probably fucked close to one hundred or more women but never had this reaction. I could say that it's because I'm in love with Rory, but I was in love with Lily and never felt this way. Maybe I wasn't really in love with her the way I am now. Rory is like a glove that fits over my hand perfectly. Lily never was; we were too different.

CHAPTER 20

The short drive home has me fidgety, but I see that Rory is too. I'm hoping that no one is in the house, but if they are, we'll manage. I wish we were back in the city because I want to make her scream with delight the way she did when we first had sex.

At a stoplight, I can't help but reach out to stroke Rory's exposed knee. Her tanned skin is so soft and smooth. I startle her from staring out the window, and when she looks up at me, I can see how dark her sapphire eyes have become. The light changes, and I don't move, stuck on her gaze until the car behind me blares its horn. My feeling is to pull over and take her in the backseat, but we're not sex-starved teenagers. Well, sex-starved maybe, but not teenagers.

My heart sinks when I get to the house and hear voices filtering from the deck. The guys are there with some of Rory's roommates, and the aroma of hotdogs and burgers hits me as I exit the SUV. I walk around to let Rory out, and my hand brushes her breast as she slides from the seat. Her nipple is straining against the peach cloth, just begging for my mouth or fingers.

She gives me a look of regret when we round the corner, and everyone is sitting at the redwood picnic table on the deck.

"It's the birthday girl," Jamie yells.

"Thanks, Jamie," Rory calls.

"Where were you two?"

"We went to lunch," I said.

"You should have waited since we barbecued."

"That's okay. What are you all doing this afternoon?"

"Well, now that lunch is finished, back on the beach for some tanning. Gotta look good for tonight, right girls?" Jamie said.

"So, everyone is going to the club tonight?" I asked.

"Unless you have a better idea."

"Nope, just checking."

I take Rory by the hand, and we go inside, heading to my bedroom. The shades are still down from this morning, and my bed is unmade. I sit on the window seat overlooking the beach and pat the place next to me. The sexual tension between us crackles, and I stroke her hair, gently pulling on her ponytail.

"How long until they leave?" Rory asked.

"Looks like they were just about done, but we don't have to wait."

I jump up and lock the door then pull off my polo shirt as I head back to the seat next to her. She's already taken off her sandals, and when I sit, I pull her onto my lap, so she's straddling my legs. Four buttons are between me and her sexy cleavage. I concentrate on unbuttoning them while she plays with my hair.

Once they're undone, her cleavage is exposed, and I stick my tongue in-between her breasts. She tastes slightly salty, but the scent of her skin is making me hard. Her bra is the same peach color as her dress. I push the skirt of it up and reveal a tiny pair of peach lace panties. The sight of them causes my breath to stutter. I'm finding it hard to control myself.

I need to kiss her and start at her neck, biting the delicate flesh, then move to suck on her ear. She softly moans before I claim her mouth with a hard kiss, forcing my tongue into her mouth, tangling and curling around hers.

"Take your dress off," I murmur.

For a minute, she looks frightened and gives me a questioning look.

"Sweetheart, we don't have to do this, but I want to."

"I need this. But they haven't left yet."

I realize that it's not me she's afraid of, but that her friends and mine will hear us. I start to slide her off my lap to check outside, but then clomping of feet and fading of voices tells me they're leaving.

"Better?"

"Better," she said with a lazy smile.

I grasp the skirt of her dress and pull it up to her waist, then chest and finally over her head, depositing it on the floor next to us. My hands skim her ribs and along the sides of her breasts while our mouths find each others again.

I can't resist, and I moan into her mouth. My erection is straining against my shorts, and she rubs herself against it, causing me to gasp, breathing in her warm breath. She does it again, pivoting her hips and riding my length. The only thing between us is the ultra-thin layer of cloth that covers her lower half and my shorts and boxers.

Two can play that game, and I wiggle my fingers between us until I'm touching the sodden panel of underwear. I press my fingers against it, searching for my quarry. When I find it, that swollen nub of nerves, I circle it. Rory mewls into my mouth, a feral sound, and no one would doubt its origins.

I need to touch her and not through the lace. I'm frenzied as she begins to tug at my leather belt, managing to open it before I can assist her. She begins undoing my button and zipper. If she touches me, I'm going to explode. I have no control; I'm lost in the depths of Rory.

"Do you want to continue this on the bed?" I said into her mouth.

I hear her say something that sounds like no and remove my

hands from her to lean back against the windowsill. I want to watch as she releases me, and she does as she forces down my boxers, tucking them under my balls.

"Now what?" I said with a seductive grin.

Rory says nothing and slides off my lap, reaching back to release her breasts from the confines of the peach lace. She slips off her panties, letting them fall to her ankles, and I'm mesmerized as she steps out of them, flicking them toward me. I catch them and bury my nose in the panel, feeling and smelling her arousal.

She stands there with her arms crossed. "Well? Do you want me to undress you, too?"

Rory doesn't have to say another word. Her panties are forgotten as I drop them and slide off my shorts and boxers in one movement. I look up, and her arms are still crossed. That won't do since her breasts are perfect, and she's hiding the rigid peaks I want to suck.

I scoop her up in my arms and lay her down on the bed. I place my knee between her legs and join her, holding myself over her body as I decide my plan of attack. There is so much I want to do to her. We spent such a short time together that I wasn't able to show her all I can do to make her feel good.

"Hunter?"

"Shh, I'm thinking."

Rory reaches up to touch my face. "Stop thinking and fuck me."

"That's it? I wasn't planning on just that."

"Plan on it now because I need you. I need to feel you inside me."

I get off the bed and pull my gym bag onto the window seat, going through pocket after pocket.

"What the hell are you doing?"

"I need a condom."

"Have you been tested?"

"Yes, I'm clean. Have you?"

"Yes, I have the all-clear; I got it the day before I left. You're ruining this."

I jump back in between her legs. "Oh, am I? What about pregnancy?"

"I take my pill religiously. Are you worried?"

I shake my head. "Not one bit."

I watch her bite her lip as I'm poised at her entrance, teasing her by pressing and then withdrawing.

"Stop it," Rory breathes.

She continues biting her lip, and I hover above her, then dip down to run my tongue over them, causing her to release from her bite.

"You don't like to be teased?"

Rory doesn't answer me, but I feel her shift her hips against me, and I push in a little deeper. She bites her lip again, and I smile wickedly at her, which makes her close her eyes. The truth is that I can't hold off, I need to be inside her. The heat and tightness of her slick tunnel is driving me mad, and I end my misery by thrusting hard into her.

Rory's eyes open like a shot and fix on mine. She wraps her legs around me tightly as I begin to move my hips. I'm inching ever so close to climaxing too soon, I don't want that, and I slow to almost a stop.

"No, don't stop, please," she mewls.

"Rory, baby, I have to."

"Why? You feel so good."

"I'm so close, and I need you to come first."

I don't wait for her answer. I lower my head to her breasts and suck on her nipples, hollowing my cheeks as I take the first one, then the other in my mouth. Rory massages my scalp with her nails, and it sends shivers to my core. I can see the pulse in her delicate neck beating, and it's the next spot my lips go to, sucking.

"Please, Hunter."

"Shh, baby, be patient."

I unlatch her legs from behind my back and bend her knees, then kneel. My cock is still deep inside her, but I have better access to her clit, which I begin to rub with my thumb. Rory moans loudly and starts playing with her nipples, which is so erotic to watch that it's going to send me over the edge.

She keeps clenching as I move slowly. I know she's close because she keeps arching her back with each stroke.

"Come for me, baby. Don't hold back."

I feel her tighten around me, and she explodes with a loud cry of my name. It makes me smile, and I remove my thumb and plant my arms on either side of her stomach, pounding into her. My release is close, and I'm done when she rakes her nails over my chest. I fall apart and spill into her. It seems like my orgasm is endless, but I finally finish.

We're both panting, and she reaches up to wipe beads of sweat off my brow. I take her hand and kiss it, sucking on her fingers.

"You're beautiful," I say, and it's not because I'm caught in the moment.

"Why do men always say things like that after they fuck you?"

"Rory, I'm not just saying that. You're beautiful, and I've told you even when we aren't having sex."

I pull out and stretch my body next to her. I'm still hard, and I see her reach for me. She thumbs my glistening tip with fascination, and I suck in my breath.

"I'm sorry. Did I hurt you?"

I grin. "Hurt? No. I'm sensitive."

"You're still hard."

"Give me a minute, and I won't be."

Sure enough, my erection begins to disappear until I'm flaccid. She turns to me, and I kiss her on the tip of her slightly freckled nose.

"Did you enjoy that?"

"I came, so what do you think?"

"That's not what I asked you. I asked if it was enjoyable for you."

"Yes, but I expected you to come first and then get me off later."

I'm shocked because that is not how I do things, and she knows it. What did that fuck, Derek, do to her? Fuck her, come, and leave her to her own devices?

"Rory, we've made love before, and have I ever done that? Have you ever left my bed dissatisfied?"

"Well, no. But it's all that I'm used to."

"Well, get unused to it. I'm not him, and I know how to treat a woman in bed, especially one that I love."

I guess the tone of my voice frightens her because her apology is swift and meek. She doesn't understand that I don't need an apology. All I need is her love. I gather her in my arms and pull her against my chest, kissing the top of her head. She hugs me back, and we fall asleep in each other's arms.

I'm awakened by voices coming from the kitchen. The light has begun to soften, and I see oranges peeking through the sides of the shade. It must be early in the evening, and we have a club to go to tonight for Rory's birthday.

"Sweetheart, you need to wake up."

"Don't want to," she mumbles into my chest.

"You need to, or your friends will be disappointed."

"Can't I just stay here with you?"

"I'd love nothing more than to have you in my arms all night, but I'm sure your friends wouldn't be very happy. We can shower, and then you can go home to dress."

She yawns against me, and I can feel her warm breath, bathing my chest. I lean back and kiss her forehead. Rory takes it as an invitation, and her lips find mine, soft and sweet. Fuck, I wish I could stay in bed with her.

"I promise you can sleep here tonight."

"Suppose I don't want to?"

"That is entirely your choice, but you are welcome to share my bed."

"Always?"

"Always, period."

She turns on her back and sits up, glancing at the clock.

"Shit! My mother said she would call at 6:30. It's now after 7:00. Where is my phone?"

"Probably in your purse. I think it's on the chair in the corner."

Sure enough, her purse is there, and she claws as the zipper to retrieve her phone, softly cursing as she hits the power button.

"She called at 6:30. What am I going to tell her?"

"Tell her you were in the pool and didn't hear the phone. Don't get upset. Call her now."

Rory dials the number and turns her back on me, so I get an awesome view of her posterior. I would love to bite it, but I think she would have my head, especially since she's talking to her mother right now. Her voice raises, and she's arguing about Derek. I bet that fucking charmer made some bullshit story for why they broke up. She ends the call with a curt "goodbye, mother" and hangs up.

"What happened?"

"Derek came to my house with a gift and told my parents that he needs to talk to me. He wants to get back together."

"Why do they want you with him so badly?"

"My parents love Derek. They think the sun and the stars rise and set with him. I never told them the truth about any of what he did to me."

"Sweetheart, maybe it's time that you did. They need to know how abusive he was to you. I don't know your father well, but what I do know of him, I assume he would be very angry and upset."

"I know he would be. Ever since I met him, he's treated me so well. It's been wonderful to have a father. My grandfather wouldn't let him near me, and I never looked for him. I heard horror stories about how he left me. His parents wanted nothing to do with me until he came back into my life."

"I'm sorry, but you should tell him. Derek needs to answer for the things he's done to you. Maybe this will push him to get some help."

"I doubt it. He's an arrogant fuck."

"Be that as it may, you still need to tell everyone. If he loses his job because of it, he deserves what he gets. Didn't you say he doesn't even need to work?"

"No, he has a large trust fund, but his parents want him to work. They're trustees on his fund until he's twenty-five, which is in a couple of months. I'm sure he'll quit working at Wilton once he gets full control."

"It's always the assholes who have all the luck."

"His luck is about to run out. I decided I'm going to tell my parents when I get home."

Rory starts gathering up her clothing and pulling them on.

"No showering with me?"

"We can shower tomorrow. You're taking me home, aren't you?"

"Of course. What time are we going to the club?"

"I think at 10:00 PM."

"That's three hours from now. You can spare another hour."

"If I stay here, it won't be another hour, and you know it. Besides, I have to wait my turn for mirror space. The house has three bathrooms, but with eight women, it's going to be hard."

"Fine, I'll be dressed and ready to go in a little while. We should have some drinks over here before we go. A toast to your twenty-first birthday."

"I'll ask everyone."

Rory kisses me on the cheek and is out the door. I hear her talking to the guys in the kitchen before she leaves. Matty comes strolling into my bedroom after she's gone.

"So, is this on now?"

"It is. We're seeing each other."

"I would never have pegged you for a long-distance relationship."

"It won't be. She's moving back to New York after she gets home from here."

"To your place?"

"No. To her apartment with Ellie."

"Oh."

I can see he's deep in thought, and I decide to ask him what's going on.

"Matty, something you want to say?"

"It's just that the last time you were together, she destroyed you. You were the mopiest son of a bitch I ever had to deal with. I don't want that to happen again if she breaks up with you."

"She's not going to break up with me. We love each other."

Matty holds up his hands. "Okay, I get it."

"On a different note, I have the cake for Rory in the refrigerator. I would like to have a toast before we leave for the club and give her the cake. Can you talk to the girls and see if they want to do that? Oh, and please do it while Rory isn't around. Don't broadcast it."

"Geez, Hunter! I know how surprises work."

"Good. Now go over there and humor me."

He picks up my towel from a chair near the door and throws it at me. I catch it and give him a big smirk. Matty exits my room and slams the door. He can be a pain in the ass, but he's my best friend.

CHAPTER 21

I lie in bed for another hour because I have a feeling I'm going to need sleep if Rory stays with me tonight. I finally haul my ass out of bed at 8:15 and go into the shower. As I'm washing, I think about what Rory did to me when we were together in here, and I start to harden. I can't resist, and I stroke myself with soapy hands thinking of the sex we just had a few hours before. I come hard, and my legs fell weak enough to need to sit.

I hear Matty's voice at the door, and I get up to peek my head out of the shower enclosure.

"The girls will be here at 9:45, so get the cake and candles ready."

"Great. I'll be out in a little while."

I quickly finish up and wrap a towel around my waist while I style my hair with a little gel. My hair is getting long, and I need to have it cut, but I'll get Rory's opinion since she likes how my hair curls just above my shirt collar.

Tonight I feel like going commando, and I slip on a pair of black jeans. I brought a light pink oxford with me, and I put it on, leaving the shirttails out. I'm one of those guys who's secure with his manhood to wear pink.

By the time I come out of my room, it's after nine and the girls should be here soon. Jamie and Dario already had a couple of beers, and Matty is drinking a glass of wine. I guess I get to drive, which wouldn't be a problem if I didn't want to spirit Rory away early so we could make love in an empty house. Truth be told, I want to hear her when I give her pleasure; it's a major turn-on.

I prep the cake and rummage around the drawers until I find a small lighter for the candles. As soon as I hear them coming, I'm going to light them and turn out the lights; then, when she comes in, she'll see the cake. I'm nervous and start chewing on my nail. Dario looks at me and starts laughing.

"Dude, why are you so nervous?"

"Hunter is in love," Matty says.

"Shut up, Matty, don't be a dick."

All three of them start laughing, and I want to kick their asses, but there is no time. I hear the girls talking as they walk onto the deck. I quickly shut out the kitchen light and fire up the candles. The guys stand around the counter, and Matty lets the girls in. We all launch into the worst off-key happy birthday song, but Rory is smiling ear to ear. My stomach does flip flops just watching her.

When we finish singing, and Rory blows out the candles, I hand out forks, and everyone takes some of the cake. When we're finished indulging, I cover the cake and put it back into the refrigerator. I can think of a few things Rory and I can do with the frosting later.

I'm elected to drive to the club, and with twelve people in the SUV, it's a bit of a tight squeeze. There is a huge line waiting at the door to The Dockside, but Dario is a club promoter and knows the owner, so we head right inside. It's crowded, and I take Rory's hand and lead the way to an empty table in the corner that Dario had reserved. It barely fits all of us, but soon, the girls have gone out onto the dance floor with Matty, Jamie, and Dario, all except for Rory, who stays with me.

Unfortunately, the music is so loud we can barely talk to each other. The waitress stops by, and we order two bottles of champagne. I can't resist kissing Rory's neck. She smells so good, and she looks fantastic in a dark blue strapless body-hugging dress. I didn't say anything, but it's so short that it barely covers her ass.

I'm not thrilled about how revealing it is, but I don't want her to think I'm like Derek. While we wait for the champagne, I feast on her shoulders, neck, and lips. It's hard to control myself when she looks like this. I keep telling her I love her, but she can hardly hear me even when my lips are pressed against her ear.

Everyone comes back to the table just as the champagne gets there, and we toast Rory, then we all head to the dance floor. I can see several guys looking at her, and I plan to keep her close to me. We dance together, and when she rubs her ass against me, I begin to harden. Where she's concerned, I'm like a teenage boy.

We keep going back and forth, dancing, drinking, and enjoying the music. I stick to one glass of champagne since it seems like everyone else is getting drunk. If I don't, then we might have trouble getting home since taxis can be scarce late at night on Montauk.

We've been here for over two hours, and I'm tired and sweaty, but everyone seems to have more energy than me. Some of the girls have found guys in the club they keep dancing with, and Matty seems to have latched on to Rory's friend, Carla, a cute little brunette.

Rory wants to keep dancing, but I tell her to go ahead and dance with some of her friends, I'll watch. I sit back, drinking ice water and relaxing in the booth until I see two men approach her and her friend, Deborah. They start dancing, and I tense up, especially when I see one of the guys put his hand on Rory's bare shoulder. I can see her glancing over at me, and I have a feeling she's uncomfortable, so I head onto the floor to save her.

I tap the guy on the shoulder. "Hey, buddy, thanks for keeping her warm for me."

"Get your girl," he growls.

"She is my girl. She's my fiancée."

He forgets Rory and turns to me. "Where is her ring, then?"

"Look, she doesn't want to dance with you any longer, and frankly, I don't want you dancing with her anymore. We can handle this two ways. Either I kick your ass, or I kick your ass. So which will it be?"

He looks me up and down, then smiles at me and holds his hand out for me to shake. I reach to shake it, and he hits me hard in the stomach, enough to double me over. Matty sees what's going on, rushes over, and drops the guy with one punch to the chin. It's nice to have a boxer for a best friend.

By the time I regain my composure, the guy is being escorted out of the club, and Rory is clinging to me and telling me how sorry she is that it's her fault.

"For what? For being beautiful, desirable, sweet, and kind?"

She looks at me puzzled and then smiled, kissing me softly on the cheek.

"Can we go home?"

"That's a problem since there is no one to drive these drunk bastards."

"Deborah can drive. She only had one glass of champagne, and that was two hours ago. She's been drinking ice water."

"Go ask her."

I head back to the table and wait for Rory to come back. She's all grins when she does, which means that Deborah has agreed. Now, all we need is to find a cab. It's almost 1:00 AM, and we might be stuck here until everyone wants to leave. I lead her from the club, and luck is on our side when we find a taxi passing by as we step out onto the street. I whistle for him, and he stops.

As soon as we're inside the car, I pull Rory onto my lap. We're both sweaty, and I plan on getting sweatier when I get her home. I can't keep my hands off her and stroke her legs until I'm touching her inner thighs. I place her on the seat next to me, and we start to kiss, I can taste her lip gloss, it's raspberry. How many flavors of lip gloss is there?

Once again, I stroke her thighs, and she slightly spreads her legs so I can get between them. I don't know if her panties are wet from my stimulations or her dancing, but they're sodden. I stroke her most sensitive spot through the damp panel, and she moves her hips forward. I take this as a cue and move the covering over and slip a finger under.

She's slick, and I insert a finger inside her. She quietly moans, and I smile against her mouth before I press my lips to her ear.

"Do you dare me to get you off right here?"

"Please." The word is barely audible.

I slowly plunge my finger in and out of her, using my thumb to work on her clit. The driver startles us by saying he's almost to our destination, and I grunt my okay then continue with Rory. I move my thumb faster, hard circles around her clit, and she bites my lip, holding on with her teeth as she orgasms. I can feel her pulsing around my finger, which I remove just as the cab enters the driveway of our house.

I quickly pull out my wallet and hand the driver a twenty. He tells me to wait for change since the bill is only twelve bucks, but I say to keep the rest as a tip. I think Rory is still coming down from her orgasm because I need to prod her a little, so she gets out.

"Did you enjoy that?" I said with a wicked grin.

"More than you know. I needed to come all night."

I chuckle. "You're going to come a lot more than that by the time I'm done."

I take her hand and lead her up the deck to the front door, punching in the code to the electronic door lock. The light turns green, and I pull her inside, shutting the door quickly and scooping her up into my arms.

"I'm tired. Can we go to sleep?"

I guess the look on my face is disappointment because she

begins to smirk, and I know she's kidding. In my bedroom, I slam the door, throw her purse on the chair and push her against the wall. I'm rock hard from our little session in the car, and I need to fuck her soon.

I wrench her panties down and push them past her knees. They slide to her ankles, and I kneel to help her take her heels off. On the way back up, I pull her dress up to reveal her naked waist. The scent of her arousal is intoxicating, and I slide my tongue against her clit. She whimpers loudly and curls her fingers in my hair.

"What should I do with you? Should I tease you or take you hard?"

"Take me hard."

I'm surprised because I would think that Rory would want to be teased, but I'm game because my balls are beginning to ache. I stand up, and her hands deftly work my pants open, which is when she discovers that I'm not wearing underwear.

I spring free of my jeans, which are loose on my hips, then lift her against the wall, positioning her above me while she wraps her arms around my neck. In one swift motion, I let her sink to my base and push her legs around my waist.

"Hold on, baby."

I secure her against the wall and begin moving my hips hard. I have my hands laced under her bare ass, and though my biceps begin to burn, I continue to move her up and down. She begins to suck on my neck and then buries her head against it.

"Fuck, Rory, you're so tight. I can feel you pulsing around me."

"I'm going to come soon," she murmurs.

I secretly thank God because I'm going to come soon, too. I move more frantically, and she holds my neck tighter. I feel her clench around me and loosen her grip against me as she begins to come. I follow quickly, thrusting hard several times until I'm spent.

I hold her against the wall, steadying my legs for the walk I'm going to have to take to the bed with my jeans pooled around my ankles. It will be a miracle if I don't fall on the way. I think Rory read my mind.

"Hunter, you can put me down."

"Are you sure?" I say hoarsely.

"Yes, let me down."

I lift her, and she slides down my legs until her feet touch the floor. I kick my jeans off, and we walk to the bed where I undress first her, then myself. We fall into bed together, and I hold her close to me. She's bewitched me, and I'm totally under her spell. It's a feeling I find hard to describe.

CHAPTER 22

The entire rest of the week is a blur because we spend most of it in my bed or on the beach. July Fourth comes, and we make it outside to see the fireworks before we go back inside to make love again. I'm dreading the next day because we need to pack up the SUV and head back home. Our rental week is up.

Rory is going to spend another week on Montauk and then go back to Boston to make arrangements to move to New York. She already talked to Ellie, and they renewed the lease on the apartment for another year. Her parents are going to be upset that she's leaving Boston, but she's an adult and needs to make her own choices.

I'm hoping she decides to visit me in the city for a few days instead of staying on Long Island. I don't think I can handle being away from her for two weeks. I'm truly in love with Rory. It's not just the sex that I'll miss, but her.

We spend the morning of the day that I'm leaving together. I take her to breakfast in a small diner not far from the houses. We hold hands the entire meal, and I can't stop kissing her. On the way back, she says something that makes my heart leap.

"Suppose I left Montauk a few days early and stayed with you? Would you mind if I did that?"

I pull the SUV over to the side of the road, unsnap her seatbelt and practically pull her over the console and into my lap.

"Do you know how happy that would make me? I want to see you. I'm not sure I can handle two weeks without you in my arms. Don't you understand how you make me feel?"

"I think so because it's probably exactly how I feel."

I give her a long passionate kiss, and her hands start to roam below my waist.

"Hey, don't get me all hot and hard. I have to leave in a little while."

"Why can't you just stay with me until tomorrow?"

"Rory, sweetheart, I have to get back to the city. I have a bunch of things to do before I go back to work on Monday."

I put her back in her seat and wait until she secures her belt, then I pull back out into traffic. She has her arms crossed, and I can see that she's pouting.

"Come on, baby; I have so much to do. Don't make the last hour we have together a bad one."

"I want you to stay just one more day."

"I can't, and anyway, where would I sleep?"

"With me."

I laugh, and she hits me in the arm, "Your bed is a twin, and you share a room with two other girls. What's the point?"

"The point is that you would be with me another day."

"Sweetheart, I really can't do it."

Rory goes back to pouting and looking out the window. I pull into the drive, and she hops out of the car and practically runs over to her house. I stand there like an idiot watching her as she goes in the door. Now what? Should I go after her? I don't want our last interaction to be negative.

I decide to let her cool down while I head into my house and pack my bags, giving the room a once over. I find a pair of Rory's panties under the bed, and I slip them into the pocket of my shorts. That's the second pair of hers that I have.

"Hunter, ready to go?" Matty calls.

I am, but I need to make it right with Rory before I leave. I don't want to fight with her. As I head out the door with my bags, I see her climbing into the SUV.

"What's going on?"

"We have another passenger."

I shove my bags into the cargo area and climb into the third row, which is where she's sitting. Rory smiles at me, and I stroke her face with my knuckles.

"I thought you were staying for another week?"

"I'd rather stay with you another week. Do you mind a roommate?"

"Not if it's you."

"Ugh, will you two love birds shut up. I have a headache," Jamie said. He's lying across the seat in front of us while Matty and Dario are in the front. I'm glad because I want some privacy with Rory. In no time, Jamie and Dario are asleep, and Matty is listening to the radio, so they don't hear our conversation.

"I wish we were home right now."

"Oh? What would you do to me if we were?"

"Sweetheart, you're going to find out soon enough."

"You could give me a preview."

I don't wait for her to tell me twice. I begin kissing her neck, gently sucking and nibbling her earlobe. My hand is splayed across her stomach, and I move it up slightly to skim the underside of her breasts. She inhales while I kiss her, taking my breath inside her mouth.

Her fingers wander between my legs, cupping my balls and move upward to my hardening cock. I wish we were home too because nothing can be done for me in the car, but I can do something for her as long as she's quiet. I move my hand down until it's resting on her upper thigh. She did the right thing by wearing short shorts.

It's easy for me to slide my fingers up her almost non-existent pant leg and slip under the panel of her lace panties. Rory is wet, and I'm able to move through her slick folds with ease. She softly moans in my mouth, and I break our kiss to shush her silently. Her sapphire eyes are dark with wanton lust. I move my mouth to her ear and whisper.

"I'm going to make you come, but only if you promise to do it silently."

She nods her head, and I take my fingers out of the leg of her shorts, opening them and pushing my hand down into her panties. Her clit is swollen, and when I slide my middle finger over it, she shifts her hips, meeting my touch. We continue to kiss, our tongues tangling and exploring each other's mouth. I wish I could taste her.

Her breathing is heavy, and fingers clench my forearm as she nears release. I can see the hard peaks of her nipples pressing against her bra and shirt. I want to free them and take each one in my mouth. I press her mass of nerves a little harder, and I feel her break apart as her orgasm tears through her.

Rory is true to her word; she keeps quiet as she comes. Not a word or sound from her lips, though I can see that she is close to saying something. As soon as she finishes spiraling down, her grip on my bicep weakens and falls away as she goes limp. I take my hand out of her shorts and close them, then pull her against me.

"You're a naughty girl," I whisper.

She looks up at me, sighs deeply and kisses me on the cheek, then places her head on my lap. I'm uncomfortable because I'm rock hard, but I ignore it with the satisfaction that I made her come. In a few minutes, I hear even breathing that only comes with sleep.

Somewhere between Nassau County on Long Island and the Manhattan Bridge, I fall asleep. When I wake, we're on the FDR Parkway heading toward Central Park. Since Matty and I live so close to each other, everyone is getting out there, and the SUV will be taken back to the rental place by Jamie.

Rory is still sleeping on my lap, and I take the time to check out her soft features. She's so petite and small. For some reason, my mind drifts to the bruise that was on her wrist, and I start to feel angry. She still has the cast on her arm at least for another couple of weeks. I can't wait until it's removed. Making love with that clunky pink piece of plaster is no fun, and taking a shower together is even worse.

I stroke her hair, and she turns onto her back, giving me a view of her perfect full red lips. I bend down to kiss her, and she wakes.

"Where are we?"

"Almost to my place. Matty will drop us off."

She sits up and yawns, then stretches.

"Did you have a good sleep, my love?"

"It was wonderful. I had a dream about you."

"Oh God, can you two knock that lovey-dovey crap off?" Jamie said.

"Shut up, Jamie. You should get yourself a girlfriend."

"Not if it turns me into a big lump of Jell-O."

"Ignore him."

Rory laughs, and I'm glad that she isn't offended by Jamie's remark. Matty double parks in front of my building, and we hurry to retrieve our bags. Dario gets out, deciding to take a cab the fourteen blocks to his apartment. We tell everyone goodbye and enter my building.

I take Rory's bag and wheel it into the elevator. She has this sleepy look on her face, and it's too adorable for me to ignore. I let go of the bags and put my hands on either side of her face to kiss her.

"Your fingers smell like me."

I put them up to my nose, and sure enough, her scent is still on them. I would never wash my hand if I could smell that all day. Of course, I would never get a thing done because I would dream about Rory all the time and the things I want to do to her.

The elevator dings, and we part as I let Rory get out first and follow behind her with the bags. She moves aside so I can open the door to my apartment. Once we're inside, I can't resist pulling her to me. She molds against my body as I hold her tight against me.

"Hunter, what's the matter?"

"Nothing. I just wanted to hold you."

"Are you sure?"

"Yes, sweetheart, I'm sure."

I let her go and think about where I should bring her bag. I don't want to assume that she's going to sleep in my bed with me, but I'm sure she will. I decide to ask.

"Are you sleeping in my bed?"

"Why would you ask that?"

"I don't want you to feel pressured. I want you to sleep with me."

Rory raises an eyebrow, "Sleep or sleep?"

"Aren't they one and the same? If you don't want to have sex, it's entirely up to you. I won't pressure you into anything."

"I think we need to have a discussion."

This doesn't sound good, and my heart starts to pound. I must look nervous because she takes my hand and leads me to my bedroom.

"Let's sit on the bed and have a talk."

"Rory, are you not interested in having a relationship with me?"

"Stop speculating. I want to tell you about Derek."

"I really don't want to know. He's an asshole. I should've kicked his ass when I had the chance."

"I was foolish. I was heartbroken, and he picked up the pieces."

"You didn't have to be. I would've welcomed you with open arms. I just needed an explanation."

"I know that now but back then, I was afraid of being rejected once I told you I'd been pregnant."

"You should have told me, but I understand why you didn't."

"I decided to stay in Boston and take the semester off. I'd been working so hard the entire three and a half years. I needed a break. So I went to work at Wilton Properties, and that's where I met Derek again. He was kind, and we enjoyed our time together. But then after a few months and shortly after we got engaged, it turned dark. He started to control me, even in bed and the things that I wore. He was cruel at times, telling me I couldn't eat certain things because he didn't want a fat wife."

"Rory, he is nothing but a bully. He wanted to keep you under his thumb."

"He would get angry if I wore something he thought was too revealing or if I spoke too long to a male coworker, then he started to grab and push me. He would verbally abuse me."

"Why didn't you tell your grandparents or parents?"

"I was scared. Derek said if I did, they would never believe me. They thought he was wonderful. It was getting worse, and the day you saw the bruise on my arm was one of those times. He never broke anything until my wrist. He called me a few times, asking for forgiveness, and like a fool, I gave it to him."

"You could have come to me," I said quietly.

"I know that now. I knew he was up to something the night I went to his place and found him with that girl. I was horrified when he asked me to join them. It was the end for me."

"You should've ended it much sooner. You never should've started with him. I loved you. I wanted you."

"I know. I corrected my mistake and want you to know that this is for real. On Monday I'm letting my parents and grandparents know that I'm moving to New York for good. I'm done with Derek."

"Have you thought about taking me up on the offer to work for Lawson?"

"I want to, but I don't want any special favors."

"You fill out an application, give me your resume, and I'll have HR check to see if we have any openings. I know with the expansion that we do. Also, we didn't find many diamonds in the group we just had interning. Joe was kept on, and he works for me, but I could use another sharp mind."

"So, you want me to work directly for you?"

"Don't you want to?"

"But it seems so, what's the word I'm looking for...sordid."

"Sordid! I'm not asking you to sit under the desk and blow me. I'm asking you to work for me. Handle things you probably have done at Wilton. I need someone skilled. If you want to know, in the short time you worked for Lawson, my father was impressed with you. You would've been offered a position after your internship was done."

"If I work for you, do you promise to keep your hands off during the day? Keep it professional?"

I smirk. "Of course. I wouldn't have it any other way unless you requested different."

"Then, I'll give you my resume and fill out the application."

"Great. Then you can start work after this week."

"You don't even know if I have the job."

"I'm the boss. You have the job, so you have a week to get your fine ass moved into your apartment again."

Rory starts laughing, and I pull her onto my lap and lean against the headboard while I cradle her in my arms. I've never been this happy.

"There is one thing."

"Shit, I knew there was a catch."

"You're going to have to meet my parents."

"I already know your father, and I met your mother at the hospital."

"But once I tell them we're together, they're going to want to meet you again."

"I'm not great with parents."

"How many parents have you met? You've only had one girlfriend."

"I met Lily's, and they didn't seem to like me very much. Probably because we weren't as compatible as I thought, and they knew it before we did."

"I'm sure my parents will be fine with you."

"I'm not so sure. A few years ago, I hung out with your father and said some things that he might remember."

"It was a few years ago. People can change. I don't care what they say. I love you, and they're just going to have to deal with it."

"So when are we going to do this?"

"How about next weekend? I have to go back to get my clothes and other things that I took from the apartment. I never took my furniture, so it will be a fairly easy move. My bedroom is still the same there."

"I can help since you want me to meet your parents. Please give them a heads up. The last thing I want is to spring it on them when I walk through the door."

"I'm calling them Monday after you leave for work."

"Are you telling them that you're staying here?"

"Absolutely not. My father would have a fit if he knew I was living with a man, even if it was for a short time. What they don't know won't hurt them."

"I hope you're right."

I claim her mouth with my own, sucking on her bottom lip.

Rory wraps her arms around my neck, and I hold her against my body. She feels so good in my arms, and I know I want this to last.

"I'm hungry. Do you have anything to eat in this place?"

"Let's get up and check. I didn't leave much in the refrigerator, but the pantry is pretty stocked up with snacks."

We go to the kitchen, and I pull open the pantry door, which is basically a large closet with a bunch of shelves lining the walls.

Rory searches the shelves. "You have a ton of cereal in here."

"I know. I love it. It's my favorite meal."

"When?"

"All the time, breakfast, lunch, dinner."

"That's going to stop now that we're together. I like to eat food, and I haven't been cooking that much lately."

I bet. That idiot probably kept you on salads and yogurt.

"If you want to cook for me, I'm not going to say no. Where did you learn?"

"My mother and I took cooking lessons when I was a teenager. We had a maid who cooked, but on the weekend, she was off, and we had to fend for ourselves. I was getting sick of sandwiches or pasta.

You have Nilla Wafers? I love those. I haven't had them in a while."

"Help yourself."

Rory takes the box and hops up on the granite island. I can't stop watching her nibble at the cookies. Her lips are so inviting that I want to devour them. She notices me, and I see her face pink with embarrassment.

"Stop watching me. You're making me self conscious."

"You're beautiful. I can't stop watching you."

"Aren't you going to eat something?"

"I'd love to, but I'm not sure if it's on the menu."

"Oh, you mean me?"

"You're very tasty, especially certain parts of you."

Rory giggles and I take the box of cookies from her and get between her legs. She closes her eyes as I kiss her neck, moving my lips softly over her ears, chin, and cheeks. I stop when I reach her mouth and glide my tongue over her lips. She moans, and I slide her further off the counter, pushing her legs around my waist.

"Take me to your bed."

"Gladly."

I lift her off the counter and slip my hands underneath her ass to hold her up. Her arms circle my chest, and she tucks her head under my chin while I bury my nose into the fragrant scent of her hair. I gently lay her on the bed, and she let's go of me as I stare down at her.

"What should I do with you? Any ideas?"

She seductively licks her lips and smiles at me. Her sapphire eyes have grown dark with desire. I pull off my polo shirt and discard it on the floor. I'm already erect, and my shorts are tented because I neglected to put on boxers this morning. Rory sits up and unzips me, reaching in to release my swollen length. Her touch makes me rock hard to the point where I ache.

"It's my turn to play with you."

I stare down at her, mesmerized as her full lips take my head into her mouth. Her tongue swirls over the tip, making me gasp. She takes me deeper, wrapping her fingers around my base. She works me in and out until my breath is ragged, and my legs become weak.

"Fuck, Rory, that feels so good."

She looks up at me innocently. It's too much, and my orgasm comes screaming so quickly through me that I barely have time to warn her. But she doesn't pull back when I shoot my load; she takes me so deeply I could almost feel the back of her throat.

After I'm finished, my legs are like rubber. She releases me, and I stumble to the bed, plopping down next to her. Rory has a look of satisfaction on her face and a smile to match. My heart is pounding so hard that it feels like it's in my throat, and I lie back until it slows down.

"How was that?"

"Incredible. You're very good at that."

"Is that all I'm good at?"

"No. I need some time to see all your talents."

She lies back next to me and turns on her side, placing her head on my chest. I stroke her long hair, playing with her wavy blonde curls.

"I'm good at a lot of things."

"I bet you are. I think that I'm going to be a very spoiled man."

"If you play your cards right, you will."

"I plan on it."

I stand up and undress, then undress her. We spend the rest of the afternoon, making love and napping. She has me under her spell, and it's a nice place to be. I do have my doubts about her parents, though. I'm not sure they're going to like me, and that could be a problem.

∽

Sunday, I teach Rory the benefits of cereal. Fortunately, the milk I had in the refrigerator survived my week away even though it's three days past expiration. So for breakfast and lunch, we each have a big bowl of Apple Jacks mixed with Frosted Flakes. I know a lot of sugar, but I loved it, and it seemed that Rory did too.

I need something more fortifying for dinner, so we ordered Chinese food, and I went downstairs when it was delivered. When I came back up, Rory had plates, silverware, and napkins laid out on the breakfast bar. I feel a little shiver when I see that because it means we're in sync. I didn't ask or expect her to do it, she just did.

"You didn't have to set out plates. I would have done that."

"I wanted to."

"Thank you."

I hand her the food and watch her open everything. She would make the perfect wife. Whoa, am I already thinking about marriage? There is no way I'm, we're, ready for that. We barely know each other.

"You got a ton of food. Why did you order the big portions?"

"Because you're gorgeous, sexy, and appealing just the way you are. In fact, if you gained a few pounds, I wouldn't care. I want you to be comfortable and not afraid to eat. I'm not going to treat you badly if you're not perfect. No one is, and I'm sure in time you'll find I have plenty of faults."

Rory smiles at me, but I see that she's still only eating a little bit of food. I think that it's going to take time for her to get it through her head that I'm not Derek.

Because she laid the plates out, I clean up and pack the leftover food in the refrigerator. I'm exhausted, and tomorrow, I have to work. I had a wonderful vacation with Rory, and I'm going to miss her when I'm away, but by next week, we'll be in the same office. I probably should speak to JC and find out if I should alert Dad that Rory and I are together. I don't want the rumor mill to get started.

As soon as we're snuggled in bed, I asked Rory what she plans to do while I'm away tomorrow.

"I have to speak to my parents. I want to discuss you, and I'm debating whether to tell them about what Derek did."

"Sweetheart, they need to know. Would your grandparents want someone like that working for them? Someone who hurt their granddaughter? I doubt it."

"I don't want them to be angry that I didn't tell them sooner."

"It's over. What happened, happened. But you can't let Derek get away with what he did. You can't keep it a secret. He didn't deserve you, and he doesn't deserve you keeping his secret. He's an abuser, and he needs to be stopped."

"I guess you're right."

"I know I am. Please don't be afraid."

"Thank you."

"For what?"

"For being you."

CHAPTER 23

Monday, I'm in a foul mood. Not only is there a ton of work for me to do, but I miss Rory. I snapped at my assistant more than once and had to apologize. Even my father is staying away from me. I'm this way until about 11:00 AM when Rory calls me. It lightens my mood to know that she's thinking about me as much as I'm thinking about her.

Unfortunately, I have to cut the call short because I have a call from the contractor for building one — some shit about a problem with the plumbing. So I need to straighten out the issue before my father bitches that I'm not doing my job.

By lunchtime, I have a free moment to call JC. I need his advice. I already turned in Rory's application and resume that we printed up last night. I told them I want her position expedited with a start date of Monday the following week. The woman, Andrea, in HR, gave me a look that could kill.

"Hey brother, what's up?"

"I need your advice."

"You've been doing that a lot lately. I feel used."

"Okay, then forget it. I'll call Lexi and see what she thinks."

"I was kidding. What can I help you with?"

"I'm back with Rory."

I count the seconds that go by until he answers. "Oh."

"Is that all you're going to say?"

"I'm sorry. Go on."

I explain to him how we met and the decisions we made. How she's going to work for me and if I should tell our father that she's my girlfriend.

"Hmm, I think you should tell him. You know what will happen if the rumor mill starts, and he finds out that way. Especially when her start date is after you were already dating, see the problem?"

"Yeah, I do. I don't want him to torpedo this whole hire thing. Rory is very capable and would be perfect for assisting me in the development department. She has plenty of experience."

"Can I tell Lexi?"

"You might as well. You know Rory was very sorry for the way she talked to her. It was when she was a kid, a stupid teenager. Please let her know that. We want to get together soon so she can apologize in person."

"I think Lexi would appreciate that very much. I hope this girl is worth it."

"She is. I promise."

"I have to go. Conference call at 1:00."

"Thanks for the advice."

I hang up with JC and head to my father's office. I might as well get this out of the way. Most of the conversation, he stares at me. I'm waiting for him to start yelling, but he is strangely calm.

"I must say that I'm glad you're settling down. Your mother and I were very happy when you were spending time with Lily."

"Rory isn't Lily. She's better. What about her working for me?"

"You understand that this is a professional environment. Somehow business and pleasure can get mixed up. I've seen her credentials, and she is very good, however, maybe she should work for someone else in your department."

"No, that's out of the question. I want her working directly for me. I want her expertise. She has the experience and will be an asset to me."

"I'm going to trust you on this, but don't let your personal lives get mixed up in the office. If I see it, then she will be moved to another part of the department where she won't report directly to you. I also expect you to introduce this young woman to your mother, especially if you consider her to be a permanent part of your life."

"I'm working on it. It's early yet to be thinking about that. I don't want to scare her off. She's only twenty-one."

I feel lighter than air for the rest of the day. Rory is going to work here, and my father didn't give me a hard time about it. On the way home, I stop at the florist and pick up a huge bouquet of red roses. I'm in a wonderful mood, and it gets even better when I walk into my apartment, and I smell the most delicious aroma. Rory is in the kitchen cooking.

"What are you making?"

"Salmon with a lemon dill sauce, roasted asparagus, and potatoes au gratin. I hope you like that."

"I love salmon, but you didn't have to cook for me. I didn't expect you to."

"I told you that I was going to start feeding you better. I hope you don't mind that I did some cleaning. You needed laundry done, and so did I. I folded everything. I also cleaned the master bath and changed the sheets on your bed."

"Sweetheart, you're not my maid."

"I know. I wanted to. Are those roses for me?"

"They are. I hope you like them."

"If they're from you, then yes, I love them, and I love you."

Rory takes the roses from me and puts them in a vase that I had sitting on a shelf in the living room. I don't want to tell her it's Lalique crystal and very expensive. I really don't care. I change out of my suit, and when I come back, she's just taking the fish from the oven.

"Did you talk to your parents today?"

"I did."

"And?"

"They thought I would get back together with Derek. That this was just a spat even though we've been apart for almost three weeks."

"Did you ask why they thought that?"

"He spoke to them and my grandparents. He told them that it was a misunderstanding. I told them it wasn't."

"Did you tell them the exact reason why you're done with him?"

"No."

"Rory, I thought we agreed that you would."

"I want to, but it's better said in person. I told them that and said that I want them to meet you. My father didn't seem happy that I was dating you."

"I can understand his feelings, but I'm not that person from a few years ago. I want to settle down, and I would never cheat on you. I could never hurt you that way."

Rory comes over to where I'm sitting and gets between my legs before she wraps her arms around me. Her touch gets me heated, and I feel myself stir in my shorts.

"I missed you today. I wish you could've stayed home."

"I know, baby. I was in a foul mood until you called. I can't wait until you start working, then at least I can see you periodically during the day."

"So everything is good? I'm hired?"

"Of course, you're hired. I spoke to HR and my father."

"Your father? I thought you didn't need to run it by him."

"I don't. I spoke to him because I didn't want rumors to get started around the office without him knowing the true nature of our relationship."

"Is he angry?"

"No, quite the opposite, but he did warm me to make sure our personal business stays out of the office. I agreed. We can't bring our problems to work."

"I'm hoping we have no problems to bring there. My parents are expecting us on Saturday to discuss things. I'm going to need your support when I tell them what Derek did to me."

"You know I'll always support you. I'm sure when your parents hear what Derek did, they will be done with him. He should be fired."

"That is entirely up to my grandparents. They have affection for him, so I don't know what they will say."

"They should believe their granddaughter. Not some cheating playboy who only works for them because his parents want him to have a job."

Rory silences me by pressing her lips against mine. She's aggressive, and her tongue spears into my mouth. I can feel the heat of her body seep into mine as we become one. I start to roam her body with my hands, slipping them under her shirt.

I caress the flesh of her back and move higher so I can unclasp her bra. I want to feel her breasts in my hand. In turn, her hands slip under my shirt, stroking the muscular ridges of my abs. Her movements send shivers up my spine, and I shudder in her arms.

"Are you cold?" she mumbles into my mouth.

"No, anything but."

I'm quickly become aroused, and my erection is uncomfortably pressing against my boxers. I'm too confined, and I shift my legs to try to release some of the pressure, but it doesn't help. Rory reaches down, stroking my length, which doesn't help. Thoughts of burying myself inside her make my balls ache.

"We should go to the bedroom."

"Why? We're alone."

I don't wait for an explanation but quickly tug at her shorts. The thong she's wearing is incredibly sexy and unbelievably tiny.

A strip of lace held together by string. I bunch the waistband in my hand, and it snaps away, fluttering to the floor.

"Those were one hundred twenty dollars."

"Yeah? I'll replace them with anything you want."

I skim my hands to the front of her as we kiss, cupping her breasts under the bra she's wearing. Pinching her nipples and rolling them between my fingers causes her to gasp in my mouth. I break our kiss to strip the rest of her clothing off, tossing it to the floor. Rory stands before me naked in my kitchen that smells of lemon and dill.

I pick her up and seat her on the cool dark granite of the island counter, then quickly remove my clothes. The counter is the perfect height for me to make love to her here. I push her knees up, so she is wide open for me then tease her by rubbing my swollen head through her slick folds. She moans loudly and closes her eyes. Rory lies back, and I hear her hiss as the cold of the stone makes contact with her skin, but I don't want her that way. I want her touching me with her hands as we make love.

"Sweetheart, sit up. I want to hold you."

She does as I ask, and I pull her to the edge of the counter while she grips my shoulders. In one swift thrust, I'm inside her, and it's heaven. She's so wet that if not for how tight she is, there would be no friction. Rory wraps her hands and legs around my body as I pump. I can feel her pulsing as I move.

I tangle my fingers in her hair and gently tug so that the underside of her chin is exposed. It allows me to bite and kiss the tender flesh as I trail my tongue down to the hollow in her throat. I'm so caught up in the delicacy that I'm barely moving my hips.

"Hunter, why are you stopping?"

"I'm not stopping; I'm enjoying our oneness."

"I'm enjoying it too, but I want to come. I've been thinking about it all day."

"Have you now?" I say wickedly.

"Please."

As much as I would love to tease her, the sensation of being inside her is too delicious. I start pounding her, and I know that she's getting close when I feel her shudder around me just before she explodes with a loud moan of my name. I follow seconds later, thrusting deeply, giving her everything I have until I'm spent.

Rory holds me tight even after we both finish. I feel so overwhelmed. It was never like this with any other woman I've been with. I feel scared because it's happened so quickly, even though my love for her has been months. These are feelings I never had for Lily.

I don't want to let her go and tell her to hold on tight while I carry her to the bedroom. I sit down and lie back on the bed with her on my chest until I soften and slide out.

"Do you want to take a quick shower?" I ask.

"Not particularly. I want to lie in bed with you all night."

That's exactly what we do, dinner long forgotten. We fall asleep in each other's arms and wake up together shortly before ten. Now I'm starving. My long day and our sexual activity have piqued my appetite. We head to the kitchen, where cold fish and soggy vegetables greet us. Rory immediately starts to clean up, and I stop her.

"Sweetheart, it's okay. You don't have to clean; I'll do it."

"Why don't we both do it together?"

The two of us work on righting the kitchen, and the funny thing is that we're doing it naked. Once we finish, I get together my go-to dinner, cereal. Rory laughs as I prepare a couple of bowls with milk, and I stack four different kinds of cereal on the counter to choose.

After we finish, we head back to my bed. This is the way it goes the entire week. By Wednesday, I tell her not to bother with dinner since we never seem to get that far, and it goes to waste. Privately I feel bad because her food looks wonderful, but there will be plenty of time for me to sample her cooking.

Saturday is a perfect day for a long drive to Boston. We wake up at five in the morning to get ready. I want to leave by six since the trip will take close to five hours. I'm hoping we don't hit traffic. I rented a car the day before, and all we need to do is put the bags in, and we're all set.

We're only staying overnight, and Rory's parents have offered for me to stay at their home. I hope it all works out. I'm still not quite sure how Noah is going to handle me dating Rory.

The trip takes less than four and a half hours, which we spend most of it silent. I'm not sure what to think of it, but I know Rory is nervous. She has so much to tell them, and I hope that her parents are supportive since they seem to love Derek so much. Secretly, I'd love to see that asshole so I can show him what it's like to be abused. He beat Rory down until she made excuses for his behavior.

We pull up to Rory's parent's home just after 10:00 AM. It's a large brick home with thick wooden double doors at the front. She tries to open the door on her side, and I can see her hands are shaking. I stop her, take her hands in mine, and kiss them.

"I'm here. Everything is going to be okay. You tell your story."

Before we can get out of the car, Noah opens the door. He looks the same as I remember him from three years ago, except his hair has some gray in it. He eyes me but offers his hand, which I vigorously shake. Rory's mother, Vivian, is waiting at the door and welcomes me with a warm hug. I start to feel at ease.

"Would you two like something to drink before we get started?" Vivian asks.

"No, mother, we're fine."

"Then let's sit at the table and have a discussion."

We follow Vivian to a large dining area and sit at a long mahogany table with twelve chairs around it. Rory sits on the same side as me, facing her parents. I squeeze her knee under the table and see her inhale deeply as if she's trying to calm herself.

"Derek abused me."

Probably not the right way to start a conversation, but I can see the effect, like a shot to the gut. Her parents sit with their mouths hanging open.

"Excuse me?" Noah says.

"Derek verbally and physically abused me," Rory holds up the cast.

"When did this start and why didn't you tell us before?" Noah said.

I can see Noah's face is starting to turn crimson, and Vivian is holding her hand over her mouth as Rory's story unfolds. She tells them when it started and why she never said anything. She was too afraid he would hurt her further, and no one would believe her.

"What made you finally decide to end it?"

"He cheated on me. I'm sure it wasn't the first time, but he got caught. I was so stupid and foolish. I let him do this to me."

Rory starts crying, and I put my arms around her shoulders. I feel so powerless, and I wish that I could've helped her. She's been through a lot. Noah turns to me.

"Hunter, were you aware this was going on?"

"No, sir, not until after she broke up with him. If I had been aware, I would have intervened immediately."

I would have beat that bastard to a pulp.

"We need to speak to your grandparents. They can't keep him employed. We should press charges."

"No, Daddy, I don't want to do that. Please don't make me. It's too embarrassing, and I want to put it behind me."

"He should pay for what he's done."

"I know, but I don't want to go to court and admit how foolish I was."

"Are you sure? I want him to pay."

"I know, but he'll lose his job, and that will be enough. He isn't getting his trust fund for months. He will have to find another job if he wants to keep living his playboy lifestyle, or his parents won't give him his monthly stipend."

We discuss a few other things until lunchtime arrives. While we go wash up and the Wilton's staff prepares to serve, Noah takes me aside.

"Rory seems to like you. I hope you're not the same as you were when I first met you."

"Noah, I understand your concerns, but I've changed. That was a few years ago, and I'm not the same person."

"I hope so. Rory has been through enough the past few months."

I don't want to tell him that she could have avoided all of this if she had just stayed with me in September. I loved her then, and I love her even more now. I have a feeling that she hasn't dropped the bomb yet about moving to New York.

CHAPTER 24

Lunch is Caesar salad with grilled chicken and homemade lemonade. I'm not much of a salad person, but it was delicious. It must be nice to have staff that cooks and cleans for you on a daily basis. I watch Rory, and she picks at her food. I'm concerned that she's worried about telling her parents about moving.

After we eat, Rory insists that she shows me the grounds of her parent's home. It's a large parcel with a well-manicured lawn and beautiful planter beds with all kinds of flowers. A large saltwater in-ground pool dominates the patio just outside the French doors of their home.

She pulls me along until we get to a greenhouse, and we enter. Long tables hold all kinds of plants, some in large hydroponic cones. I'm fascinated until Rory skims my balls with her hand.

"What are you doing?"

"Loving you."

"But your parents…"

"I need you."

"Sweetheart, we can't do this here. Someone is going to see us."

"We're too far away for them to see us."

"Later. I promise to make it up to you."

Rory is insistent and continues to massage me until I'm semi-hard. I think this is about something else other than sex, so I stop her.

"Want to tell me what is going on?"

"I can't desire you?"

"You can, but frankly, I'm a bit shocked that you would want to do this here."

"I'm so hot for you. Please?"

I'd prefer not to be discovered, making love to her among the flowers and vegetables. So instead, I kneel and open her pants, pulling her shorts and panties to her ankles.

"Hold onto me."

I spread her legs as far as I can get them to go with her shorts at her feet, then I thrust my tongue against her clit. She is soaked and tasting delicious as I lick her. As soon as I insert two fingers inside her, she begins to moan. Her grip on my hair is tight as she tugs. I gently circle her swollen clit. It doesn't take long, and I feel her orgasm take hold as it squeezes my digits.

When she starts to come down, I slide her shorts and panties up, buttoning them just as I hear her mother calling for her.

"You see what I mean. I could be bare-assed and fucking you hard when she walked in. Wouldn't that not only be embarrassing but scandalous?"

"In here," Rory calls.

Her mother comes in just as she finishes zipping up her shorts, and I wipe my face.

"What are you two doing?"

"I was showing Hunter the hydroponic towers. He was curious."

"Oh. We're having dessert now. Would you like some? Grilled peaches with fresh whipped cream."

"Mmm, yes, we'll be right there."

Rory chastely kisses me and grabs the hand that contains the fingers that were inside her, not more than five minutes ago.

"Are you going to tell them about New York?"

"Tomorrow. I think one revelation a day is enough."

"Remember, you have to work on Monday."

"I'm going to tell them. I'm not a child. I want them to see I can make my own decisions."

∼

For the rest of the day, we spend it with her parents. I haven't spent this much time with parents since I was a teenager. Noah is nice to me, but I have a feeling he is still unsure. I want to tell him that it would tear me apart to hurt his daughter, but I keep it to myself.

In the evening, Rory shows me to my bedroom. It's a large room with a balcony that overlooks the backyard. Her bedroom is right next to mine, and her parents are right down the other end of the hallway. The most surprising thing to me is that we share a bathroom. Either her parents are very trusting, or they hadn't thought of what that could mean.

I'm exhausted from the drive and the events of the day. By nine-thirty, I let everyone know I need to go to bed before I nod off and snore. They laugh at that, and I bid them goodnight, kissing Rory on the cheek before I go upstairs. I'm in bed when I hear her in the bathroom. I debated whether to lock the door that leads to my side. Rory was so hot for me this afternoon that I have a feeling she's going to want to have sex under her parent's roof.

I wait, holding my breath, but she doesn't enter my room, and I see the light under the door switch out, and her footsteps fade away. An hour later, she wakes me with a soft kiss on my lips.

"Rory, you can't be in here."

"Why not?"

"Because your parents will hear."

"I doubt it. I think they're busy."

"Are you serious? I don't want to think about your parents having sex."

"Then don't. Think about having sex with me."

She peels her short robe off, and she's naked underneath. I can see her entire body in the bright moonlight filtering through the windows. I neglected to pull the shades when I got into bed.

"Sweetheart, I'm so tired. Let me sleep."

"You promised me."

She's right, I did. But I also thought she understood that was to be when we got back to New York.

"I can do all the work if you're tired."

This is intriguing, but it's also not my style. I prefer to be an active participant, but I decide to play devil's advocate.

"Really? What are you going to do to me?"

"I'm going to ride you."

That's it. Any residual sleepiness has disappeared, and my cock is starting to rise to the occasion. I fling the sheet off me, and she tugs at my pajama pants. I lift my hips, and she slides them off me. She takes my length in her hand and rubs her thumb over the bead of dew that has pooled at the head.

Rory climbs on the bed and gets in between my legs, bending down to gently suck my head into her mouth. I groan as she takes me deeper. She stops and straddles me, positioning herself over my aching erection. I can feel her heat, and seconds later, she's running her slickness over my length with her hands flat on my stomach.

"Fuck, what are you doing to me?"

She says nothing and continues to tease me. Her long hair brushes against my chest, and I reach to cup her breasts, then with me positioned between her folds, she lies on my chest. I run my fingers over her spine, and she whimpers, then sits up and gets on her haunches. Rory positions her opening over me and sinks slowly.

Rory's heat sears into me, and I want to take control, pounding her hard. But I let her do what she wants. She begins to move slowly, then speeds up a bit. The bed quietly creaks as I move my hips to meet hers. My heart is pounding in my ears, and I stroke her legs, moaning her name. This causes her to smile. I think she likes being in control of the situation.

I reach over and rub her clit with my thumb. She's torturing me, varying her speeds, flexing herself against me. I'm going to explode, and as hard as I try, I'm going to lose it before she comes.

"Rory, I have to come. I can't wait."

"Come. Fill me."

Her words cause me to fall and break apart as I explode. I grabbed her hips and thrust upward as I spill into her. I can't stop saying her name, and I continue to move and rub her until I feel her climax take hold. When she's finished, she lies next to me, and I kiss her for all I'm worth.

"Are you going back to your room?"

"No. I want to be with you."

"Are you sure that's wise?"

"It might not be, but I don't care. I love you."

It's then that I realize we're in the same boat. We've plunged so far together that we can't dig ourselves out if we tried. However, I don't want to, and I don't think she does either.

Rory fades to sleep in my arms, but her sleep is uneasy, and I feel her stir. I know anxiety about telling her parents about New York has her in knots. I think it also had something to do with her insistence that we have sex. Rory needs to be supported and loved by me.

∽

The next morning she's grouchy, and when I hear her parents moving about the hall, I wake her. She snaps at me, but I tell her to go to her room and meet me downstairs for breakfast. We have to leave by noon so we can get her settled in her apartment. She hasn't even packed, and that needs to be done. Fortunately, most of it is clothing.

When I get downstairs, she's still in a mood and picking at the eggs that the maid has cooked for her. The closest thing to cereal they have in the house is granola, so I settle for that, watching Rory as I eat. I reach down and stroke her leg, which she pulls away. I'm bewildered by her behavior, but I leave her alone and wait for her to speak up. Just before everyone finishes, she does.

"I have something to discuss with you."

Her parents look up and wait in anticipation while the granola I've been consuming sits like a rock in my stomach.

"I'm moving to New York."

"You're doing what?" Vivian said.

"I'm moving to New York…today."

Both Vivian and Noah glance at me. "When did you come to this decision?" Vivian said.

"A couple of weeks ago. I can't work for Wilton forever. I love Manhattan, and I want to move there for good."

"Hunter, will you excuse us. We'd like to have a family discussion."

I nod as they get up and head to the study. The door is shut, but I can still hear bits and pieces of the conversation. I also hear my name mentioned, and I expect that I'm going to have to defend my position as her boyfriend. By the time they come out, Rory and Noah are red-faced, and Vivian looks pale.

"Hunter, can you please help me pack?" Rory said.

"Uh, sure."

I try to avoid looking at either one of her parents because I'm sure they hate me and think I'm the reason why she is leaving Boston. Upstairs, Rory doesn't talk to me; she just shoves clothing and personal items in her suitcases. I can hear her sniffling, and I know she's trying to be brave and not cry. I go to put my arms around her, but she pushes me away.

"Rory, will you stop for a minute?"

"I want to get out of here. They don't understand."

"You can't leave here with them pissed. Should I talk to them?"

"You can try, but I doubt it will change their minds. They think I'm too young to be out on my own."

"I'll try to offer them some insight."

I head out the door and down the stairs. I hear her parents talking in the dining room, and I give them a sheepish look as I enter. I explain Rory's decision and that I had nothing to do with it.

"We worry about her after what happened with her arm," Noah said.

"That was a result of Derek. She has friends, and she'll be working for Lawson. We've offered her a great position."

"She never told us that she already accepted a position somewhere. We thought she was still looking."

"She's hired with a start date of tomorrow. My father was impressed with the work she did in the short time she interned for us. The fact that she spent several months working for Wilton Properties only strengthens her worth to our company.

I promise to take care of her. If she ever needs anything, I'm there for her."

Vivian says something that shakes me. "You love her, don't you?"

"Is it that obvious?"

"Yes, and so is her love for you. We're glad that she found someone, but she is fragile, so you need to be careful."

"I'm not fragile." We all turn to see Rory walk into the room with a suitcase in one hand and a bag in the other.

"We just worry that you might not be able to handle living away from home full time."

"I can, and I'll be fine. I'm living with Ellie, and Hunter will be around if I need anything."

I nod and take her suitcase from her hand. We say our goodbyes to her parents, and we're on our way.

"I heard what my parents said. They know you're in love with me."

"Yes, and it didn't seem to bother them. Your father told me to be careful when it comes to you, and I promised him I would."

∽

The end of the second week, and we've settled into life together, working, and personal. I've never been happier. It's funny that Rory renewed the lease on her place because she's seldom there. She spends most of her nights with me, but I wouldn't care if she wanted me to stay at her apartment.

Her parents spoke with her grandparents, and Derek was fired. He was told that if he ever bothered Rory again, they would report him to the police. Apparently, word got out what he did, and he's having a hard time finding a job. He sent some pretty nasty texts to Rory, and I told her to get a new number.

We were invited to JC's home for dinner on Saturday. I know that Rory is a bit agitated that Lexi is not going to let her off the hook, but I told her to relax. Lexi isn't holding a grudge and wants to see her. We stop by a bakery to pick up a cake before we go over.

"I know this is going to be awkward," Rory said.

"It's not. I guarantee everything will be fine. Lexi is happy now. Wait until you see the kids, adorable."

"You really like children, don't you?"

"Sure, I do. I love kids and can't wait to have one of my own. I never told you this, but after we split, I spent a lot of time with Johnny."

"I remember seeing you at the picnic. You were so good with him, so patient."

"He's a great kid. I've been teaching him how to play soccer even though he's barely three. My friends, Henri and Claude, hold a soccer clinic for children a couple of Saturdays a month. I should take Johnny back. I took him a few times, and he loved it. I think you'll like him. Do you like children?"

"Yes, I do. I want to have at least three when the time comes."

I understand what she's saying. She wants to be a mother, but not until she's ready. I guess the pregnancy that she lost scared her. I want her to be ready, and I won't push.

When we arrive at JC and Lexi's, Rory seems to be afraid, but as soon as the door opens, the fear disappears. That's because Lexi takes her into her arms and give her a big warm hug, even before me. I can't stop grinning.

"Welcome, you two. Come in. Johnny is around here somewhere."

My nephew comes barreling around the corner and runs right into Rory, who picks him up. He doesn't struggle, and she hugs him.

"This is my friend, Rory. Can you say hello?"

Funny, but the kid buries his head against her shoulder rather than look at her. He's in her arms, and he's shy. I try to take him from her, but he says no.

Lexi smiles, "He must know you're friendly because he never did that to anyone before."

I hand her the cake, and we all walk toward the kitchen, where my brother is putting the finishing touches on a tossed salad. It's amazing how two kids can domesticate you.

"Little brother, nice to see you. Hello, Rory. I see you've met Johnny, and he's taken a shine to you."

"Daddy, she pretty."

"Yes, she is. You be nice to her."

Rory puts him down, and I grab him for a hug, but he struggles, latching his tiny hand into hers, pulling her along to his bedroom.

"I think he loves Rory as much as I do," I said.

"Looks that way. The little charmer."

We can hear Johnny showing Rory his toys, and then he tells

her about his favorite book. It goes quiet, and we all tiptoe to his bedroom. He's sitting in her lap, and she's reading to him. I feel so much love for her right now that my heart is swelling.

"It's almost time for dinner, you two," Lexi says.

"No, book first."

"I'm sorry, Rory, that my son has taken you hostage."

"It's quite alright. I don't mind being in the company of this handsome, young man."

I sit on the bed and watch her finish the story. As soon as Rory puts the book down, Johnny is off her lap and out the door for dinner. I kiss her and say how sweet she is to read to my nephew. Rory makes like it's no big deal.

Dinner is wonderful and not just because of the food. I feel such a sense of family being around their dinner table. When Arabella cries, I tell everyone to stay seated, and I check on her. She's lying in her crib and cooing when I get there. I pick her up and smell her baby scent, taking her out to the table and putting her in the bassinet that Lexi keeps there.

On the way home, Rory tells me how nice it was to spend time with my family. She lays her head on my shoulder and is half asleep by the time the cab pulls up to my building.

"Are you staying with me tonight?" I ask her in the elevator.

"Of course. I might as well move in here."

I raise my eyebrows. "Would you if I asked?"

"I haven't decided yet. I kind of like having a place to go just in case."

"Just in case what? We fight?"

"No. Just having my own space. You never know. There could be a time where we need a break."

I'm puzzled by what's she's saying, but I don't want to have this talk in the hall, and I wait until we're inside my apartment.

"Rory, am I too much for you? Is this too much? I can pull back if you need me to, just let me know."

She puts her hands up. "No, no, I love you. I didn't mean to imply anything. I like what we have, but it's so new for me, different."

"Different how?"

"I don't need to be afraid with you. I can speak my mind; I have control."

"Because that is how it should be. I don't want to take anything from you. I want you to give yourself freely, and if it gets too much, say so. I don't want to lose you."

Her cell rings, and she ignores it. A minute later, it rings again. She's too busy to answer it because I have her body in my arms, and we're heading for the bedroom. I don't want to be interrupted by anything, including the phone.

∾

The next morning, Rory is fast asleep when I wake up. We made love several times, and sleep has been limited the past few nights. I'm in the mood for freshly brewed coffee and hot bagels. There is a wonderful deli around the corner who makes their own baked goods. I quickly jot off a note for Rory and leave it on the nightstand.

I hope she doesn't wake up before I come back because I want to do that. I love to kiss her awake. To see those beautiful sapphire eyes open and see me first thing. I whistle as I head to the deli. It's a nice hot late July morning. I can't believe how well things are going in my life.

Work is keeping me tied up, and my father is in the midst of purchasing a fourth building. This will keep us with work through the next two years. Rory has been a great help to me, and she's even better than my assistant, Andrea, in some areas.

The line at the deli is long, and I grab a coffee to sip while I wait to order fresh bagels and maybe a couple of chocolate croissants, which are Rory's favorite. The bagels are warm in the bag as I walk home, and when I get into my apartment, Rory is gone. Usually, she makes the bed, but today it's like she just ran out of there.

CHAPTER 25

I feel a sense of panic as I hunt to see if she left me a note. My phone has no texts from her, and when I call her, the phone goes right to voicemail. I call downstairs to the desk, and they tell me that Rory left over twenty minutes ago. Why didn't she leave me a note or text me, and where did she go?

My phone rings as I think of what to do and it's Ellie. She's panicked and not making sense.

"You need to get to our apartment. Please, it's Derek, and he has Rory and me."

As I move towards the door, I hear banging and the cracking of wood, then a gruff voice tells Ellie she better come out, or she'll watch Rory die. I'm sick, and I can hear the entire nightmare unfolding. I wonder if I should call the police, but how long will it take them to get over to the apartment? If I lose her…

I keep listening on the way to Rory's place. Derek sounds frenzied, and the phone must have been left in the bathroom because it's hard to figure out what is going on. Rory and Ellie are begging Derek to put something down, and I can't be sure what it is. I beg the cabbie to drive faster and tell him there's an extra twenty in it for him. He starts flying along the streets,

ADDICTED BY LOVE

taking shortcuts. It's early on Sunday morning, so the traffic is light.

On arrival, I shove money in his hand and fly out the door. In the lobby, I tell the guy at the desk to call the police and that it might be a hostage situation. He blinks at me, and I bark at him to pick up the phone as I jump into the elevator.

The elevator dings and I can hear a muffled conversation. The door to Rory's is slightly open, and I peek in. There are blood droplets on the floor in the foyer, and I see Derek standing near the kitchen with a knife in his hand. I can't be sure whose blood it is, but I slowly push the door open and duck down.

Derek doesn't see me, and he's crying. I see a small pool of blood forming below the hand that holds the knife. He's cut himself. Rory and Ellie are sitting on the floor against the wall of the entrance to the hallway. The fear on their faces is heart-wrenching.

"You bitch. I should slit your throat," he said, pointing the knife at Rory. "You got me fired, and now I have nothing. My parents cut me off, and it's your fault."

"Derek, you're cut. Let me call an ambulance," Rory said.

"Don't act like you want to help me, you fucking cunt. You did this to me."

I bob my head up and see a momentary look of relief on Rory's face as she sees me. I keep inching ever closer to Derek. If I don't do something, he's going to hurt them. I'm not paying attention, and I kick the plate that a large houseplant sits on. It skids across the tile a short way, and Derek wheels around, holding the knife. I have no choice but to lunge at him.

He slashes at me, and I jump away, then kick him in the wrist, which dislodges the knife. It skates across the floor out of his reach, and I throw a punch that grazes his chin when he ducks. He pushes me hard with his body, and we slam into the wall. He's hard to get hold off because the blood on his hands is slippery.

Derek gets the best of me when I slip on blood droplets. He

climbs on top of me, and I keep moving my body to push him off. He rains punches down, and I'm lucky because the police barge into the apartment and pull him off me.

"Are you hurt?" one of the officers said.

I don't know because I have so much blood on my body. I'm not sure if any of it is mine, but I don't feel hurt except for where he punched me. Rory becomes hysterical, and I see Ellie and a female officer comfort her. I want to go to her, but I think the sight of me would be traumatic.

I hear the officer call for an ambulance. Derek can't be handcuffed because of the actively bleeding wound on his wrists. He is ranting and says he wanted to end it. I think that he's going to needs some psychiatric help, which might be in line for Rory after this situation. I look over at her as I tell the officer what happened. She looks catatonic, and she's stopped crying. Her eyes are staring off into space, and it tugs at my heart.

Even though I decline medical treatment, one of the paramedics looks me over to make sure I have no serious injuries. I tell him that I'm just sore and probably bruised. My ribs hurt from where Derek planted some well-placed punches, but I doubt there's anything broken.

I head to the bathroom to wash my arms and face. There is nothing I can do about my clothing, and I'll have to wait until I get home to change. By the time I get out, the police and paramedics are escorting Derek out of the apartment. A group of neighbors has gathered outside the door, and when the emergency personnel leaves, I close the door.

"Ellie, is Rory alright?"

She's about to answer, and Rory looks up at me. "Don't talk about me like I'm not here."

"Sweetheart, are you okay?"

"Why won't you hold me?"

"I'm sorry. I didn't think you wanted me to touch you; I'm a mess."

"I need you."

I walk over and take both Rory and Ellie in my arms. The apartment is a bloody mess, and there are wrappers left all over the floor from the paramedics. They wrapped Derek's wrist with gauze before they took him away.

"Why don't you two change, and I'll clean this place up. Just point me to the cleaning supplies."

"You don't have to do that," Ellie said.

"I'm already dirty, so let me do it."

Rory has already gone to her room, and Ellie leads me to the kitchen, stepping over the bloody mess on the way. Fortunately, only the floor and some of the wall has gotten any blood on them. The tile needs a good scrubbing. After Ellie hands me the cleaning items, I grab her hand.

"Are you seriously, okay? I mean, this was so fucked up."

"I knew he was crazy, but I didn't think he would do this. He's been calling Rory on her cell, sending her emails, and calling here. I told her to get an order of protection, but she said she would be alright."

"How did he get in here?"

"He had a key. I came home this morning, and he was here waiting. Derek threatened me and said to call Rory. I did and told her she needed to get over here and bring the police. He grabbed the phone from me and said if she called the police, that I would be dead when she arrived."

"So, she came to protect you."

"She thought she could talk some sense into Derek, but he just got worse when she arrived. He knew she was with you all night, and it just seemed to agitate him more. He slashed his wrist in front of us and began to bleed. He was losing so much blood that I thought he would eventually pass out."

"How did you get into the bathroom?"

"I told him if I didn't go, I would pee on the floor. He had the decency to let me go. I slipped my phone off the kitchen counter, and I guess he realized I was up to something when I didn't come out quickly enough. He told me that Rory would die and began to bang, then run into the door. It started to crack, and I opened it before he finished the job."

"Go change. We can talk in a little while."

Ellie steps into her bedroom and closes the door to change. I fill the bucket with hot water and start wiping at the dried blood until it's completely clean. The last thing I do is spray disinfectant on the areas and do a final wipe down. Ellie comes out of her bedroom, but Rory has not.

I remove my shirt, which has a majority of the blood, my shorts are barely stained, and I knock at her door.

"Rory, can I come in?"

"Yes."

I pop the door open, and she has a suitcase on her bed. She's taking things out of her drawers and closet and stuffing them into the case.

"You can't leave me."

"I'm not leaving you. I'm leaving here. I can't live in this apartment after what just happened."

"Where will you go?" I ask with alarm.

"To stay with you if you'll have me."

I feel relief wash over me. "Of course you can stay as long as you need to. But what about this place?"

"Ellie can have it to herself. I'll pay my share of the rent until the lease is up."

"She's not going to be happy you're leaving since you just signed the lease for another year."

"I know, but she'll understand. It's not like she didn't live here by herself before."

"You should talk to her now."

Rory brushes by without touching me, and I sit on the chair at her desk, not wanting to expose any of her linens to remnant blood I have on my shorts. I hear her talking with Ellie and wait for her to come back. It starts to hit me, the magnitude of what we all just went through. It makes me wish I got in more shots on Derek. He created his misery and tried to blame Rory for his circumstances.

She comes back and tells me that Ellie is going to stay with her father for a while since she doesn't feel comfortable here either. I feel sorry that I couldn't prevent what took place, but it will take some time for us all to get over it.

∼

Four weeks later and I've been giving Rory as much space as she needs. She's had some nightmares about the incident. It turns out that Derek had a far more sinister plan based on a journal that was found in his hotel room. He planned on committing suicide and taking Rory with him. Ellie was the one factor that prevented him from carrying it out.

It seems that he became rattled when she was in the apartment instead of Rory. His plans went to shit after that, and he sliced open his wrist in a desperate attempt to gain sympathy. He thought that Rory would fall into his arms and profess her love for him.

Derek is now back in Boston at a psychiatric facility getting the help that he needs. I can't feel any compassion for him because he almost destroyed the person I love the most in this world.

I've been patient with Rory because love and support are what she needs, and I admire her strength and resolve. She barely missed a beat and went back to work three days after the incident. Her parents wanted her to move back home, but she declined, saying she needed to work this out on her own.

I know we're going to make it, and as each day goes by, little by little, I see the old Rory coming back, the one that I first met on the beach over a year ago. The one that I was in love with before I knew what true love was.

EPILOGUE

Four Months Later

I'm so excited that I can't contain myself. I keep checking my pocket to make sure it's there as we head to Rockefeller Center. Rory keeps eyeing me, and I'm afraid she's figured out the surprise. It's a few days before Christmas, and I wanted to take her to see the grand tree that they put up each year.

Once she told me that she'd never been there, it became my mission to plan every minute detail. Each day, I fall deeper in love with her, and I know that all my former playboy ways were because I was looking for her. Rory is my soulmate.

It's not a typical December day. The sun is shining brightly, the wind is calm, and the temperature is a balmy fifty-two degrees. I'm glad because I don't want anything to ruin this moment.

When we get to the tree, I see Rory's sapphire eyes shining. She gazes at the lights on the tree; her head tilted to the clear sky. She's not paying attention to me when I get down on one knee, open the black velvet box, and propose.

"Aurora Kathryn Barton, will you do the honor of marrying me?"

She turns to me, and I see tears in her eyes as I wait for her answer. Rory can't get the words out, and I see she's mouthing yes, over and over. I stand and take her in my arms, then step back to slip the two-carat emerald cut diamond in a platinum setting on her petite ring finger.

People standing around us are clapping and taking pictures as we kiss. I'm so happy that my heart is going to explode and she finally speaks.

"I thought you would never ask."

"I was just waiting for the right moment."

My life is complete, and there is so much more to follow.

The End

Look below for an excerpt from the next book in The Full Circle Series, Twisted by Love

TWISTED BY LOVE

I pulled up the sleeve of my lab coat and glanced at my watch, 4:02 PM. I had fifty-eight minutes until my work week was over. The lab was quiet, not the usual Friday afternoon banter that took place as it got close to quitting time.

I was pretty sure that had to do with the new chief administrator, Chase Pearce. He had arrived on Monday from the Atlanta office of Nolan Pharmaceuticals. The former chief, Doug Bannon had been transferred to the California office in Los Angeles. It made me sad to see him go since for the last two years, I had risen through the ranks under his tutelage.

I was now early shift lab supervisor, but I deserved it. I had spent plenty of late nights and even some weekends working on research. I put in my time and was rewarded.

"Megan, have you met Pearcy?" my coworker Cindy asked.

"Who?"

"Pearcy, you know, Chase Pearce."

"No, he hasn't had the decency to show his face. You would think that he would want to introduce himself to the staff instead of calling us in, one by one. I hope he doesn't bother until Monday. I'm tired."

I had been clued in by a colleague in the Atlanta office that Chase could be hard to handle. He was an arrogant taskmaster but brilliant and passionate about medicine. I had been told he held a medical degree from Harvard. The intercom crackled.

"Megan Stanford, can you please go to Dr. Pearce's office."

"Fuck, I had all of less than an hour."

My coworker, Edgar Pilar, gave me a sympathetic look. He had seen Dr. Pearce earlier that morning and by his depressed mood, it hadn't gone well.

"I guess I'll have to face the music sometime."

I packed up the reports that I had been working on and stashed the folder in my top drawer. I would have to compile the results on Monday. I removed my lab coat and straightened my dress before I headed to Chase's office.

I walked down the hall and took the elevator to the top floor. All the heads of the company resided on the top floor of the Nolan Pharmaceutical building including the chiefs of each department. Standing in front of the door, I took a deep breath and knocked. I was greeted by a deep baritone that told me to enter.

Chase Pearce sat in his high-backed leather office chair paging through a medical book. His back was turned to me, but I could see he had a thick neatly combed inky black hair.

"Please sit, Miss Stanford. I'll be with you in a moment."

I took the seat in front of his desk and arranged my dress, so it covered my legs. It was just above my knees when I stood up but when I sat, it moved to my thighs. I should have kept my lab coat on. I didn't want to make the wrong impression on the good doctor.

Several minutes went by and I began to grow annoyed. Why call me up here if you I was just going to sit and wait? I began fidgeting and bouncing my knee which made my heel clack on the floor. Without turning around, Dr. Pearce addressed me.

"No need to be nervous Miss Stanford. This is only an informal meeting. I'll be with you in a minute."

What do I say to that? "Uh, thank you."

A few more minutes and he finally turned around to face me. I took a small gasp as I saw his face. He was, well, gorgeous. His blue eyes were the color of the Mediterranean Sea framed by long thick black eyelashes. They alone were enough to draw you in but the square jaw line, cleft chin and patrician nose didn't hurt either. All at once I felt my belly clench as I thought about running my tongue up and down that chin of his. I must have been gaping at him because he called my name.

"Miss Stanford? Is there something wrong?"

"No, I'm sorry," I could feel my face starting to heat up with embarrassment.

He smiled. Was he laughing at me?

"I've been going over your records. You've moved up pretty quickly since you've been here. I respect my predecessor, but I don't reward employees that easily with promotions. I have a certain protocol I follow. Looks or charm mean nothing. So, your past performance means little to me. It's what you do from here on that counts."

I didn't know if I should be angry or upset. It sounded like he was implying that I got my promotions due to my looks and not the work I've done. My tongue was tied and lucky for that because I wanted to tell him off. What a fucking jerk. Did he think I slept with Doug to get where I was? I was about to reply when the intercom buzzed.

"Doctor Pearce, you have a call on line four."

"Miss Stanford, I need to take this. I'll see you Monday. You're dismissed."

I stood up and straightened my dress. I caught him watching me from the corner of my eye as I turned to leave.

"Oh, and by the way, I like my employees to look professional.

The neckline of that dress is far too low. Please wear appropriate clothing to the office."

He picked up the phone as I was about to exit so I couldn't reply to his comment. My dress was not inappropriate. It was a scoop neck and barely showed a hint of cleavage. I had never been told my clothes were not proper for an office. This was the third job I had. I was fuming by the time I got back to my desk.

It was past five and all my coworkers had left for the day, so I wasn't able to vent my frustrations to them. Dr. Chase Pearce had a hell of a nerve saying what he did to me. I was mortified but the hell with it. It was Friday and I wanted to go have a drink at McKinnon's bar across the street.

I went to my cubicle and gathered my purse and coat. It was late April but there was still a bit of a chill in the air. I stepped out onto the street and breathed in the fresh smell of spring. It was still light out and I relished the coming of longer daylight.

McKinnon's was busy as it usually is on a Friday. I waved hello to Samuel, the owner and he came right over to take my order.

"Martini, extra olives."

"How are you Megan?"

"A little worse for wear. Met my new boss today. A real stickler."

"Sorry to hear that," Sam said as he placed the Martini in front of me.

"Me too."

I scanned the bar to see if any of my coworkers were here, but I didn't recognize anyone. Whatever. I'll just finish my Martini and head home. I started to check my emails while I sipped my drink. Nothing of importance except my sister Lexy wanted me to have dinner with her and her family. She lived not far from me with her husband, JC and two children. Maybe I would go one of these evenings.

I didn't notice the man that sat next to me until I pulled the hair band that was tight at the back of my head to release my ponytail. I shook my blonde hair out and heard someone say something.

"Your hair looks much better down."

The voice sounded familiar and I looked up to those beautiful blue eyes of Dr. Pearce. He smiled at me.

"I beg your pardon?"

"Your hair, it looks much better when it's down. I like it."

What a jerk. I had no intention of doing anything to satisfy him so I promptly put my hair back in the ponytail. It was a childish thing to do but I was angry from his comment about my dress.

He didn't say anything, but I could see his mouth turn up into a smirk then a smile and then he started to laugh. Though I tried to control myself, I smiled at him and chuckled, then pulled my hair out of the ponytail again.

"It's been a busy week for me and you must let me apologize if I offended you earlier. Though your dress is a bit lowcut."

"You can just apologize without the negative comment. My dress is not that low cut. I barely show any cleavage. If you want to see low cut, I'm sure I can oblige."

His eyes were drawn to the ivory flesh of my upper chest and then they fixed on my mouth then up to my eyes.

"Why would you want to cheapen yourself in such a way? You don't need to convince men you're beautiful by wearing revealing clothing."

What the hell was this man saying? He thought I was beautiful?" I was too tongue tied to ask and then a guy who seemed a bit tipsy bumped into me and spilled some of his beer on my coat. He didn't apologize and Dr. Pearce grabbed his collar.

"You owe this woman an apology. You spilled your beer on her."

"Get bent preppy."

"Apologize please."

The guy handed his beer to friend and wrenched his collar out of Dr. Pearce's grip, then pushed him in his chest.

"I'm not gonna apologize and if you got a problem with that, I can meet you outside."

"Have it your way."

I shook my head, but Dr. Pearce twisted around and picked up a pair of arm crutches, securing them in his hands before he stood up. He was disabled? Why didn't I see the crutches earlier when I was in his office?

"You can't go out there. He's an idiot."

The man was waiting for Dr. Pearce to follow and I put my hand on his arm, summoning Samuel at the same time.

"What's up Megan?"

"That asshole spilled a drink on me and when the doctor asked him to apologize, he wanted to fight."

My eyes pleaded with Samuel to do something and he pointed at two of his security guys then to the troublemaker. They escorted him out of the bar along with his friends.

"You didn't have to do that. I'm perfectly capable of handling myself."

"But you're, you're…"

"Disabled. You can say it. It's not a bad word."

"I'm sorry. I didn't mean to offend you."

I picked up my purse off the bar and got off the stool.

"Megan, don't go. It's perfectly fine. You didn't offend me. I'm used to it. I can protect myself when I need to, and I'll surely protect the honor of a lovely woman."

I sat back down, and he smiled which disarmed me. I felt defensive and foolish until that gesture.

"Let me make up for my rudeness earlier by buying you dinner. I'd like to get to know my staff a little better since I'm new to Manhattan. I have no friends here and who can't use some friends?"

"You want to be friends?"

"Of course. I'd rather be friends than enemies, don't you agree?"

"Yes, I'd agree."

"I don't know the area very well so why don't you choose where we should eat."

"I haven't said yes."

He stared at me, "Then let me formally ask. Would you let me take you to dinner Miss Stanford?"

"Yes, I'll accept your invitation. What type of food do you like?"

"Anything really though I am in the mood for a good steak."

"I know just the place. The Bull and Brew. It's a few blocks away from here. We should take a cab."

I would have suggested we walk since it was a fairly nice evening but with his disability, I didn't want to embarrass him by suggesting it.

"We can walk."

I raised my eyebrows in surprise but turned away quickly so he wouldn't see me. I picked up my purse and Dr. Pearce secured his crutches in his hands. He gestured for me to go ahead of him and I held the door so he could pass through.

We were silent as we walked to the restaurant. I could see that he used the crutches only for balance, slightly leaning on them. I was curious what type of injury he had sustained but it would be rude to ask so I would wait until he offered.

When we arrived at the Bull and Brew, it was crowded. I gave my name and looked around for the owner, Steven Tidwell. He and I had been friends for a few years, rather, friends with benefits but it had been awhile. I asked the hostess if she could tell him I was here.

She nodded and called him on the intercom that was attached to the station she was at. In a few minutes, he came out, giving me a tight hug and pressing his lips to mine. I noticed Dr. Pearce scowling at him.

"How are you Megan? I haven't seen you in a while," he purred.

"I've been busy with work and life. You?"

"Single again. We can get together if you're interested."

"I'll let you know. Do you still have the same cell number?"

"Yes. Same as before."

Behind me I heard Dr. Pearce clear his throat and introduced him to Steven.

"And you are?"

"This is Dr. Pearce, my new boss."

I could almost hear Steven breathe a sigh of relief. We always had a good time in bed and if I was dating, that would be off the table.

"Pleasure to meet you doctor. I can seat you and the meal is on the house, anything you want."

"Thanks, Steven."

He grabbed a couple of menus from the hostess station and we followed him to a booth in the back of the restaurant. I kissed him on the cheek and felt his hand caress my ass as he left us.

"Are you close to him?" Dr. Pearce asked, a deep frown marring his features.

"Close enough. We've known each other for a few years."

"Intimately?"

"Dr. Pearce, I don't see how that is any of your business."

"It's obvious by the way he was looking at you that you are or have been."

"We have a mutual understanding."

"You mean friends with benefits?"

I could feel my face turn crimson, the heat of my embarrassment pushed from my neck up.

"You're very forward, aren't you?"

"It's as I said before, you don't need to cheapen yourself. I can see that you are intelligent and worthy without that type of behavior."

I didn't look at his face, rather concentrating on my menu but I could feel those blue eyes boring into me.

"It's a coordinated satisfaction. Why is it that a man can sleep with many women and it's not a problem but if a woman does it, she cheapens herself?"

"Because women are delicate, lovely creatures who should be worshipped, not used. Excuse me for my old world thinking."

"Everyone is entitled to their opinions. I just prefer to remove myself from permanent entanglements. I'm not interested in marriage."

"Why?"

"Because they cause hurt. I've been there, gave my all and got screwed over. It's not worth my time or emotions."

"Well that man deserves a horse whipping. You are worthy and you should let go of your previous emotional damage to try again."

Dr. Pearce made me feel like a child who was being scolded by his parents. He wasn't that much older than my twenty-eight years, maybe he was thirty-five, but his stern voice made me feel younger.

"What about you?" I countered.

"I've been there, and I let it go but I have no time for relationships. I'm married to my work and it keeps me busy."

"What happened?"

"It's not important unless you quid pro quo."

"You first."

The waitress interrupted us to take our orders and when she was gone, I stared at Dr. Pearce, waiting.

"Dr. Pearce?"

"This is an informal setting, please call me Chase."

"Chase."

I see him take a deep breath and he starts, "I was once married, it ended a couple of years ago, shortly after I was injured in a car accident. I couldn't give Carrie what she needed during my recovery or even before that. In retrospect, she was superficial, and I suspected she was cheating. She wasn't the right woman for me. We were very much in love when we first married but my work stole time with her. What I took away from the marriage is never marry someone who doesn't have their own interests."

"I'm sorry. She didn't work?"

"Carrie was born into a family of blue bloods. She didn't need to work. She was beautiful and rich, that was enough. I lived for my work and when I refused to quit, our relationship started to degrade. The accident was just the last straw."

"It sounds like you were drawn in by her looks, not her character."

"Carrie had her charms. She was generous with her money to charitable organizations but that's as far as it went. She didn't give of herself. I was blinded by her philanthropy, hoping it would morph into something else. It turns out I was wrong. Your turn."

"I dated Jeremy for a little over two years. He was sweet and worked for a Hedge fund. We lived together for a while and our relationship just seemed to go stale. I know he loved having me on his arm. He wasn't the typical guy that I go for but he had a great sense of humor. Then he just ended it. He said we needed space. I thought we were heading for marriage."

"Did he break your heart?"

"Yes and no. I was in love with him but not like I was when we first dated. I was blindsided by him breaking up with me. He just came out one day and said it wasn't working out. No discussion, no nothing. That was it. I didn't want to stay in New Jersey after that. I applied at Nolan and was hired so I decided to move to Manhattan."

"Sounds like he didn't realize what he was giving up."

Again, I feel the creep of a blush working its way up my face. Thank God the waitress comes with our food, so I had something to distract from the conversation. We're both quiet while we ate and when we both reached for the salt at the same time, our hands touch and we both withdrew as if burned.

"I'm sorry, you can use it first," Chase says.

"Thank you."

After I lightly salted my steak, I slid it over to him. I could see him watching me and his eyes were hypnotic. Those damn blue eyes.

"That's a large steak for someone so small."

"You'd be surprised at what I can pack away. Unfortunately, I let it get out of control when I was with Jeremy and gained about twenty pounds. I think deep down he was insecure and wanted me to gain weight so his friends wouldn't look at me so much."

"Did it work?"

"If anything, they looked more. I became curvier than I am now."

Chase laughed. I liked his deep rich laugh; it was somehow disarming. I felt so comfortable with him that I thought I would ask about his accident and what was wrong with him.

"Chase, can I ask you a personal question?"

"It depends on what it is but ask."

"How did you get injured?"

He looks at the ceiling while chewing a piece of steak and I start to think I made a mistake prying into his personal business.

"I was hit by a car. It was late one night, and I was crossing the street to the parking garage after work. The driver hit me and broke my pelvis and both my legs. I have nerve damage. I'm actually part of a special trial that's stimulating the nerves to regenerate. I'm hopeful but if it doesn't happen, I can live with it."

"What were you like before the accident?"

"I was active. I played sports, was a center fielder on a softball team during the summer. I played basketball and ran each morning. When it was colder, I spent time weightlifting. I was in pretty good shape and that's what I think attracted Carrie to me."

"Do you? That's all?"

"I don't understand what you mean."

"Chase, you're very handsome. I'm sure you get plenty of female attention."

"I don't notice."

"You don't notice women looking at you?"

"I don't because I'm not interested. I'm married to my work."

"Is that going to be forever? Won't you ever change your mind about marriage?"

"Will you?"

"Probably not but my circumstances were more damaging than yours. Your wife was just a jerk. My boyfriend dashed my hopes by breaking my heart."

"I would say that he was a jerk too. He didn't see what he had in front of him."

"You're very different from when you're in the office."

"You've only met me once in the office, how do you know?"

"I have my sources."

Chase raises one eyebrow, "You mean you spoke to some of your colleagues at the Atlanta office? Look, I know I can be a hard ass but that's only because I'm passionate of what Nolan is doing. If they can improve the lives of people through their drug therapy, then I'm all for it."

"I didn't mean to imply anything."

"Yes, you did and that's fine. I like to know how people view me. It won't change how I am because I'm just doing my job."

I don't know how to respond and we finish the meal in silence. When the waitress offers us dessert, we both decline. The mood has become uncomfortable and I prefer to go home. Out on the street, I say goodbye to Chase, and we go our separate ways.

"Megan?" he calls.

I turn and he gestures for me to come over to him not knowing what to expect. He leans in and gently kisses my cheek without explanation and turns to leave. I'm a bit stunned and stare at his retreating figure. As I walk home, I think about how soft his lips felt on my skin.

It's still early when I walk into my apartment. I wonder if Olivia is home. She's my sister Lexi's best friend and lives downstairs from me. Olivia is single still and fun to go to a club with especially if she talks her brother Matty into joining us. But lately, he's been seeing some woman so he might be out. I dial Olivia's cell, but it goes right to voicemail.

"Oh well, I guess I'm on my own for the evening."

No big deal, one Friday night of sitting home and relaxing is fine. I change into shorts and a tank top. My apartment is very warm even though I've shut of the heat a few days ago. It always gets like this in springtime. I plop down on the couch and start scrolling through the movie menu on my television. There must be something good to watch. My phone chirps with an incoming text.

How was your meeting with Pearce?

It's Cindy and she probably wants to know if I survived since most of my other coworkers got an icy reception. I decide not to mention that we had dinner together but tell her that he was not so nice in his office. It's what she expects me to say. Why should he show me preferential treatment?

Even with his steely exterior, he is gorgeous, don't you agree?

Yes, he is very handsome but remember, he's our boss.

I wonder if she knows that he has a disability. I didn't know it until I saw his crutches in the bar. It doesn't mean anything to me but sometimes people get the wrong idea about someone who is disabled. They feel they need to act a certain way around them. They're people, a disability doesn't change that.

I know, but he is still very fuckable.

CINDY, are you serious? You have a boyfriend.

So? I can dream, can't I?

I'm busy so enjoy your dreams tonight when you go to bed. Make sure you don't scream out Pearce's name when Ian is on top of you.

Very funny. I would never. I'll talk to you later.

Cindy might have a master's degree in biology, but she sometimes acts like a teenager. I bet that despite Chase's denial, women look at him all the time.

End Chapter 1

Printed in Great Britain
by Amazon